ORDER OF THE STEEL ROSE BOOK 1

DARK
MASQUERADE

R. SLATER

A catalogue record for this book is available from the National Library of Australia

Dark Masquerade: Order of the Steel Rose Novels – Book 1 -- 1st ed.
ISBN Paperback 9781764138604
ISBN Ebook 9781764138611

*Dedicated to the memory of my mother, Katrina,
without whom I wouldn't be here, in more
ways than one.*

Contents

Author's Note

I would like to commence by stating that I do not in any way support or believe in *racism*, *discrimination* or *misogyny*. However, these ways of thinking were prevalent and customary to the people of the Victorian era, so form a core part of the events that unfold.

The Victorian era (June 1837–January 1901) was one of dramatic change. It was one of those pivotal times in history where the flow of humanity was fundamentally altered.

Although changes had been occurring for quite some time, with people moving into cities from rural areas and family structures evolving, these differences accelerated during the Victorian era. New technologies sprang up, sometimes almost overnight. It was – after all – the *Industrial Revolution*. Many of the things we take for granted today originated in the Victorian era; for example, factories, mass production and department stores. It was also when leisure time and public hobbies first became available to the masses. Even what we so think of as a twentieth century creation – *marketing* – began its explosion into what it has become during this period, and it would be instantly recognisable to anyone today.

The Victorian era, however, also had many ideas and beliefs that would be at odds with today's world. For example, a young lady of good upbringing was not allowed to walk down the street unaccompanied, even though she may well have had a full-time job (which she was expected to give up, once she *inevitably* got married). Likewise, if a young man, who knew said young lady, saw her in the street, he could not simply go up to her and talk to her. She had to acknowledge him first. And then, it was considered rude on her part to do so if he were smoking – particularly a cigar – as young men were not supposed to smoke around young ladies, and he would be forced to discard that cigar! And he certainly could not ignore her, either!

This period was also considered the most glorious point of the British Empire. It was known as 'The Empire on which the sun never sets', and this was actually accurate. People and lands across the world came under the auspices and stewardship of Her Majesty Queen Victoria, and more directly, the Foreign Office and the government of the day.

During this time of colonial idealism, which it is important to point out, was not something exclusive to the British – certain beliefs were deeply held regarding the various citizenry of the empire. In this narrow view, foreigners were often regarded with contempt, and particularly native peoples were seen as lacking – in intellect, wit and civilisation. They were considered in desperate need of the guiding light of the empire to bring them out of their quagmire of ignorance and into the enlightenment of the modern world. As such, non-white and non-British people were very often treated abysmally.

Likewise, the attitudes towards women were less than ideal. While women were held to be treated with the utmost respect in society, they were still seen as weak and more or less incapable. This being despite the fact that both Elizabeth I and Victoria – the monarch at the time – were amongst the most influential in the history of Britain, and were both *women.* History and the stubbornly lingering attitudes still evident in the western world contain more than enough evidence of these attitudes. But to put it in context, women in the United Kingdom did not receive equal suffrage with men until *1928*!

Class was another characteristic of society in this era that showed a great divide. People of the lower classes lived crammed into slums and in conditions that would have been considered abhorrent by the upper classes. They were forced to labour long hours in factories for a wage so low it was not realistically sufficient to support their often-large families. Even though reforms did improve some of these conditions, in realistic terms, they remained less than ideal. People were often compelled to resort to whatever means available to them to survive. As an example, during the Victorian era the levels of prostitution in the East End were so high that some authorities considered them *epidemic*.

Also, while western attitudes towards 'the world's oldest profession' may not have largely changed in this day and age, the fees charged by sex workers today would have been *inconceivable* during the Victorian era. The sad reality is that the few coins earned in a night *may* just have been enough to pay for a place to sleep, and *perhaps* a meal. Furthermore, the food usually consumed by the lower classes at that time would in this day receive a large rubber stamp that said: 'Not fit for human consumption.'

A final characteristic of Victorian society worth mentioning is the 'stiff upper lip'. Widely derided and satirised during the twentieth century, this paradigm stemmed from the Ancient Spartans, and from Classical Stoicism. It was enshrined in Victorian education, particularly that provided to the upper classes. Practically, this entailed gentlemen not making excessive and expressive displays of emotion. Challenges or dangers were to be met with a cool, indifferent demeanour, or understatement. While ladies were not necessarily beholden to such stoicism, they *were* expected to display poise and dignity, often through tranquillity and agreeability. Ladies were to sit or stand still and upright, not fidget or wave their arms about, and at most, smile, nod or take very composed actions. This detached reserve in a confronting situation would seem odd to us. We would expect shouting, expressive actions and even profanities. Such behaviour would have been seen by Victorian ladies and gentlemen as acting without restraint, and therefore ill-mannered, uncivilised or unreasonable.

To many readers, none of the points above would be considered astounding revelations, so why do I discuss these here? To put it simply: *authenticity*.

While there are characteristics of Victorian culture that could improve today's society, such as manners and courtesy, many of the ideas and beliefs discussed above would largely seem ignorant and offensive today. However, in recounting the events in these novels, I cannot ignore these aspects of Victorian society. To do so would depict an inaccurate and idealised version of that world, and it would be just as ridiculous as saying that the participants here cruised the streets of 1890's London in a sports car, or that they googled the information they needed on their smartphones!

That being said, I *have* taken some small creative liberties for the sake of practicality and convenience. The main one being changes to the spoken language. People – from the upper class, in particular – would have spoken, socially, in a rigid and roundabout manner that would seem overly formal to us, and devoid of a lot of the expressiveness that 'feels' natural to us. Therefore, I've modified the spoken language to still convey formality or distance as required, but to be far less verbose and much more accessible for readers.

I — Overture

'I have seen the dark universe yawning

Where the black planets roll without aim,

Where they roll in their horror unheeded,

Without knowledge, or lustre, or name.'

— **H.P. Lovecraft, 'Nemesis'**

Prologue
A Perfect Prey

Somewhere in London, sometime in 1891

The room moved in a dizzying whirl of colour and sound. Light, music, silk gowns, laughter, the banter of conversation and the strong scent of cigar smoke all bombarded him as he turned on his heel and scanned the room.

Heartbeats, desires and the secret, lustful thoughts of those around him pressed themselves on his psyche. As always, he could not hear the exact thoughts, but he knew what they were thinking and feeling. And wanting.

And he knew what he wanted. He would have it tonight. The impulse would not be denied again.

A beautiful young lady in teal silk, wearing a large square-cut sapphire necklace that dazzled in the light, crossed his path and smiled graciously, bowing her head demurely – as only a proper lady would – and he replied with a small formal bow and a smile of his own.

Light sparkled in her large ebony-dark eyes as they widened in response to his smile; he saw the lock of her raven-black hair, loose and dangling obscenely at the side of her neck, contrasting against her pale skin. The hunger grew within him. How easy it would be to bite there; to sink his teeth in and hear the blissful moan of equal parts pleasure and pain. He watched her glide gracefully away and stop at a nearby table. Within the pretence of mundane action, her eyes surreptitiously flickered to his, and they held each other's gaze for a fleeting moment of eternity. Was this what he was looking for this evening? Perhaps. But this one would be all too easy. This one dulled the fire within him. To be sure, there was nothing wrong with her, he thought, as he regarded her with the gaze he had mastered: a gaze that spoke of forbidden acts of lust, and freedom in passion. A gaze that set afire the hearts of all the ladies he cast it upon; indeed even now, he saw the recognition in her eyes, the sudden flush of colour in her cheeks and the involuntary parting of her lips as her breath quickened. As he caught the rise and fall of her breasts in her gown, she turned away, embarrassed by her body's betrayal of her lustful thoughts. He smirked to himself. All too easy.

Glancing around the room, he sipped the champagne in his hand and wondered whether he would be there when she invariably turned back for more? While he knew his possession of her was now a foregone conclusion, he did not regard himself as some sort of starving animal. No. He was a connoisseur, a patient and masterful hunter, and like all hunters he savoured the thrill of the chase as much as the satisfaction of the kill itself. The thrill was in the inflammation of the senses, the anticipation of a favourite dish, the impending gratification of satiation. His eyes swept the room again, looking for the perfect prey.

Suddenly, there she was. He stiffened and went still, like a pointer on the set. All his attention focused on her. The music, the people in the ballroom, the other dancers all subsided to a grey meaningless fog like that which beset the docks so frequently; like that in which he used to hunt once upon a time. She was dancing with some handsome fool, who no doubt had no idea what he had within his grasp, other than a beautiful lady. Her flowing red hair was woven into a thick and complex braid that nestled on her shoulder like a snake, with two strands of ringlets hanging down on either side of her face. A face with pale skin, smooth like polished ivory, a small nose, full cheeks and full, sensual lips, currently drawn back in an alluring smile, showing off perfect white teeth. Her eyes – green like a turbulent, storm-wracked sea – sparkled with fire and excitement in the chandelier-scattered light as she stared up at the fool with whom she was dancing, fully engrossed in the banality spewing forth from under his carefully maintained moustache.

Likewise, her entire demeanour spoke of absolute attentiveness to her dance partner. This alone spoke of impeccable breeding: clearly, she had been taught to dance properly, her movements unthinking and automatic. Only the highest noble ladies danced in that manner. And yet, he was not immediately familiar with who she was. Her body was neither slim, nor voluptuous, but just the right shape of curve and tautness to appeal to his tastes. The form-fitting, sleeveless crimson gown with an almost scandalously low neckline accentuated the curve of her hips, the slimness of her waist and the fullness of her breasts. The fabric was so sheer against her body that he could see this was not a woman who crammed herself into a corset; on the contrary, corsets were designed to emulate women such as this.

Her delicate fingers and hands were sheathed in gloves of the same colour and material, which insinuated themselves against her creamy flesh to past her elbows. Instantly arousing, this seemed to him more exciting than seeing her bare skin. The finishing touch, and the *pièce de résistance* to his mind – the blatant obscenity and perversion that flamed his desires even further – was the dark silk choker she wore, drawing focus to her long and shapely neck. A small metal object – a flower or star, or some such thing – hung from the front of the choker, bobbing and swaying rhythmically as she danced, just like the way that a woman's body moved during acts of passions.

No, he was no mere *starving animal*. He was, of course, still *a connoisseur*. And yet, he felt the animal rising within him. Base, clawing, salivating urges raced through his mind, threatening to overwhelm him, and his heart pounded, beyond lust or desire, to the cadence of an ancient, long-forgotten rhythm. How was not every eye in the room on this beauty? How was every man not paralysed by their primitive need to possess such a creature and draw gratification from it? Oh yes! This would be a glorious night. Truly, a night to remember. The hunt, the *true* hunt, was now on. By the end of the night—

Again, his thoughts were intruded upon. The grey fog receded, and rest of the room came back into focus as everything rushed in around him, and he found himself hyper-aware. In the periphery of his vision someone was approaching. It was the young woman in the teal gown with the raven hair and eyes like midnight. The brazen and shameless creature! She smiled at him shyly, betraying her nervousness. A thought penetrated the clouded hunger of his mind: an appetiser? Yes, why not? Something to get the juices flowing for the main course. Oh, what a glorious night indeed.

He turned his gaze on her, afire from the thoughts of his perfect prey, and smiled his most dashing smile.

<h1 style="text-align:center">One</h1>

<h1 style="text-align:center">An Offer</h1>

Shadwell, East London, 13 February, 1891

Richard Carnby stared off into the distance, lost in thought, the letter held lightly between his fingertips.

He had slept deeply after the revelries of the night before, and had awoken in a state of alarm. He was almost thankful that he had awoken alone, and that she was not still here. He had felt as though he had been caught napping, as it were. In actions that had seemed too graceful and fluid for such a stocky man, he had leapt up from his bed as he unconsciously checked that his weapon was loaded.

His small and degenerate second-floor rooms were most definitely empty, aside from the mean furniture that occupied the space. Moving silently, he had pressed himself against the wall and slid up to the window. Gently moving the tatty dark curtains no more than necessary, he had peered out into the pale light: the usual denizens of Spencer Street had been going about their business, such as it was: there were the urchins, those children who played in the street all hours of the day and night; the old mum who took in washing in order to eat; and that pretty flower girl – what was her name again? Not that she had much to sell this time of year as winter flowers were expensive. And a few others had been moving to and fro about their business, shivering, wrapped in tattered clothing that did little to protect them from the freezing cold.

Snow covered the narrow and dirty thoroughfare, and more was falling from a typical London sky, greyed by clouds and smoke. No one who would cause alarm had been on the street. Letting the curtain fall back in place, he had moved silently to the door. That was where he'd seen it, outlined against the dirty darkness of the floor was a rectangle, almost radiant in its whiteness. A letter. He'd ignored it at that moment and listened at the door, hearing only silence. Subtly, he'd checked the handle – good girl, he'd thought, she had locked it as she left.

Richard Carnby's first weapon of choice was a 'sawn-off' double-barrelled shotgun, which had had the stock and most of the barrel cut off, making it the size of a very large pistol. It was most devastating in close quarters. He'd opened the breach and checked the loaded shells before closing and cocking the weapon, oblivious of his earlier check. Holding the shotgun against his leg, he'd cracked the door open a fraction with his other hand and peered into the dark hallway. Nobody. Nothing. There had been no sound from the neighbouring rooms; his neighbours were either also resting off the night's follies, or they had, as usual, made their way through the pre-dawn haze to the crushing despair of the factories for but a pittance of a wage. He'd stuck his head out and peered around carefully, listening for the slightest noise: breathing, or the creak of a floorboard. Yet, again, he'd heard nothing. When he had finally been satisfied that he was alone, he'd quietly slipped back into the room and shut and locked the door.

Still ignoring the letter, he'd moved to the small dresser, de-cocking his weapon and placing it on the small, rickety table as he went. He'd knelt and pulled out the lowest, shortened drawer, and reached into the secret space in the back. His hand had closed around the bag, and he felt its shape and weight, and grunted in satisfaction. The loot was still there.

Replacing the drawer, he'd stood and cast his pale blue eyes around his meagre demesne: the bed, the table, the dresser, complete with a cracked wash basin and broken, cloudy mirror, a chair, a broken hat stand, and a small black stove, in which the fire was slowly flickering out. Finally feeling the cold through his scruffy and worn undergarments, Carnby had drawn his coat around him – being of little general means, he often donned his coat in the night for additional warmth – and moved to the stove. Opening the front, he'd grabbed a handful of wood with his meaty and powerful hands, and tossed it in, stoking it to feed the flames.

'Wood,' he'd snorted to himself; these were the remains of someone's chairs, bought and sold cheaply, no doubt to recover some debt. Likely, the former owner had died, perhaps from some misfortune such as consumption, or from not paying the rent.

Once the fire had been crackling to his satisfaction, Carnby had turned to the table. He'd run a hand through his dirty blond hair and rubbed his stubbly face. Creeping up on forty, Carnby felt his age, and then a few more years on top for good measure. His joints ached mercilessly, his muscles were cruelly stiff and his head was pounding like a carpenter's hammer. And he'd needed a drink, 'the hair of the dog,' and all that. Pouring cheap gin into a dirty glass, he'd slammed the drink down, and poured another, as he'd felt the hot fiery liquid burn through his insides, waking his body. He'd sniffed, coughed, and spat onto the floor, before gulping down the second. Pouring the third, he'd caught sight again of the white rectangle in the gloom.

He had turned to regard it. Richard Carnby had been expecting a visit. A visit from the Cable Street Boys. After he had 'politely' refused their offer a week ago, and 'politely' commented on their guv'ner's mating habits, he had been expecting – what the rich folks called – a 'social call'. But so far, they had not come. But someone had. And had caught him sleeping. Richard Carnby did not like to be caught sleeping. In his part of London, sometimes, if you failed to wake when you had to, you never woke again.

Still regarding the letter like some sort of bomb, he'd moved carefully and picked it up. Turning it over in his coarse hands, he'd seen that this was a quality envelope, which must have cost a fair penny. His name was written in fine handwriting on the front, with no return name or address on the back. A puzzle indeed. Returning to the table, he'd lit the small oil lamp that sat there, and taking a seat, he'd torn open the envelope and pulled out the letter. Turning it to the dim light of the lamp, he'd begun to read the fine handwriting. Richard Carnby *could* read; he had learned, but he'd still needed to read the words out aloud as he went.

'My Dear Mista Carnby,' he'd begun, and immediately grimaced at the contrast between his nasal Cockney drawl and the obviously educated way in which this letter had been written. In his mind, he could almost hear a proper gentleman speaking the words, but he could not reproduce the sound. He'd continued reading with a twinge of self-consciousness, despite being alone in the room.

'Allow me to begin by con-grachoo-la'in' yew on the foine manna in which yew comple'ed your last job.' An immediate sense of alarm had grown within Richard Carnby. He had been bloody careful, and he was sure he hadn't been seen. Had someone *blown* on him to the *Peelers*? But who knew? Unconsciously, his eyes had flicked to the bottom drawer of the dresser, as if the loot needed checking again. He'd continued reading:

'Please do not be alarmed Mista Carnby, Oi 'ave no desire to cawse yew any concern.' He'd paused a moment. 'Oh well then, that's bluddy all-roight then, i'nit?!' he'd muttered caustically.

'Oi ahssure yew, we do not—' he'd struggled with the next word, trying a couple of times, '—rep-reez-ent the police force, nor a 'ostile criminal organ-i-zay-shun. *So, 'oo th' blummin' 'ell are yew then?'*

'My asso-cee-yates were also most im-pressed wiv your last job. Yew 'andled yourself with great sub-tl-tea...*Subt-letea? Sub-tuh-letea?* and discre-shun.' *An' so Oi did! Well, discre-shun, any-way.* He wasn't too sure about this 'subtlety' business, but he'd guessed it meant something along the lines of discretion, or outright deviousness. 'In fact,' the letter continued, 'we 'av been wotchin' yew for sum toime now.' *'Av yew now, in-deed?'* His mind had raced, but nothing struck him as out of the ordinary. Whoever these people were, they were better and sneakier than he was, and apparently also half the East End. It had troubled him as how could these toffs be roaming the East End watching him, unless—? The thought had filled him with dread, and an almost overwhelming sense of paranoia had washed over him, making his hair stand on end. *Unless the people watching him were Eastenders.* Which meant—

He'd paused, not wanting to complete the thought. Which meant that they could be anybody – his neighbours, that pretty flower girl, or even those urchins who hung about the bloody street all bloody day – absolutely anybody could be a *blower*, an informant.

His first instinct had been to do a bolt, to grab his gear and run. But where would he go? If these people were as good as this letter suggested, they would be watching him now. They would know when he left, and where he went. And they clearly knew of his most recent job, meaning they could dob him in to the fuzz, or worse, to the Cable Street Boys.

At a loss for what else to do, he'd stared back at the letter. It went on: '…an' in-deed, this last piece of wurk 'as con-soli-day'ed…*wot?*…our desi-zhun: we are most keen to offa yew a job; we 'av need of a man wiv your skills and tal-ents, an' we pro-pose a sort of biz-ness par'-ner-ship.

'Oi must warn yew, there are sub-stan-shul risks, but a man ov your calibur must surely revel… *revel?*…in the challenge. *Revel mast be like, en-joy, or sumthin.* And the rewards are most ahssuredly com-men-syew-raite…*bluddy wot?*…to the dangers faced. There is a guaran'ee of on-going wurk, so in-come will be of no con-cern. *Th' Guv' 'as my atten-shun!*

'If this offa seems of interest to yew, please be at the address indica'ed at the bottom of this let'er, no lay'a than two o'clock to-morrow afta-noon.

'If yew choose to de-cline this offa, we will unda-stand from your non-atten-dance at the spe-, spekifaid…spesifaid?…*Wots this blummin' word?*…toime, and in that event we will trouble yew no furtha. In this case, all we ask is that yew de-stroy this let'er completely. Re-gards, A Po-ten-shul Fu-chur Friend.'

There was an address at the bottom for Belgrave Square, which was somewhere in the hoity-toity part of the West End as far as he could recall, and the symbol of a rose, coloured in silver at the bottom of the page. The rose was raised, and he could feel the bumps of the petals and the stem. There was a word for this, but it had escaped him. He knew, however, that this was expen-sive work; in fact, everything about this was expensive: the rose, the address, the paper, the envelope, even the language was ex-pensive. These people clearly operated on a whole other level than he was familiar with. Even a criminal gang like the Cable

Street Boys, who thought they ran Shadwell, were a minor outfit compared to this.

And that was how he found himself staring off into space. He noticed his gin going unloved, and gulped it down like the others, quickly pouring another to help himself think. *If* these people were on the level, then it seemed he could hope to make a fair quid out of this. If not? Well, who could say what would happen, but he would certainly go prepared…*if* he went.

That gin disappeared in an instant, and he poured his fifth. When he weighed up 'income will be of no concern,' against invariable, eventual starvation and freezing – and perhaps, not just for himself – it seemed a decided argument. But still, he hesitated: what would he be getting himself into? And if he got in, would he be able to get out again? Carnby was under no illusions that the people of his station in life were usually viewed by their social betters as tools, devices by which to fulfil their unsavoury needs, and then cast aside like filth. He felt an anger welling within him. It happened to the working girls around here every night: the toffs, the lords, they came down here and did things with and to these poor girls that they would never dare to suggest to their good lady wives, and once their shameful needs were satisfied, threw some coins at them, and left. And if that were the worst thing that happened to these girls, they could count themselves lucky. Not that men such as Carnby – burglars, *cracksmen* and the like – often fared much better when employed by those of higher standing. Depending on the circumstances, they often found themselves floating face down in the Thames, or worse, a guest of Her Majesty.

We're good, decent folk, he mused unhappily, *but when rich folk turned up and started talking sweet words and offering money, it usually ended with something bad happening to you in a dark alley…*

He thought of the recent Whitechapel murders and shivered. A wave of sorrow washed over him. 'Ah,' he sighed, 'Poor Liz; poor Annie. They was gud gurls. They was all gud gurls.' He raised his glass in a solemn toast, 'Oi 'ope their souls are at rest.' And the fifth gin went down the hatch. He poured another. Of course, it didn't matter that they were good girls; they were poor, so it had been allowed to happen.

As he pondered his options and the consequences of either accepting or refusing – both seemed rather bleak – the mystery of this offer intrigued him. *If Oi go*, he thought again, *Oi'll bluddy well go prepared.*

Two
Homecoming

Lambeth, 13 February, 1891

Everything about the return trip had been a shambles. Quite frankly, he was surprised to be sitting in a Hansom, rattling through London, and not at the bottom of the Atlantic Ocean.

Terrence Alexander 'Axel' Hastings was, much like his father, tall and handsome; standing at 6'1', he was broad-shouldered and trim waisted. At twenty-one years of age, everything about him spoke of physical fitness and a life of action. Even his long, elegant fingers were now hard and calloused. He had dark brown hair, neatly cut, and parted on one side for his return. Deep blue eyes regarded the world coolly and laconically from above a sharp, straight nose. His moustache was carefully trimmed and styled in one of the several current fashions. The dirty and scraggly beard he had worn for so long was now gone, revealing a strong, square jaw, which framed a dashing smile.

His looks, particularly his height, were no doubt due to the distant Viking influence in his family that no one willingly discussed.

Two and a half years, he thought. And even though everything looked different, it still looked the same. Some things never change. And perhaps, he hoped, some things do.

When his father had passed six years ago, his eldest brother Warner had – according to the mandates of primogeniture – naturally stepped into the role of fifteenth Earl of Huntingdon. Warner, himself still a young man of seventeen at the time, had set about establishing himself as the patriarch of the family. Invariably, they had clashed. Repeatedly. It wasn't so bad while Axel had been at school, but whenever he'd returned home, it was...uncomfortable...to say the least.

He remembered that summer, in 1888. Axel had stormed into his rooms, pulled out that old valise, and packed. Something Warner had said in their last argument rankled with him. 'What exactly *do* you know about the world, Axel? After all, you're just a boy. You've not experienced anything of life! So, I'll thank you to refrain from commenting on matters you could not possibly grasp!'

It didn't matter that Warner was scarcely two years older than him; the incumbent responsibilities of their family title meant that he had been compelled to grow up and deal with worldly matters all too fast. It rankled because, of course, thanks to this necessity, Warner was right. Now, with the perspective of hindsight, there was naturally nothing to their arguments but for the friction of two strong-willed young men growing up and butting heads. But at the time, it had been the end of the world! Determined to resolve this knowledge deficiency and prove Warner wrong, and despite the heartfelt entreaties of his mother, Mary, and his younger sisters, Evelyn and Katherine, he had found himself on a steamship, and much like his repudiated forebears, on a voyage of discovery to the New World.

He had floated around New York, Boston, Philadelphia and Washington for some time, but these places reminded him too much of London and Paris, albeit with their own distinct flavours. Looking for something more, in the late autumn of that year, he had taken a commission from the nascent so-called 'National Geographic Society', where some insightful person had foreseen the inevitable destruction of the various Native American cultures and deemed it important to catalogue their traditions.

So he had found himself, simply known as 'Axel Hanson', on a train to St Louis, and then on various dusty 'stagecoaches' travelling to the heart of the west, where he'd met up with a photographer named Grabill.

The next two years had been spent in remote border towns, and amongst those tribes of the natives with whom they were able to negotiate a peaceful welcome.

At the fringes of civilisation, the rule of law held little sway; life was cheap, and fraught with danger. Mr Darwin's recent contentions seemed apt: the quick, strong and smart were the ones who were rewarded with survival, while the others...were not so lucky.

He had come to learn that life was most often indifferent, and far too often, unjust. And so, he had become proficient with the American style of shooting, taking to the renowned Winchester repeating rifle, and the Colt 'Peacemaker' pistol, as made notorious by the so-called 'cowboys' and others. Many times over, the fact that he was still alive today came down to the reliability and stopping-power of his Winchester and Colt. Even now, he had brought them with him on his return – along with his large 'Bowie' knife – unwilling to part with what had for so long been necessities of basic survival.

All the while, the native people were indeed being driven to seeming extinction. The insatiable need for land; the same colonial desire for conquest that drove his own great empire, drove the white man ever north and west – and the red man ever closer to the verge of oblivion. Though they fought back bravely, Axel could see the inevitability of superior numbers, training and firearms.

Axel remembered the end all too well. In the December of 1890, he and Grabill had found themselves in the infant South Dakota, travelling with Chief Spotted Elk of the Lakota, as well as the Medicine Man, Black Elk, amongst others. The chief and his people were travelling to Pine Ridge to answer some official summons, and Axel and Grabill had planned to take leave there of the Indians.

Despite there being tensions, having approached the tribe respectfully, neither he nor Grabill had ever encountered hostility, and he was sad to be leaving these ingenuous and warm people.

Just before the new year, their group had been intercepted by cavalry near Porcupine Butte. He remembered a sense of unease and foreboding when he'd learned that these were the 7th Cavalry – the same men who had been involved in the Black Foot debacle, and the regiment to which Custer had belonged.

Instead of being allowed to continue to Pine Ridge, the group had been redirected to Wounded Knee Creek and ordered to encamp. By expectation, he and Grabill – they were white men – were *forced* to join the cavalry camp.

The next day...the next day... The next day still haunted him.

The day after the next day, he had parted company with Grabill. Axel had then found himself heartsick and alone. He could see all too clearly the future of this country, and the directions in which it was headed. Not that his indictment of America was unique; it was something universal to man, and his own supposedly 'great' empire was guilty of much the same. And much worse.

He'd realised he was no longer the bright-eyed and naïve boy who had come west in 1888, looking for experience in life. He had it now. Far too much of it.

A month later, by the end of January this year, he had been back in New York, boarding a steamer to Liverpool. He had wired his family, and the response he'd received – from Warner, no less – was warm and favourable. Shaved, trimmed and neatly dressed, he'd felt like a new man – a gentleman – for the first time in far too long.

The return trip was supposed to take a little under a week. It didn't. After the second day, they'd hit a fierce North Atlantic winter storm. Their ship had been tossed about in massive waves, and was driven alarmingly close to titanic drifting icebergs. Axel remembered an acute sense of dread every time one of those frozen monoliths heaved into sight between the wildly bucking waves. It was only thanks to the admirable seamanship of the captain and crew that they were not driven head-first into one and pulverised.

It had struck Axel that misfortune, in the shape of an unyielding mountain of ice, would one day catch up with some unlucky vessel and its passengers, and as a result, many lives would be lost. As it was, finally, even their valiant little steamer ran out of luck, for the most insidious aspect of these floating behemoths was that a portion of them remained unseen below the surface. On one particularly close shave, the steamer's port propeller had struck one such portion, suffering substantial damage.

Reduced to a fraction of their full speed, the captain had been forced to veer sharply southward to escape the fury of the storm. Frustratingly, they'd had to detour as far as France, limping finally into Calais. There was a palpable sense of relief amongst the passengers, which frankly, Axel had shared; though, while most were happy to have a few days of solid ground beneath their feet, he'd found himself restless. The weather had still been poor; there was, of course, fog on the channel, meaning he could not look across and see his homeland. Cabling home to apprise of the current situation, he'd booked a ticket on the next day's channel ferry, not wanting to delay any longer.

The ferry trip had been thankfully uneventful, as was the train from Dover to Waterloo Station. However, he had been alarmed to find a messenger awaiting him at the station when he arrived. He'd feared some grave news from Warner, but was puzzled to be handed a letter addressed to him in name only, and written in a fine hand. There was no return name or address, and the messenger was, of course, no use.

Half an hour later, on his way to The Savoy to take a room, he reread the letter in the dim light of the Hansom:

13 February 1891

My Dear Mr Hastings,

We are most pleased at your safe return to our shores. Let me begin by expressing my condolences on the passing of your late father; I had the great pleasure of working with him on various matters, and I know from first-hand experience he was truly a fine man.

I understand that your elder brother, Warner, is acquitting himself in his duties as the current Earl of Huntingdon admirably. You should take comfort in the knowledge that your family seat is in good hands.

I can only imagine the emotions of being home after two years in the 'Wild West' of America. London must seem a vastly different place. I am most keen to hear a first-hand account of your adventures in that great and untamed land. In fact, my associates and I have been following your adventures for some time now; and indeed, you have shown yourself to be a man of considerable courage, resource and aplomb. As such we are most keen to make you an offer: we have need of a man with your skills and talents, and we propose a sort of partnership.

I must warn you, there are substantial risks, but a man of your calibre must surely revel in the challenge. The rewards of forgotten lore, and artefacts long lost, are most assuredly commensurate to the dangers faced.

I, of course, understand that a man in your position has little concern for the trivialities of finances, but you may draw comfort to know that income will be of no concern.

If this offer seems of interest to you, please be at the address indicated at the bottom of this letter no later than 2 o'clock tomorrow afternoon. If you choose to decline this offer, we will understand from your non-attendance at the specified time, and in that event, we will trouble you no further. In this case, all we ask is that you destroy this letter completely.

Regards,

A Potential Future Friend, 30 Belgrave Square

The writing spanned two pages, and at the bottom of each was embossed a rose, finished in silver-grey.

There were several troubling things about this letter, with no return details being only the first. These people knew an alarming amount of information about him, or at least appeared to know. While it was reasonable that others had come to learn of the diversion of the sea route, he alone had decided to continue travelling, and he had only wired Warner with the details, in any case. And yet, this letter was dated today, and was waiting for him at the station.

Then there was the implication about his interest in archaeology. It was, as yet, an interest; he hadn't formally studied it for there to be a record. Of course, Axel had spoken about it with friends, but that in itself implied a disturbing degree of intimate access.

He stared out the Hansom window at the people moving in the falling snow: the rich, comfortably nestled in luxurious winter attire, moving at ease; the poor wrapped as best as possible, scurrying, shivering. He turned back to the letter; the paper was white like the falling snow, very good quality. He sniffed it quickly. There was a trace of cigar smoke, scotch, and something else, familiar but elusive. The penmanship and the language used suggested a well-educated writer.

Finally, the address: Belgravia. That in itself spoke volumes. It spoke of affluence and means open only to the privileged few of society. He knew the area well, though he had never visited regularly. Thinking back, he seemed to recall that the French ambassador had a residence in the area, at Belgrave Square, specifically. Also, he vaguely remembered that one of the townhouses had recently – well, not long before he left in 1888 – sold for nearly £8,000!

He pulled his Colt from his club bag and turned it over, watching the pale light glint dully off the barrel. Once, not long ago, this had seemed to be the universal solution to all of life's problems. He worked the empty cylinder. But one could not go around shooting off a pistol in the West End of London; it just wasn't done.

And yet, the people behind this letter indicated a level of power that could be dangerous, and he wasn't going to ignore that, particularly given the level of familiarity with him that they showed. Axel slipped the revolver back into his bag and leaned back to take in the sights of dirty, crowded old London.

If they thought he would come unarmed, they were surely mistaken. And, if, as they claimed, they knew of his 'adventures' in America, it was folly for them to underestimate his capabilities.

Three
Belgrave Square

Belgravia, 14 February, 1891

Richard Carnby felt terribly conspicuous standing on the snowy south corner of Belgrave Square. In his drab, dark grey attire, with his common cap and coat, he thought he looked like a dirty soot stain, besmirching the pristine white façades of the town-houses. Snow was piled into neat rows, having been shovelled aside. The road and pavement were clean, wide and spacious, and worst of all, there were no shadows. Shadows were safety; light and open spaces were exposure and almost invariably, danger and capture – a lesson he had learned all too well in his criminal endeavours across the East End of London. The shadows had often been the very difference between life and death.

He was filled with apprehension as he peered across the bare trees in the Square's central park at all the townhouses and all the windows. Dozens and dozens of windows. Too many windows. All looking down at him. Watching him.

He could turn back, but these people who had 'invited' him no doubt already knew he was here. Still, coming to Belgrave Square had given him an excuse to try something he had wanted to experience for some time now: the railway system. He had little call to take it anywhere normally, but seeing as he currently had a little spending money...

Getting on at the conveniently located Shadwell Station, he'd travelled to the current end of the line at Fenchurch. Bypassing Cannon Street, he'd made for Mansion House, there boarding the District Line direct to Victoria Station – the nearest to Belgrave Square.

Despite having consulted his Bacon's Map, he had gotten turned around at Chester Square. Forced to ask a Bobby for directions, he'd gotten a strange look until he'd lied about seeking a position as a household servant. Set on the right path, he'd soon arrived at his destination.

He now trudged north-east along the southern row of the Square. The toffs who inhabited this area paid him little or no mind, presuming him to be from below stairs. For his part, he bowed his head deferentially whenever he passed these hoity-toity folk.

Two white stucco pillars supporting a porch framed the door of Number 30. After a moment's hesitation, he stepped up and rang the doorbell.

Presently, a distinguished silver-haired butler answered. Taking one look at Carnby, he stated, 'The servant's entry is to your left.' Indicating the stairs down, he began to close the door.

'No...' Carnby called, giving pause to the door closure. 'Oi...er...Oi was invoi'ed.'

The butler regarded him a moment in silence, then spoke, 'Have you a document, sir?'

Sir? Carnby thought. *What's all this then?* He drew out the letter from his inside coat pocket and hesitantly handed it to the butler.

Casting an eye over it, the butler opened the door and invited, 'Do come in, sir.'

Carnby entered and found himself in a rectangular hall, in warm dark colours, populated with a heavy mahogany table and a plant in a pot. Carnby saw that there was a fireplace in the hall; not a stove, but a proper built-in fireplace. In the hall. *Bloody hell.*

The butler was speaking, 'Your hat and coat, sir?'

Carnby doffed his cap quickly – even he knew that was bad manners – but almost panicked about the coat. He couldn't take that off. One look at all the hardware strapped to his body underneath it, and they would have him arrested on the spot! 'Er...Oi'd rather not...'

The butler regarded him again. 'As you wish, sir.' He took Carnby's hat and went into an adjoining room opposite the front door, then returned in a moment without it.

Carnby took the opportunity to regard the area: this entry area – or whatever it was – was almost as big as his entire Spencer Street flat! Was it any wonder the rich looked down on the lower classes?

'This way, if you please, sir.' The butler led him through a small hallway into a cavernous open area dominated by a staircase that began opposite the passage he had just passed through, and then followed the right-hand wall up, before turning back on itself. Through the large open area in the middle, he could see that it went up several floors, ending in a roof made of glass, to let in the light, such as it was. *Blood-y-hell!* Carnby thought.

The butler led him to the stairs and began to ascend. They passed a door to the right; Carnby glanced in and saw rows and rows of books. The number of books was mind-boggling. It could keep a family in his neighbourhood in warmth for probably two years. He caught a trace of perfume – heavy with flowers he could not name – wafting from within, and tried to get a glance at the owner of the heady scent, but saw no one from his perspective.

Continuing up the stairs, they came to a large landing leading off in three directions. They turned left, towards the front of the house, and came to white double doors, which the butler opened, ushering him in.

Carnby found himself in a vast room, populated with large, soft-looking settees, armchairs, side-tables and lamps. The room was finished in bright airy shades like beige and cream; the up-holstery in shades slightly darker, to complement, with dark tables for contrast. There were more books here, and *two* more fireplaces, on opposite walls, both lit. *Must be a bastard to clean,* he thought, as the room was spotless. *Blood-y-blood-y-hell, these people were rich!*

'Please make yourself comfortable, sir. Lord Renfield will not be long.' He paused. 'Would sir desire some refreshment?'

'Er..?' Carnby replied. He wasn't even sure he understood the question.

'Would sir like some tea?' The butler asked; but clearly seeing that was not to Carnby's taste, he continued, 'Or scotch?'

Scotch? Whisky? Stone-the-crows, these toffs lived well. And it was probably the good stuff too. 'Er...yes...' he replied slowly. 'Scotch would be vury noice, thank yew.'

The butler bowed and exited, closing the door behind him.

Carnby walked to the middle of the three massive windows opposite the double doors. As he approached, he realised they weren't windows, but doors themselves, opening onto a narrow balcony that looked out onto the Square.

Lord Renfield? So that was the name of his 'potential future friend,' then?

He studied the room. Even the knick-knacks sitting on the side-tables and mantles were very expensive. He thought briefly about pinching a few, but resisted the temptation.

The butler returned in a few moments, carrying a silver tray with three bottles and several glasses. Was he supposed to use another glass every time? He wasn't sure.

Placing the tray on a side-table, he asked, 'Would sir like water or soda?'

Carnby was at a loss. 'Er...jast playn, thank yew...'

The butler poured a straight scotch without missing a beat. Carnby noticed he only filled the glass part way. *Must be running out,* he thought. He was then presented the glass on a tray. 'Would sir like anything else?'

'No. Thank yew.' Carnby had no idea whether he was saying or doing the right thing, but he guessed – that is, he *hoped* – basic politeness would be acceptable.

The butler seemed unfazed by anything he said. At that moment, there was a distant ring drawing his attention. 'Please excuse me, sir. Do make yourself comfortable,' he repeated, gesturing to the seats. Giving a slight bow, he departed.

Carnby looked at the drink in his hand and gulped it down, reeling from its heady fire. Quickly making his way to the side-table, he poured himself another, larger drink, and gulped that one down as well. *Better get some before it's all gone.* He looked at the other bottles – one was clearly just plain water, but the other was an odd hourglass-shaped thing with a wicker mesh and top on it like a water fountain. He was about to examine it when he heard footsteps from outside. Quickly pouring a third drink, this time to the same low level as he had received, he hurried to an armchair in the front corner of the room that faced the door and sat down, feigning ease.

Axel arrived at 30 Belgrave Square with little fuss. He was dressed in a coat, morning suit, top hat, vest and trousers all grey in colour, with a white shirt, grey tie and black shoes. Ringing the doorbell, he was greeted by a silver-haired butler in austere black and stiff, starched whites. 'How may I help you, sir?'

'I received an invitation,' he replied, 'requesting my presence at this address, today, at this time.'

'Ah, yes sir. Do you have the document?'

Axel presented him with the letter. After glancing at it, the butler stepped aside, 'Do come in, sir.'

His top hat and coat were taken to the cloak room, and Axel was led through a lobby into a large staircase hall and towards the stairs. There was a lingering scent of perfume, heady and cloying, though not overwhelming, as though a lady had just passed through. It was a delightful, almost hedonistic scent, redolent of flowers – the names of which escaped him – that made him want to linger, just to take more in. He glanced about for the lady, but saw no one.

They ascended a flight of stairs; Axel looked up the spacious stairwell, beyond three floors above ground, to a great skylight that was doing its best to serve its purpose under the leaden sky. *The top floor must only be accessible by the back stairs,* he thought.

The butler led him to the first-floor front drawing room, and ushered him in. There was a man – seemingly of the working classes – still wearing an overcoat, tucked into an armchair with a glass of scotch in his hand.

'Lord Renfield shall attend you presently,' the butler was saying. 'Would sir like a refreshment while waiting?'

Axel glanced at the bottles on the side-table. 'Scotch will be fine, thank you.'

The butler nodded and moved to oblige, 'How does sir take it? Water, soda or neat?'

'Soda.'

Quickly preparing the drink, the butler offered it to him, and excused himself, parting with, 'If sirs require anything else, please ring.' He closed the door as he left, leaving them alone.

Axel regarded the other man present, and met his cool, appraising pale blue eyes. He moved across the room and feigned interest in a periodical on a side-table. The other man continued to observe him attentively. He was a few inches shorter than Axel, and stockily built. Though dressed as a commoner, Axel had no doubt that there was nothing 'common' about this man: he didn't miss a thing. Having spent enough time sizing up other men in order to determine the degree of threat they posed, Axel knew well enough what he was seeing. Beneath the coat that he wrapped around himself defensively, this man was armed to the teeth. '*Si vis pacem, para bellum*,' he said at last, looking at Carnby.

'Beg' par-dun, sir?'

'Do forgive me, please,' he said sincerely. 'It's Latin, from Renatus' "*De Re Militari*". It means, "If you seek peace, prepare for war".'

'Oi see,' Carnby replied blankly. 'Oi must'a missed readin' that one, sir.'

Despite himself, a smile crept across Axel's face; there was something immediately likeable about this man's gruff defensiveness. 'As in, sir,' he explained, 'You must clearly be seeking peace, from the look of you.'

Carnby studied him carefully for a moment, and nodded. 'Yew seem t' be quoite well pre-pared your-self, sir.'

Axel became very conscious of the heft and bulk of his own revolver in its holster under his arm as he strolled to the window and looked out onto the snowy square, sipping his scotch. He smiled. *Not common at all.* He looked back to the other man. 'I merely come prepared for unknown circumstances; you sir, appear to have come prepared for the line-of-battle.'

Carnby grinned. 'My fatha taught me t' always be pre-pared for *any* cir-cum-stances!'

Laughing, Axel replied, 'Yes, my father taught me much the same thing.' He indeed liked this man. He walked over and held out his hand. 'Hastings. Terrence Hastings. But please, call me Axel.'

The man rose quickly and took his hand. 'Carnby,' he replied, 'Richard Carnby. But please don' call me Dick!' He gave an impertinent smile.

Axel burst into laughter.

'That's a good 'an'shayke yew got there. Yew dun sum 'ard graft, ay?'

'Graft?' Axel was confused.

'Oh.' Embarrassment and hesitation crossed the other man's face. 'Er…yew wurk'd 'ard, ay?'

'Oh! Yes, I spent quite some time in…er…the wilderness.' He saw the approval in Carnby's face. 'I take it you were "invited" also?'

They moved to the end window and took in the snowy scene. Carnby nodded, 'This Lord Renfield…'e's a friend 'a yours?'

Axel shook his head, 'Don't know the man. His name doesn't ring any bells either. Do you know him?'

'Oh yesss!' Carnby exaggerated. 'We tayke lunch at th' Savoy most days!'

Axel smirked. 'No doubt with Her Majesty and the Home Secretary, as well?'

Carnby made a face suggesting such an event was a mere trifle.

It really was rather hard to escape Carnby's roguish charm. Though, Axel was under no illusions of what this man was likely capable.

The door opened then, giving pause to the conversation. The butler led in two more men, and before Axel could wonder if one of these was the mysterious Lord Renfield, he gave these two the same message of the lord's impending arrival.

One man was of a height with Axel, well dressed in much the same manner as the young nobleman: morning suit, vest, tie, trousers, but all done in light shades – beige, light grey, a mustard tie and brown shoes. He had about him the easy manner only the very affluent possess. Axel judged him to be about thirty, and he had light brown eyes, flaxen hair parted to one side, and a rather long and stylish moustache. His pale skin substantiated his life of ease, and while Axel's body was powerful, his was lithe and graceful. He moved with a fluidity akin to that Axel had witnessed in his brief observation of Carnby. His face was longer than Axel's, the jaw less square, though he was still very handsome; his smile was disarming, and his manner affable in general. He carried a rather finely crafted black cane with a silver handle, fashioned into a shape resembling a lion's paw. No doubt as an accessory, rather than as a necessity.

The other, Axel noted, was far more dour and conservative. Very short dark hair, and a neat 'short boxed' beard outlined a round face, accentuated with an aquiline nose and furrowed, brown eyes framed with round horn-rimmed spectacles. He was dressed in brown trousers with black pinstripes and a black morning suit; his ascot tie was also black. Though the attire was seemingly clerical, it was obvious to Axel that the cut and material indicated substantial wealth. This man was a professional of some sort, Axel thought; a lawyer or doctor perhaps. Certainly someone with a no-nonsense academic bent, and an attitude created by a life of entitlement. This man appeared to be in his late thirties or early forties.

The butler was enquiring about refreshments.

The tall man glanced at Axel and Carnby holding their scotches, and said, 'Scotch seems to be the order of the day; scotch and water, there's a good fellow!'

His diction and casual manner with staff cemented it for Axel: this was undeniably a man accustomed to comfort and being waited-upon.

The dour man, without so much as glancing at the room replied curtly, 'I take tea at this time. Black. No sugar.'

This is the one that is going to be difficult, Axel thought. Aside from knowing people like this his whole life, he had met several such men in the cities along the eastern American seaboard. They occasionally seemed to find their way west. When they did, they never lasted long. Axel sighed internally, reminding himself he was in Belgravia now, and not Denver or Salt Lake City.

The butler bowed deferentially, and after providing a scotch to the tall one, departed the room.

The tall man strolled over in a jaunty manner and offered his hand to Axel. 'Percival Wallace.'

Taking the offered hand, he replied, 'Terrence Hastings. But call me Axel.'

'By all means!' He smiled. 'And do call me "Percy", old chap!'

Axel gestured to Carnby. 'And this is Richard Carnby.'

He noticed that Percy did not offer Carnby a hand, though he did smile charmingly and nod. Carnby gave a slight bow. 'Truly a ple-zhure, your lawd-ship.'

'Oh, I'm no lord!' Percy replied showing surprise.

Liar, thought Axel, though he remained silent. He could see immediately that Carnby did not believe that claim either, though he smiled and gave another short bow.

Axel turned to the dour man, who was slowing approaching the trio. 'And who might you be, sir?' he asked, offering his hand.

The dour man shook his hand perfunctorily. 'Doctor Stanthorpe Cunningham Whitehall the Third. Doctor Whitehall will suffice.'

'A pleasure, sir,' Axel replied graciously, ignoring the ill-mannered answer. 'And I am Terr—.'

'Yes, yes,' Whitehall interrupted irritably, 'Hastings; and you may be called "Axel". And this is Percy,' he summarised, shaking hands with Percy. He ignored Carnby.

'And Oi'm Richard Carnby!' Carnby added, impertinently.

Whitehall made an exasperated noise and rolled his eyes, turning away and moving to find a seat.

Axel cringed internally and met Percy's gaze; the other man's expression matched exactly what Axel was thinking.

Axel saw the expression of intense irritation plastered across Carnby's face. He quickly stepped in front of the man to prevent any rash words or actions. Talking rather loudly, he addressed the other man, 'I see you've emptied your scotch, Mr Carnby. Allow me to get you another!' Taking the still-full glass from Carnby, he made his way across the room and filled it to a double and returned. Handing it to Carnby, Axel gave him a meaningful look in the eye and a quick shake of the head.

Carnby regarded him in silence. Clearly swallowing his pride with a gulp of scotch, he nodded grimly.

Percy took a seat and gestured to Carnby. 'Please, Mr Carnby, do sit down.'

'Thank yew, sir,' he replied, and obliged, sinking into an armchair.

'Where the devil is that man with my tea?' Whitehall grumbled. Turning to the others, he asked, 'Do you fellows know why we've been invited here?'

The group looked at each other and shrugged. 'This mysterious "Lord Renfield" is obviously the key to it all,' Percy offered.

'Well, he certainly likes to keep people waiting.' Whitehall drummed his fingers impatiently on the arm of his seat.

Axel sat back in the sofa. 'Perhaps there are other invitees we are waiting on?'

Ignoring him, Whitehall continued in his lamentation. 'It really just isn't good form! One must be punctual in all matters! I see the attitude has filtered down through the household. *Where is this man with my tea*?'

Percy began, 'Come now, man. I'm sure—'

'A lax and unpunctual master will invariably instil such habits in his staff!'

Percy rolled his eyes and lounged back as well. Twirling his cane casually between his fingers, he turned to Axel and Carnby. 'Still, rather a lark, eh what? Sounds like a jolly interesting mystery to me.'

'Oi unda-stood this to be a job of sorts,' Carnby offered, but the other two men shrugged again. Axel, at least, was just as uncertain as he was. He didn't bother looking to the doctor for a response.

The men had fallen into a moment of silent contemplation when the door again opened.

'Ah!' Whitehall began, turning to the door. 'Here's that man with my—'

But none of the other men were now paying any attention to the silver-haired butler making his way across the room with tea on a tray. They were all transfixed by the captivating and alluring woman making her way towards them.

Four
Answers

She had vibrant red hair, worn in the fashionable 'Gibson Girl' style, pale creamy skin, full cheeks and large sea-green eyes that were dizzying to stare at. Her sensual lips were drawn back revealing a dazzling smile of perfect white teeth.

Axel couldn't help but stare. He guessed her to be in her mid-twenties – but with ladies, how could one tell for sure? Her dress was the same shade as the blue in a peacock's feathers, and revealed a curvaceous outline to her figure. The heady, hedonistic perfume he had smelt earlier flooded the room, emanating from her like radiance from the sun. While she did not meet the traditional Victorian ideal of beauty, everything about her spoke of alluring oceans of reckless danger. There was something primal about her and her beauty; something that fired the most primitive urges of lust within him. Combined with her cloying perfume, he was taken back to dark, windy prairies and pine-scented hunting grounds, tribal songs and the long-forgotten hidden heartbeats of the earth, which most white men no longer heard.

The way she moved as she crossed the room was undeniably licentious, almost bordering on the obscene. But, Axel noted, there was something else: she didn't walk so much as *stalk*. It was subtle, well hidden, but it was there. He had seen Native American hunters move like this while tracking prey, so recognised it. But he had never seen a *woman* anywhere move like that.

Axel and Percy were out of their seats in an instant. Carnby hurried to follow them, while Whitehall grudgingly peeled himself out of his chair.

She approached the men and spoke, her voice rich and yet light, melodic and lilting like a song. 'I do apologise for the wait, gentlemen. I understand our host Lord Renfield's carriage has just arrived. I imagine he will join us shortly.' Offering her hand to the first in line, Whitehall, she continued, 'Please allow me to introduce myself. I am Emma Westover.'

Whitehall took her hand perfunctorily. 'Doctor Whitehall. Charmed,' he muttered, before dropping back into his chair to focus on his steaming tea.

Percy, staring into her eyes wolfishly, took her hand and kissed it. '*More* than charmed.' He smiled rakishly. 'Delighted to meet you, Miss Westover. Percival Wallace, but please, do call me Percy.'

She smiled up at him, her eyes shining with flirtatious excitement. 'A delight, I'm sure, Mr Wallace!'

Emma moved on to Axel, who took her hand warmly. 'A pleasure, Miss Westover,' he said formally. 'I'm Terrence Hastings, but call me Axel.'

'Axel?' she asked, 'Is that Nordic? Or Germanic?'

Intrigued, given his ancestry, he replied, 'No, why do you ask?'

'Oh, I knew a professor a few years ago in Hamburg who had a nephew named Axel, so it struck a chord.'

Axel laughed. 'No, unfortunately nothing that exciting, merely a nickname!'

'Nonetheless, a pleasure to meet you, Axel.'

She moved to Carnby. 'And who might you be, sir?'

He took her hand gingerly but awkwardly. 'Oh, Oi'm no "sir", my laydy. Jast your 'umble sur-vant, Richard Carnby.'

'Well, it's a pleasure to meet you, Mr Carnby.' She turned to the group. 'Excuse me a moment, gentlemen, but I need a drink.'

Both Percy and Axel moved to oblige, but she had already stalked to the side-table. They watched her pour a neat scotch, and turning, gulp it conspicuously.

Axel was unfazed. He had seen far more direct behaviour by women in America, though it amused him to see Percy's nonplussed reaction. Miss Westover's behaviour certainly was not at all *ladylike*!

She poured another. As she moved back to the group of men, the door again opened.

The man who now came into the room was tall and distinguished. Dressed in severe professional blacks, he was middle-aged, bald, except for a ring of hair running from temple to temple across the back of his head, which was brown tinged with white. He had a lean, commanding, clean-shaven face, with dark brown eyes, a strong nose and square jaw. Axel noted that even though he was dressed as a professional, his skin was tanned and weathered, suggesting either an ex-military man or a life spent mostly outdoors, adventuring.

He addressed the gathered individuals. 'Ah! Excellent. You are all here. Delightful!'

The people in the room turned to him.

He continued, 'Please allow me to introduce myself. I am Ernest Oscar Renfield, and I am most pleased that you decided to accept my invitation. No doubt you have many questions—' He paused, scanning the room. 'Hmm, I see we have one missing.'

He turned to the silver-haired butler, 'Hargraves, has Burton not returned as yet?'

'Not to my knowledge, my lord,' came the dry reply.

Lord Renfield raised an eyebrow. 'Odd.' He paused a moment. 'I'm sure he's on his way.' He seemed to be speaking more to himself than anyone else. Turning back to the group, he stated, 'Do forgive me. Where was I? Ah, yes... questions! I believe we should begin.'

Starting with Whitehall, who was most central, he moved through the group, talking constantly, shaking hands with each member, not waiting for a reply. 'My dear Doctor Whitehall! I hope your parents are *well*? Mr Wallace, we are *honoured* to have you with us today! The brave, young Mr Hastings! I *am* pleased your voyage was a safe one. Ah, the most *capable* Mr Carnby. A pleasure sir!'

He turned to the only lady in the room. 'My dear Miss Westover!' Moving to her, he took her hands in his and kissed her waiting cheek. She smiled warmly. 'I trust your stay has been comfortable? Have all your needs been met?'

'Oh yes, Lord Renfield. Hargraves and Mrs Mainwaring have been most courteous and accommodating.'

'Good. Good,' he stated, almost dismissively. Glancing around, Renfield continued. 'Does everyone have sufficient refreshment? Excellent.' Turning to the butler, he said, 'Thank you, Hargraves. That will be all. Please ensure our final guest is sent up the moment Burton returns.'

The butler bowed silently and quickly exited the room.

'Please,' Lord Renfield began, 'Do sit down and make yourselves comfortable.' He gestured to the seats. Everyone sat.

'My colleagues and I are part of an organisation named *The Order of the Steel Rose*. We have been so for a number of years, and we now find ourselves becoming a little too...worn out...to continue our activities with the gusto of younger men. We have therefore taken to overseeing affairs, and we seek a new generation of brave people to take up ranks on our front lines.

'I imagine you are wondering *what* exactly we do?' He paused, as if considering his words. 'There are, in the world, forces of...*darkness*. Evil that seeks to undermine all that is good. What we do, put simply, is combat this evil.

'After careful consideration, we have chosen you good people for your various skills. You each have capabilities that will prove useful in the fight—'

Whitehall interrupted. 'You mean we are to kill people? I am a doctor, sir!' He sat up even more upright than he had been, and stuck his chin out in righteous indignation. 'It goes against every oath I have sworn, to take lives. My duty is to save them!'

Renfield regarded Whitehall a moment, a slight enigmatic smile playing on his lips. 'Indeed, sir!' he replied at last. 'Which is precisely why we have chosen you. There will no doubt be casualties, and for that we require the foremost surgeon and physician of our time.'

Whitehall beamed, seemingly mollified. 'Well then, sir, please do continue.'

Renfield gave a slight bow. 'Thank you, my dear Doctor. No, we do not expect you to "kill people" as you put it. There are others we have invited for such purposes.'

The group glanced at each other quickly, trying to identify the murderer in their midst.

Axel wanted nothing more than to squirm and interrupt, but he maintained his composure. *If this is what these people think of me...they certainly have the wrong impression.*

Renfield continued. 'We value subtlety and discretion in our activities, and perhaps I should take a moment to identify what skills make each of you ideal for our purposes.'

There was a knock at the door at that moment. 'Oh, what now?' Renfield muttered. 'Yes?' he called loudly.

The door opened and a tall, swarthy man with dark hair stepped in part way. He was dressed in a common grey suit and held a cap in his hands.

'Ah!' Renfield exclaimed. 'Do excuse me a moment.' He walked to the waiting man.

Axel noticed the man wore a lapel pin matching the grey rose embossed on the bottom of the letter he had received. Renfield and the man whispered together. Out of the corner of his eye, he saw Miss Westover cock her head slightly at a certain point, as if she had heard something of interest. How that was possible was beyond his guessing. He turned his attention to her. She maintained the head cock a moment, before returning to her original posture. Glancing at the others in the room, she met eyes with Axel before quickly looking away. The others were watching the interaction between Renfield and the man, and none seemed to have spotted Miss Westover's behaviour. *Interesting*, Axel thought.

Axel turned back as Renfield nodded, and the man went out. He gestured to someone outside the door, and an attractive young lady walked in. She was of a height with Miss Westover – about five-foot-six – but there the similarities ended. The young lady had raven-black hair tied in a modest bun. Her eyes were big and dark like the colour of ebony wood, and glanced shyly around the room. Her entire demeanour was subdued. She had a small nose and demure, ladylike mouth, high cheekbones and a strong yet feminine jawline. She was dressed all in muted blacks, in a conservative cut, with no jewellery. *A dress of mourning, no doubt,* Axel thought. *For whom?*

The men all rose, as was customary. Miss Westover of course remained seated.

Axel was immediately taken by her for reasons he could not explain. She was undeniably beautiful, but there was something sweet and delicate about her that he found compelling.

He glanced around at the others. Carnby was regarding her much as he had Axel. Dr Whitehall was not remotely curious. Percy examined her, then turned away, disinterested. Miss Westover was regarding the young lady with the cool look of appraisal women gave other women. Axel sighed internally. More problems. He had seen this sort of thing before. One woman was fine. Then a second was introduced and something about the second threatened the first. Or vice-versa. And then the problems started. Between Dr Whitehall and Carnby, and this, he felt exceptionally exasperated. But he maintained his composure.

Renfield addressed the room. 'Please allow me to introduce the final member of our group – my ward, Miss Jane Halifax.'

The men all gave small bows. Renfield and Jane moved into the room, and introductions were completed quickly. She smiled demurely at each introduction, but spoke little.

When Axel took her dainty hand in his and looked into her big, dark eyes, he saw in the light that they were not in fact black, but such a dark shade of brown as to almost be black. Now, in close proximity, she appeared to be perhaps eighteen or nineteen years old. As she looked back into his eyes, he felt his heart race. '*Charmed,*' he said. And for perhaps the first time in his young life, he meant it.

Emma rose and took Jane's hand, smiling sweetly. They greeted each other with perfect civility. There was no warmth, but there was no malice either. *Thank Heaven for small mercies,* Axel thought.

'Please everyone, do sit down, and allow me to continue,' Renfield was saying.

Emma was in an armchair, and it would be inappropriate for Jane to sit next to one of the men, so Carnby quickly vacated his armchair, dusting it after he rose.

Axel had to smile. The seat wasn't even dirty, but Carnby made the extra effort for a lady. It was heart-warming to him, in an odd way. Jane smiled demurely again, and took the seat. Carnby dropped into the empty seat next to Axel.

'Now, as I was saying. Dr Whitehall, is of course, our physician – a life saver. Mr Wallace is a man of many connections and subtle talents in regards to the collection of information. Miss Westover, who has been our guest for the last several days, is an actress of some renown, whose skills at impersonation and...*insinuation* are unparalleled. Mr Hastings is your man of action – the one first and foremost in a heated situation.'

Axel leaned forward in his seat and cut in before Renfield could continue. 'I should point out, sir, I am no murderer or *assassin*. If that is why you have invited me here today, sir, you have the wrong man.'

'Of course not, dear sir!' Renfield appeared pained. 'If your reputation or honour were in any way doubtful, we would not have chosen you. On the contrary, sir, it is *because* you are a man of compassion and integrity that we invited you.'

'Then why do you expect *me* to "kill people," Lord Renfield?'

'I fear you misapprehend me, sir.' Renfield sighed heavily. 'Please allow me to explain for all your benefits. You have, Mr Hastings, spent the last two years or so on the fringes of civilisation in America, have you not?'

'Yes.'

'And in your time there, you were on several occasions forced to resort to less than civilised actions. Am I correct?'

Axel hesitated a moment. All eyes in the room were on him. He regarded Renfield; this man was surely a lawyer, and a canny one at that. 'Only as a matter of last resort.'

'Quite, quite,' Renfield spoke soothingly. 'And should you choose to accept our invitation, you will – unfortunately – encounter in those we face, a callous disregard for the preciousness of life that you, and we, hold so dear. At those times of "last resort" I can think of no one more capable and experienced than your good self in whom to entrust the lives of these good people, not to mention my own dear Jane.'

Axel looked to the faces around him; there was not one expression of contempt or disdain. He looked to Jane, who was regarding him with a thoughtful expression. He could have lost himself in the enigmatic midnight pools of her eyes. He looked at Carnby next to him, who smiled and gave a slight nod. Axel sighed and sat back. 'Very well,' he replied at last.

Renfield nodded to Axel. 'I thank you for your indulgence, sir. Now, where was I...? Ah, yes, Mr Carnby. While it would be most vulgar to refer to Mr Carnby as a "burglar," he has undeniable skill in accessing areas otherwise inaccessible, and gathering materials otherwise...*secured*.'

Carnby smiled. 'Oi neva quoite 'eard it put loike that, m'lord!' he said, garnering laughs from the group.

Renfield laughed warmly. 'We must do you justice, Mr Carnby. And last, and certainly not least by any means, we come to my dear Jane. Miss Halifax is a researcher *par excellence*, and is knowledgeable in all matters esoteric and *arcane*. She will prove most valuable in your endeavours.'

Jane bowed her head and offered a shy smile, fiddling with a button on her sleeve.

'What exactly do you mean by "matters esoteric and arcane"?' asked Whitehall, frowning. 'What manner of mumbo-jumbo is this?'

Renfield turned back to Whitehall. 'My dear Doctor, many of those whom we face hold beliefs that are ancient and deep-rooted, what a man of science such as yourself might call "superstition". Jane's knowledge of such topics is unsurpassed, and she will be able to relate details of lore that will undoubtedly aid your investigations. Your task as a man of science, I imagine, would be to provide a methodical interpretation of such details.'

Whitehall looked from Renfield to Jane, and back again. He frowned but remained silent, sipping his tea.

No one spoke for a time, considering all of Lord Renfield's words. The lord took a seat, making himself comfortable before speaking further. 'I understand you will still have some more questions; however, before I answer I must explain somewhat further and ask a question of each of you.'

The group nodded one by one.

'You may note I have remained particularly vague in regards to certain aspects. The reality on the threshold of which you stand is fraught with danger. It would be unfair to ask a commitment of you all without allowing you an insight to that danger. But it would also be imprudent on my part to reveal too much to those who would not continue along our path.

'We have therefore come up with a compromise of sorts. The letters we sent were the first opportunity of refusal. As you have come, I will ask you to complete a task for me this evening, which will reveal to you the nature of what we face. After that, should you wish to decline further membership within our organisation, we will not impose on you, and you will be free to go about your daily lives.

'If at that time, you choose to continue with us, I will freely reveal more. So, I must ask all of you – are you willing to engage in this task tonight? To face what lays waiting out there in the world?'

The group nodded, again one by one.

'Good!' Renfield exclaimed. 'Oh! One final point – within this organisation we do not make distinctions of class or sex. You will note we have both ladies and gentlemen present, and members of various classes. All are equal in our eyes, as all have something to contribute. It may be outside the values of our times, but we expect the same level of consideration from you. Do you agree?'

The group murmured their acquiescence.

'Excellent! Now, have you any questions? If I am able to answer at present, I shall gladly do so.'

Carnby spoke up. 'Oi unda-stood from your let'er that there would be...er...pay-ment?'

'Indeed, Mr Carnby, indeed. That is a matter I will happily discuss tomorrow, but I can assure you that the compensation for your efforts will be most generous.'

Percy asked, 'These "forces of evil" you speak of, Lord Renfield. Are we talking agents of foreign powers? Criminals? Assassins? Anarchists? And if so, are you involved with the Home Office?'

Renfield regarded Percy a moment. 'Those we defend against serve ideologies far deeper and more ancient than political ones, I'm afraid, Mr Wallace. These...factions...seek power, corruption, suffering, and the destruction of all that is good and beautiful in this world.'

'Why?' asked Axel. *Wasn't mankind evil enough as it was?*

It was Emma who answered. 'That's what unmitigated evil does.'

Axel stared at her. Her words hung like a miasma in the ensuing silence.

Five
Killing Time

Lord Renfield had left them alone for some time. He had excused himself to deal with some matters, suggesting they make use of the time to become better acquainted with each other. Before leaving, he had outlined their task: they were to travel, late that evening, to two addresses.

'The first is in Ifield Rd,' he'd explained, 'near Westminster Cemetery. There you are to briefly meet with a colleague of ours, a Rudolph von Meyerling. German fellow. A rather eccentric chap, but a brilliant engineer and staunch supporter of our cause. Over the years, he has provided us with a great deal of invaluable equipment.

'When you meet with Mr von Meyerling, you are to state, "Flowers bloom, and flowers die." To which he must reply, "But the steel abides." Should you fail to make this statement, you will find him suspicious and uncooperative. Should *he* fail to make the reply, presume the man with whom you are dealing to be an impostor.

'If all goes well, Mr von Meyerling will have for you a box, marked with the insignia of the Order, which you have all seen on the letters you received: a steel rose. What is in the box will be necessary for the second part of your task.

'From there you will travel post-haste to South Lambeth, and Hamilton Road. Burton, our coachman, knows the location. Our investigations indicate that there you will a find a number of those of whom I spoke. I would like the matter...*resolved.*'

The finality of Renfield's intonation had made it quite clear what he required. All eyes in the room had inadvertently fallen on Axel.

Observing this, Renfield had continued, 'This is a task that befalls more than just our good Mr Hastings, you understand.'

The group had regarded each other as the import of the words sank in.

Axel had followed Renfield into the hall. There, the swarthy man with the dark hair had been waiting. 'Lord Renfield,' he had begun, 'if you wish me to do as you have asked, then I will have to take my leave in order to retrieve some items from my hotel. The others may wish to do the same.'

Renfield had nodded. 'Yes, quite. I will suggest it to the group once I return. Now, if you would please excuse me,' he'd stated with no irritation or annoyance.

'Of course.'

Renfield had nodded to the dark man. 'Now, Carlo. Lead the way.'

With a simple '*Sì signore,*' they'd departed.

Axel re-entered the room and moved to pour himself another scotch, watching the conversation taking place as the group became 'better acquainted'.

Dr Whitehall was standing before Jane. 'Allow me to offer my condolences, Miss Halifax,' he was saying.

Perhaps the chap's not that bad, Axel thought.

Jane looked up shyly and spoke for, what Axel realised, was the first time she had uttered more than one word since she had joined them, 'Thank you, Dr Whitehall.' She had a sweet, innocent voice; words carefully chosen, as only a lady would, and yet betraying a deep undercurrent of emotion.

'Might one enquire as to whom you mourn?'

Jane paused a moment. 'My...my father. He passed in the summer of last year.'

'Tragic,' Whitehall said, almost dismissively. Reaching into his inside jacket pocket, he drew forth a card and handed it to her. 'Might I offer my services for the future? In the event another family member takes ill? It would undoubtedly stave off the same unfortunate result.'

Jane was reaching for the card as he spoke, and she gasped, withdrawing her hand quickly. Seeing Whitehall still holding out the card expectantly, she stammered. 'I-I have no other family. They have all passed away.'

'Oh, well then! Even more so for yourself!'

Jane gave a short cry of grief and rose from her seat, exiting the room abruptly. As she passed him, Axel could see the tears welling in her eyes. He was aghast at the doctor's callousness and glared at the man, who was seemingly indifferent to his own manners. In the American west, if he were lucky, Whitehall would have been stripped, tarred and feathered, and run out of town. If he were unlucky, the undertaker would be measuring him for a pine box. Axel was overwhelmed with the urge to give this rude cad a sound thrashing, but he clutched his glass and maintained his composure.

Emma was staring at the doctor with a look of shock on her face, and Carnby looked stunned. Percy was appalled. 'I say, man!'

'What?' replied Whitehall. The doctor became even more terse and stiff than earlier, which didn't seem possible to Axel.

'I thought you medical-*wallahs* were supposed to have a "good bedside-manner", what!'

'I was not aware of her circumstances!' Whitehall argued. He took his seat again.

Emma spoke with absolute poise and authority, sounding uncannily like a schoolmistress correcting a naughty child, 'I believe you owe Miss Halifax an apology when she returns.'

Whitehall sipped his tea. 'Very well.'

'So, you're an actress?' Percy asked Emma, to break the tension in the room. 'Have you performed in anything recently?'

'Why, yes. I had a role in the *Scottish Play* last season at the Theatre Royal,' came Emma's reply.

'Really? I saw that performance a number of times. Which part did you play?'

Emma regarded Percy. 'Lady Macbeth, of course!'

'No! Surely not! Lady Macbeth was played by...er...' He pursed his lip thoughtfully as he tried to recall the name.

'Alice Montgomery.'

'Yes! That's the one!'

'*I* am Alice Montgomery. That's my "stage name".'

'No! Lady Macbeth was much older than you!'

Emma laughed as if Percy had just told the funniest joke she had ever heard. 'It's called make-up, darling!'

'I don't believe it!'

Sighing, Emma turned to face him directly in her seat. Staring at him intently, her expression changed to one of deep intensity, bordering on contempt and anger. When she spoke, even her voice had changed: it was deeper, more mature, and filled with seething emotion.

'Infirm of purpose!
Give me the daggers. The sleeping and the dead
Are but as pictures; 'tis the eye of childhood
That fears a painted devil.'

Abruptly, she switched back to the light-hearted persona, and sat back, smiling triumphantly.

'Remarkable!' Percy exclaimed. 'You were quite remarkable in that rendition. It was the primary reason for my repeated attendance.'

'Why thank you, Mr Wallace! You are far too kind.' Putting on an air of affectation, she continued, 'It is always deeply gratifying to know one's work is appreciated. And of course, to experience the adulation of one's admirers.'

The group broke into laughter.

'Yes, quite amusing,' Whitehall exclaimed.

Jane slipped quietly into the room at this point. Axel could see her eyes were red from crying.

Immediately, Whitehall rose and approached her.

She halted in alarm, staring at him wide-eyed.

'Miss Halifax,' he said stiffly, 'I wish to apologise for the thoughtlessness of my words.' Without waiting for a reply, he returned to his seat.

Quietly, and with her head down, Jane also returned to her seat. Axel moved from the side-table back to the group, and stood, watching.

'Wot about th' otha thing?' Carnby asked Emma.

'What's that, Mr Carnby?'

'That, wot Lord Renfield said. Y'know. Yew can *'in-si'-yoo-ayte.'* Wot's that?'

'Insinuate? It means to imply, or suggest.'

'Oh? An' 'ow's that wurk?'

A mischievous grin spread across her face. 'I'll show you!' Emma looked at each of the group, and chose Axel. Getting up, she walked over to him.

Axel watched her approach, hypnotised by her sultry movements and those sea-green eyes. The scent of her perfume washed over him, and he felt like they were alone – the only two people in the entire world. She moved close, stared up into his eyes and began to talk.

'Axel, darling...' she began, softly. If someone were to ask Axel later what she had said to him, he would not have been able to answer. But it seemed perfectly reasonable at the time.

Percy watched with mild amusement as she stared up at Axel adoringly and spoke softly to him. Axel was staring back at her, listening and nodding, a sympathetic expression on his face. After a moment, he reached into his coat and withdrew his wallet, depositing it in Emma's open hand. Then, he dug into his pockets and pulled out change and passed it over. Finally, he took out the revolver that had been secreted under his jacket, and emptying the cylinder of bullets, handed that over as well, saying 'I'm afraid that's all I have on my person at the moment, but if you allow me some time, I can get you more.'

Emma laughed, and turned to the others. Smiling, she held up her prizes.

Percy and Carnby laughed. Whitehall gave a small applause.

Axel looked bewildered.

She turned back and returned his possessions. 'Thank you, dear!'

He stood there, staring at the items in his hands.

'A neat trick, Miss Westover,' Percy spoke. 'But not particularly amazing, by any means.'

'Oh?' She turned to him and raised an eyebrow. 'And why is that, Mr Wallace?'

'A young man; a beautiful woman. It's not that much a stretch of the imagination...'

She sighed. 'Not convinced, Mr Wallace? Very well.' Emma glanced about, settling on Jane. 'Let me try and show you, again.'

Axel watched intently, still trying to ascertain exactly what had taken place, as she moved and crouched next to Jane, who was sitting in her seat with a morose expression.

Emma leaned in and began to whisper in her ear.

At first, Jane simply listened. Then she began smiling. It was a radiant, yet dainty smile, Axel thought. Then Jane was grinning. And then, she was giggling; she put her hand up to her mouth demurely, trying to hold back. Emma continued to whisper. Within seconds, Jane was laughing uncontrollably. Her laugh was infectious, and shortly, everyone was grinning or laughing themselves.

Emma stopped whispering and moved away. The laughter continued for some time before dying away, though Jane continued to beam happily, her previous sadness gone.

'Satisfied, Mr Wallace?'

'Perhaps,' he replied. 'What did Miss Westover say to you, my dear?' he asked Jane.

Still smiling, but regaining the poise and reserve she had previously demonstrated, she said, 'I have no idea. But whatever it was, it was the most wonderfully amusing thing in the world, and I couldn't help myself.'

'Impressive, Miss Westover.' Percy nodded. 'Though I'm not sure I'm thoroughly convinced.'

Emma sighed again, but smiled. 'You just can't please some people. And what about you, Mr Wallace?'

'How's that, my dear?'

'Well, the doctor here is our doctor, obviously, and young Mr Axel...' She glanced at Axel, who was only just now re-pocketing his possessions. '...is our dashing hero. I am an actress with – as far as you are concerned – dubious skills! So, what of you? What secrets do you possess that makes you such a fine collector of information and man of connections?'

Carnby answered, ''E's a propa toff. An 'igh up wun, an' all.'

Percy regarded Carnby evenly, but said nothing.

'And how do you know that, Mr Carnby?' Emma asked.

'It's my job t' know people, i'nit? "Mista Wallace" is a false nayme. This one's a proper Earl or Duke, loike.'

'Is that right?' Percy maintained his relaxed posture, an amused expression on his face.

'Too roight, it is!'

'In that case, perhaps you'd be so good as to prove your skill with some further insights as to the rest of our company?' Percy taunted.

'Oi'd be de-loigh'ed!' Carnby retorted airily. 'Young Mr 'Aas-tings, 'ere, 'e's a danger-us man. 'E's kill'd plen'y 'a men. 'E don' loike th' killin', but 'e's good at it.'

Axel stared at Carnby.

'That's not really insightful, Carnby,' Percy goaded. 'It simply means you were paying attention when Lord Renfield was speaking.'

'Th' docta there,' Carnby answered. ''E's a smart man. Bat 'e's a propa toff loike yew also. That's why 'e's so rude. 'E thinks between 'is 'igh birth an' 'is brains, 'e don' need t' answer t' nobody. An' if any-one thinks diff'rent loike, then they're stu-pid, ay!'

'It's not really a revelation that the good doctor is sorely lacking in manners, Mr Carnby,' rebutted Percy.

'I say!' interjected Whitehall.

Ignoring Whitehall, Carnby replied, 'Don' think Oi don' see wot you're tryin', Mista Wallace. You're tryin' t' doi-ver' us away from wot Oi said 'bout yew!'

Still with no change in his demeanour, Percy addressed the burglar. 'Be that as it may, sir, you state that your claims about me are based on some profound insight, but I've seen nothing that suggests any more than the fact that you observed our brief interactions. Which makes those claims about me shaky, at best.

'Shall I give *you* an insight, Mr Carnby?' Percy asked, without waiting for a reply. 'You are undoubtedly a very shrewd and capable man, and the fact that you have not yet been arrested attests to this. However, sir, you feel unsure of yourself in a room full of those of better birth than you – not having the benefit of the formal or social education we received. Had you been so fortuitous, you might have been a doctor or lawyer; an engineer or scientist. But as it stands, you are unfortunately little more than a common criminal, only daring to speak to your social betters in the manner you have, thanks to the permission implicit in Lord Renfield's declaration of equality!'

Carnby leaped from his seat red-faced and stalked the length of the room, away from the group.

Axel became alarmed. Discreetly, he unbuttoned his jacket. If physical intervention was required, he wanted to be ready. He hadn't forgotten that Carnby was armed.

Turning back to the group, Carnby stared at Percy and said, 'An' yet yew 'ide be'ind that, Mista Wallace! Oi don' 'ave t' 'ave a propa ej-u-cay-shun t' know wot Oi know. Or use big wurds t' tell it. Yew want propa 'insoight' t' believe wot Oi 'ave t' say 'bout yew? Foine.' He paused. ''*Er!*' He pointed at Emma.

'I beg your pardon?' Emma exclaimed.

'She's no laydy! That posh talk o' 'ers is a *hact*! Just loike that voice she put on for Laydy Mac-... Mac-...wha'eva 'er name is!'

'*Excuse me*, Mr Carnby!' Emma interjected.

Ignoring her, he continued. 'She moight talk all propa loike, but which one 'a your mutha's or sis-tas is a hacta? Ay? None! An' why? Cos that's not propa be-'avior for a laydy, ay?'

All eyes in the room were on Emma now.

'*How dare you*, Mr Carnby!' She glared at him.

'Actually,' cut in Whitehall, turning to Emma, 'the man is quite right. Being an actress is considered most inappropriate for a lady of good birth.'

She turned her fiery gaze upon Whitehall.

But before she could speak, Carnby continued. 'See! None 'a yew toffs no'iced that, wiv all your 'ej-u-cay-shun. Jast cos she spoke propa, yew all thought she was a laydy. Oi'm roight. Th' Docta's roight. Yew'd doie 'a shame if your mutha was a hacta on stage, ay Docta?'

'Gods, man!' Whitehall exclaimed. 'If I must suffer to have you speak to me, at least speak the Queen's English, not that...disagreeable, grating racket that takes place whenever you open your mouth.'

Veins bulged on Carnby's neck. 'Oi talk th' way Oi was raised t' talk. Oi'm not pree-tend-in', loike 'er. Yew should be tellin' 'er t' drop th' false talk.'

Axel was alarmed at how quickly this conversation was deteriorating. He noticed that Jane's eyes were starting to tear up again.

'Mr Carnby, I find what you are implying to be deeply insulting,' Emma protested, the anger apparent in her voice.

'Wot's that, luv? Yew foind th' truth insul'in'? Why not stop insul'in' ev'ryone 'ere an' show us all wot'chyew really are!'

Emma was gripping the armrests of her chair so tightly, her knuckles were turning white. She was grinding her teeth. Seething, she demanded, 'And. What. Exactly. Is. That?'

'That you're th' same as me. You're nuthin' bat dead common! Yew came from th' same place as me.'

Emma gasped in outrage and fury. '*How dare you*! I've never heard such an insulting tirade in my life! *You* want *me* to claim that I'm "common" just to prove a point to Mr Wallace and to make *you* feel better about the company in which you find yourself!'

'No! Oi want yew t' stop loying t' us! Tell us th' truth an' speak loike yew was meant ta!'

Emma gave a cold, spiteful laugh. 'How's that, Mr Carnby? You mean "*Th' rine in Spine fawls minely on th' pline!*",' she retorted, mimicking the Cockney drawl perfectly.

''Ere!' Carnby spat. 'Don' *yew* mock me!'

''*Ere*?' she answered with mock incredulity. '*Here*, Mr Carnby,' she continued, 'in *H*ertford, *H*ereford and *H*ampshire, *h*urricanes *h*ardly *h*appen!'

Carnby bellowed in fury, 'I will not be mocked by wot's no more than a done-up, made-up, overly pret'y *hoa-*.'

'ENOUGH!' Axel roared, bringing silence to the room in an instant.

All eyes in the room turned to him.

He had had enough, and he had finally lost his composure. Standing now in a posture of dominance – wide stance, jacket unbuttoned and fists on his hips – he spoke with a firm and authoritative voice. 'Mr Carnby! I have no interest in your background or social status, but I *will not* allow you to speak to, or in front of ladies, in such a manner!'

'Mr Wallace, I will not be drawn into an argument with you regarding this, but Mr Carnby is quite right in stating you are not whom you claim to be. *Do not* goad him any further.

'Dr Whitehall. Your manners are most atrocious, and I suggest you make an effort at improving them, lest you find yourself censured by myself, and – no doubt – the rest of our party.'

That would do it, Axel thought. Even the suggestion of being 'sent to Coventry' was enough to give pause to anyone of good social standing.

He continued, 'If *half* of what Lord Renfield has told us is true, then we shall find ourselves in great danger this evening. In such a situation, all we have to rely on is each other. We cannot do so if we are at each other's throats. We must cooperate if we are to survive. Therefore, we will henceforth act like the ladies and gentlemen we purport ourselves to be, and treat each other with respect! Is that understood?' He glared around the room. This would either resolve here and now, or the group would collapse and go no further.

Jane was studying him with that same enigmatic, thoughtful look. Percy was regarding him approvingly. Whitehall was looking at him with an expression of shock. Emma was still glaring at Carnby.

Carnby, for his part, was staring at the group with a look of spreading horror; it seemed he realised what a profound error he had made. He straightened up, and tidying his garments, he spoke. 'Miss West-ova, Miss 'Alifax, Oi would loike t' apologise for speakin' in sach a rude manna in fron' 'a yew both. Oi am a simpul man, with a 'abit 'a speakin' straightly. Oi know that's no ex-cuse, bat Oi ask yew t' for-give me.'

Jane, maintaining her poise despite what had occurred – clearly demonstrating the quality of her upbringing – nodded and said softly, 'It's quite all right, Mr Carnby.'

But Emma continued to glare at him.

'Miss Westover?' Axel asked.

She turned her gaze to him, then away, staring out the window, setting her jaw defiantly.

'Miss Westover.'

She continued to ignore him.

'Emma!' He raised his voice.

She whipped around and glowered at him, eyes burning with rage.

'Mr Carnby has made a mistake, and he has apologised, here, in front of everyone. We need to put this behind us right now, or we'd best tell Lord Renfield that he has chosen the wrong group of people, and we go our separate ways.'

Emma stared at him before turning back to the window. 'Very well,' she said softly. 'I accept your apology, Mr Carnby,' she acquiesced with no sincerity, and continued to stare out the window.

Carnby sat down in the nearest chair and put his face in his hands.

'So,' Axel said, relaxing his stance, 'we start afresh.'

The tension in the room remained palpable as Renfield re-entered. 'Everyone getting well acquainted?' he asked lightly. 'Everyone getting on? Good! Good!'

Axel had the distinct impression that Lord Renfield knew full well that this was not the case. He had a sneaking suspicion he had, in fact, been eavesdropping on the entire interaction.

'Unfortunately, I cannot stay,' Renfield said. 'Matters call me away. However, please stay for supper and make yourselves at home. Hargraves will come to fetch you around ten this evening, and Burton will be waiting to take you about your task.

'I will, in all likelihood, not be able to meet with you again until tomorrow morning; at which time we can discuss this matter further.

'Oh! And Mr Hastings has advised that he will have to retrieve certain items he will require from his hotel. If any of you wish to do the same, I suggest this is a good time to do so.'

'Yes, I think I will.' Percy stood up. 'After all, light shades are not ideal for the evening, what?'

'And I should collect my medical bag, I think, if what you've told us is true, Lord Renfield,' Whitehall added.

'It is most certainly true, my good doctor, and that would be a most wise course of action.' Renfield paused. 'Until tomorrow, my good people, I wish you good day!' He gave a short bow before taking his leave.

Jane, Axel, Whitehall and Percy acknowledged him. Emma continued to stare out the window. Carnby was staring at the floor.

Carnby, Jane and Emma had made no comment regarding departure; seemingly, they were prepared. But the situation was untenable. Emma was unlikely to interact with Carnby; Jane would, perforce, have to remove herself if Emma were not present, leaving Carnby alone. Given what had just taken place, Axel felt bad that this should happen. He was about to go over to Carnby, but Percy was advancing on him. Now what?

But surprisingly, Percy, when he reached Carnby, offered an outstretched hand. 'Sorry, old chap! No hard feelings?'

Carnby looked up at Percy with uncertainty.

'I am sorry for antagonising you, old man.'

Carnby stood, and after what was to Axel a tense moment, he took Percy's hand. 'It's quoite all roight. After all, we're s'posed t' get on, ay? Oi apolo-gise for my rude words.'

Percy slapped him on the shoulder, 'Not at all, man!'

Six

Lunch at the Savoy

Charing Cross

Carnby decided to accept Axel's invitation to join him, and despite the fact that he was a toff, Carnby felt more at ease with this young man than he would have in that proper house, what with Miss Westover being ticked off at him and all. Separate coaches were called for Whitehall and Percy to go in separate directions, but the house's own coachman, Burton, drove them to Axel's hotel in a private hansom.

It was a relatively short coach ride to The Savoy, just off The Strand near Waterloo Bridge and Somerset House, but it took quite some time to creep through heavy afternoon traffic. They passed through the best parts of London, and tucked away in the seat of the cab, Carnby felt relaxed enough for once to enjoy the sights of the better part of the city, something he had never had the luxury to do.

'Oi neva been in a 'ansom before,' he commented to his companion.

'Oh? How do you find it?'

'Quoite noice act-chuly!' Carnby said. 'Yew toffs— Oh, sorry...rich-folk...live real comfy, ay?'

'It's quite all right, Mr Carnby, we are toffs!'

Carnby regarded the young man, shocked. He wasn't sure if he was being mocked.

Axel turned to him. 'It's true, though; we are. Just look at how stuffy old Doctor Whitehall was, fussing over his tea! And Percy was so taken aback by Miss Westover's forwardness. Not something quite so shocking to you or me, yes?'

Carnby relaxed. 'True, true!' But then the moment of ease passed, and he grew serious. 'Oi made a mis-tayke talkin' loike that, din' Oi?'

Axel sighed. 'Yes...such language is considered most inappropriate, but let's not overlook the fact that your assessment of Miss Westover is most accurate.'

'Yew reckon she's common too?'

Axel shrugged. 'I don't believe "common" is the right word. She's not one such as yourself, who grew up in, say, Whitechapel or Limehouse, with limited education and prospects – no offence, Mr Carnby. But she's certainly no "lady", no "toff", as you would put it.'

'None tayken! You're jast tellin' it loike it is. So, wot then, is she?'

'Perhaps, what they call an "adventuress"? A courtesan?'

'A wot?'

'Someone whose standing in society is determined by their paramour, even though everyone knows the truth,' Axel explained.

'Mista 'As-tings—'

'Please, just Axel.'

'Very well – Ak-sul – Oi 'ave no oidea wot yew jast said.'

'A courtesan is a lady who is well educated and well spoken. They are quite beautiful, as is Miss Westover, and are...companions...to men of excellent standing, usually high nobility.'

'So, they...' He made a nodding gesture with his head. 'Y'know...'

'Well, yes. But they're prized for their beauty, elegance, wit and charm. And for the companionship they provide. An exceptional courtesan complements a man intellectually, as well as physically. To have such a woman on your arm, even though all know who she is, is regarded a mark of privilege.'

'Oi see...' Carnby answered thoughtfully. He was not sure he did.

'But for God's sake man, don't go calling Miss Westover a courtesan! That's just my conjecture.'

No! No!' Carnby laughed out loud. 'Oi learnt my less'n good an' propa there!'

They were quiet a time; not an awkward silence, but the comfortable quiet of understanding between two people. They looked out at the city around them.

Presently, Carnby spoke again. 'So, yew a-gree with my 'ass-ess-ment' of Mista Wallace as well?'

Axel nodded, watching something out on the street. 'What was it you said?' he asked, turning back. 'A duke or an earl? I don't think he's an earl; possibly a marquess, but most likely a duke.'

'Why d'yew think that?'

'Something about his manner. I don't know, really. I've watched nobility my whole life and my instincts tell me he's, as you say, high up. A duke.'

''Ow 'igh is that?'

'Rather high. As high as one can get, without being a prince.'

'An' 'e's pre-tendin' t' be a normal fella?'

'Interesting, isn't it?' Axel paused. 'Yes, they're an interesting group. Whitehall, Percy, Miss Westover...Miss Halifax. She seems an exceptional young lady...' he finished, his voice trailing off.

Carnby eyed him slyly. 'Yes...ek-sep-shun-al all roight, is young Miss 'Alifax! Oi see yew no'iced!'

Axel snapped his head around and stared at Carnby. 'I...I don't know what you mean!'

Carnby laughed. 'No? Oi told yew, it's my job t' know people! Oi seen th' way yew two was lookin' at each other!'

Axel regarded him coolly for a minute before bursting into genial laughter.

'Wot?'

'Oh, Mr Carnby!' he replied, laughing, 'You call yourself "common", but let me tell you, sir, there is nothing common about you at all.'

Axel sat back, and drew out a cigarette case from inside his jacket. Taking one he offered it to Carnby, who happily availed.

The two men spent a thoroughly enjoyable afternoon in the dazzling opulence of The Savoy, where they had had a lunch the likes of which Carnby had never had before. They had eaten cucumber sandwiches, which Carnby thought was now his favourite meal, and salmon-something-or-other, which melted in his mouth, and which Carnby was sure they served you in Heaven. Axel had also used a telephone, something Carnby knew of, but had never actually seen used. Almost inevitably it seemed, their conversation had turned to weaponry, and Carnby was greatly impressed with the elegant design of the young man's American weapons. In turn, Carnby had shown Axel the cut-down shotgun, revolver, daggers, and bandoliers he had secreted under his coat. The young man had seen this as hilarious for some reason, though to Carnby it remained a perfectly sensible measure.

Seven

Afresh

Belgravia

The pair arrived back at Belgrave Square around quarter-to-seven that evening, to find that Percy and Dr Whitehall had returned some time earlier. They joined the two, along with Emma and Jane, in the ground floor library, making small talk.

Carnby saw that everyone was now dressed in dark colours. Whitehall looked much the same, though Percy cut a striking figure in black and white, much like Axel. They couldn't escape their whites, could they? Bloody toffs. That's why they made such bad burglars! That and they didn't need to, of course. Jane was unsurprisingly in black, and Emma was dressed in dark navy blue, with no bright bits – just as good as black in the dark – though that thick red hair made Carnby unsure. Perhaps he could have Axel convince her to wear a bonnet?

They poured scotches and sat down with the others. Carnby wasn't sure how the group would treat him, but aside from the arrogant Whitehall, and Emma – who appeared to still be annoyed at him – Percy and Jane both came and spoke with him. Meaningless waffle to be sure, but Carnby thought that it was to make sure he felt welcomed after the afternoon's unpleasantness.

It was now just before eight, and the butler, Hargraves, had come to fetch them for dinner. Carnby followed the others across the ground floor to the back of the house with trepidation. He knew nothing of the habits and manners of 'proper' dining and was apprehensive about looking the fool in front of the others. Annoyingly, in that regard, Percy had been right.

The dining room was at least as large as the drawing room they had met in earlier. Though it was still somewhat dazzling to him, Carnby was starting to get used to the space and luxury after The Savoy. They entered from a door to the left into a cavernous space coloured with rich dark red wallpaper and gold ornaments, dominated by a massive mahogany dining table with *twelve* high-backed, luxuriously finished chairs around it. There were two fireplaces again in this room, both lit. To Carnby's necessarily spartan sensibilities, the table seemed overly *cluttered*, with those large three-pronged candleholders made of silver that rich people seemed to own in excess – all lit as well – and vases with bright winter flowers, decanters of water and *bottles* of wine. Only the places on the left side of the table had been set, though the rest of the table was still ornately decorated. One of those large glass things with the lights in them – what were they called? He pondered, trying to remember: a *chandelier*, hung from the ceiling, throwing dazzling light around the room. He was pleased that he could recall such an obscure word.

Carnby waited until the others took a place; he noted that Percy, as though by habit, took the place at the head of the table, nearest the fireplace. Emma took the first seat on Percy's left, facing the door; Axel took the one opposite; Whitehall sat next to Axel, and Jane next to Emma. Carnby decided in an instant that he did not want to sit next to the rude Whitehall, and he preferred not having his back to the door. He didn't know whether it was proper, but he moved to the seat next to Jane. No one seemed to object, so he hoped it was acceptable.

Carnby looked out one of the windows to an open space dominated by an elevated terrace; snow covered the ground, and three small trees – bare and spindly in the night – stood in a row across the terrace. Beyond that was a two-storey building, with lights shining in some of the windows. 'Wot's that?' he asked Jane quietly, pointing.

She turned to look and replied, 'It's the coach-house, Mr Carnby. Mr Burton, the coachman, lives there upstairs. I believe there's a young stable-boy also. The horses and coaches are kept downstairs.'

'Oh...' Like so much Carnby had seen today, there was nothing in his experience to relate this to; he just had to accept the strange reality of it.

Carnby took his seat and stared in confusion at the excess of cutlery and crockery before him: there were bowls, plates, knives, forks, spoons, glasses – all in the *plural* of each. He didn't know where to begin. Glancing quickly at the others, he saw they were all at ease, of course. *You're goin' to make a right fool of yourself 'ere, yew old bugger,* he thought.

Jane turned to Carnby, about to speak, but when she saw the apprehension on his face, she leaned in and whispered, 'Just do as I do, Mr Carnby, and you'll be fine!'

Carnby, relieved, replied softly, 'Thank yew, Miss 'Alifax, yew are a dear.'

'Not at all Mr Carnby. And please, call me Jane.'

'Only if yew call me Richard, an' not Mista Carnby.'

'I couldn't do that! That wouldn't be appropriate!'

Carnby sighed. 'Oh, well then, Oi'll jast 'ave t' con-tin-yew ad-dress-in' yew as Miss 'Alifax!'

'Oh, Mr Carnby!' Jane laughed. 'What am I to do with you?'

'Well, it wouldn' be a-pro-pri-yate! Wot with yew a laydy, and me jast some bloke from the East End!'

'As you wish, Mr Carnby.'

There was a door adjacent to the one through which they had entered that led to some other area, and Carnby saw that servants were now coming in with steaming food. Jane took a napkin from the table, and draped it across her lap. As casually as he could, Carnby did the same.

Some discussion had been taking place between Percy and Hargraves regarding wine, and Hargraves was now moving from person to person, pouring what Carnby knew to be a 'white' wine, though he himself had never tried any. A footman was, again, starting at Percy then moving around and ladling out soup. It was creamy, and smelled good.

Jane picked up a particular spoon and toyed with it a moment, glancing sideways at Carnby. Catching her look, he acknowledged it, and chose the same spoon. He paused a moment, watching how the others ate their soup, then slowly, carefully, he ate in the same manner. There was no loud slurping or gulping here. The others took their time and ate in a refined and controlled manner. He had seen Axel do something similar at lunch. The soup was warm and tasted good. It had rice with chunks of vegetables and perhaps, chicken. Including his lunch at The Savoy today, Carnby couldn't remember the last time he had eaten so well.

While they were eating the soup, platters were brought out with what were clearly large fish fillets in a creamy sauce. Conversation at the table was light and genial. They talked and laughed about topics that meant little or nothing to Carnby, but at least they were being polite to each other as Axel had warned them. He caught Percy regarding Emma with unmistakable desire, and Axel stealing looks at Jane from time to time. He had to smile to himself when he saw Jane's surreptitious glances at Axel when the young man was occupied.

As they finished their soup, the servants came and removed their bowls, replacing the plates beneath as well. More fish was brought out, narrow little fish that Carnby recognised to be smelt, fried. Carnby had his fill of both and was satisfied. He reached for his wine, and began to gulp it.

'Mr Carnby!' Jane whispered, 'Sip your wine, don't gulp it!' As if to demonstrate, she took a little sip from her own glass. Carnby mimicked her action, and found that it was a different experience; he savoured different flavours as it passed over his tongue. No one seemed to have noticed his behaviour.

'Well,' he remarked quietly to Jane as the servants were clearing away the plates and fish, 'that was a jolly good meal!'

'That was just the first course, Mr Carnby,' she replied.

'Ay?' he blurted, surprised, though he managed to keep his voice down. ''Ow many courses are there?'

Jane reached for a little card standing on the table and read out the handwritten words. 'First Course: Rice Soup; Red Mullet with Génoise Sauce; Fried Smelt. That was what we just had. Next, Entrees: Fowl Pudding; Sweetbreads. Second course: Roast Turkey and Sausages; Boiled Leg of Pork; Pease Pudding. Third course: Lemon Jelly; Charlotte à la Vanille; Maids—'

Carnby put up his hand, gesturing for her to stop. 'Thank yew, Miss 'Alifax, I unda-stand. Oi'm full already!'

'Please don't be concerned, Mr Carnby. Just avail yourself to a little of what you like, here and there, and enjoy some wine. No one will mind.'

'Oi din' know there was gonna be so much food!' he complained.

'This is a standard dinner for six or so people, Mr Carnby,' she said matter-of-factly.

'Crikey!' he exclaimed, and sipped his wine.

The rest of the meal was a blur of dishes that Carnby couldn't begin to comprehend. He had never even seen so much food in his life and could barely consume any more. He was unaccustomed to eating so much food. Serving bowls and platters were taken out with plenty left on them. Carnby thought of asking Jane what would happen to that food, but then he realised he wouldn't like the answer. Even after the servants had had a meal, there would be so much left over. Carnby could have fed several poor families for a week. It was thoroughly disgraceful. It shouldn't have bothered him, but it did. He knew the rich lived well, but...*Bloody hell.*

After dinner, Jane quietly followed the others to the first-floor drawing room at the back of the house. Of course, she knew this house well as it belonged to the Order, and as it had rarely been used recently, she had even claimed one of the two large bedrooms on the second floor for occasional stays, leaving several items of clothing here for convenience. Her room was directly above this one, which was, itself, was directly above the dining room. This back drawing room – or the 'music room' as she called it – was done in the same light shades as the front drawing room, though the furniture was somewhat different; there were fewer lounges, but a large billiards table, a card table, a piano and a gramophone with several discs. There was also a drinks cabinet. She watched that horrible doctor move to it now, asking, 'Brandy?'

Jane paused near the door, observing the men carefully. She wasn't sure what to make of them; despite Mr Hastings being so very handsome, and Mr Wallace very charming, they all reminded her in some way of the men she had known within the Order – her father, Uncle Oscar...Carlo...and others. They exuded an authority and confidence that she found both reassuring and for some reason, a little frustrating.

Mr Hastings and Mr Wallace replied in the affirmative, and Mr Carnby followed suit. Miss Westover spoke up, 'One for me too, please!'

That startled Jane, as that was not at all ladylike behaviour.

The doctor and Mr Wallace stared at her, taken aback, but she saw Mr Hastings smirk as he leaned against a chair and lit a cigarette.

Noticing the smell, Miss Westover turned to him. 'Oh, Axel, would you mind?'

Jane stared, agog. Ladies *did not* smoke! That had been made clear to her in no uncertain terms since she was a small child.

He walked over, offering the open case to her. 'Not at all.' He looked at the other men, chuckling wryly and Jane followed his gaze to their surprised expressions.

'What, Axel?' Miss Westover raised an eyebrow, blowing out smoke.

'I fear your forthright action perturbs some of our company.' He nodded towards the others.

Miss Westover turned around to look at the two men staring at her. She laughed pleasantly, and turning back, said, 'They'll just have to get used to my "forthright actions" won't they, Axel.' She moved to a sofa and sat regally.

Mr Carnby moved over to the card table and looked at the cards. He turned to the men. 'Gen'lemen, cards?'

Mr Wallace and Dr Whitehall broke out of their stupor. 'Yes. Why not?' The former answered. 'Doctor? Axel?'

'As it should be after dinner.' Dr Whitehall replied. 'Cards, brandy and a pipe.'

'Deal me in.' Mr Hastings agreed in an American accent, drawing laughter from the group.

Jane was disappointed that she could not speak further with Mr Carnby, as she had really liked talking with him, and had wanted to do so some more. It was fascinating hearing what life was like, how different it was, just a few miles away from her own world. She had not yet spoken to Mr Hastings, and she was certain she was not nearly brave enough to do so, and certainly not in a room full of strangers. And she also hadn't spoken to—

'Miss Halifax? Come, sit,' Miss Westover called to her. She patted the seat next to her. 'Come and talk to me, my dear!' she said warmly.

A knot of nervousness tightened in Jane's tummy as she approached. She didn't know how to feel about her, as aside from her stunning beauty, the most striking thing about Miss Westover was her forthrightness. She seemed fearless to the point of being brazen. It alarmed Jane that she found herself uncertain of what Miss Westover was about to say and do. Earlier in the afternoon, the meeting had switched from laughter to near violence so suddenly that Jane found herself still reeling from it. Though Jane reminded herself that Mr Carnby had accused Miss Westover of being common, which had – she supposed, justifiably – ignited Miss Westover's fury. Yet, as she sat next to the other lady, the suddenness of it all still made her apprehensive.

'Miss Westover—' Jane began, before Emma cut in.

'Please, my dear, call me Emma. It would appear we are going to be working together. May I call you Jane?'

'Please do.' Jane nodded. 'Emma,' she continued, 'I do hope you aren't too distressed by Mr Carnby's comments today.'

Emma snorted in contempt. 'Mr Carnby comes from a class stratum that favours impulsive and forthright speech,' she stated, in a manner that suggested she did not empathise with Carnby's social situation.

'I'm sure he is deeply apologetic, and distressed about the manner in which he spoke to you.'

'Mr Carnby is distressed about having made such a vulgar blunder in polite company,' Emma replied, somewhat petulantly. 'I think it would serve him far better to be concerned with his own manners, rather than my background, before he finds himself in some very awkward situations.' It did not seem like any kind of threat, but rather an insight.

'I can't think what I should have done in your place had Mr Carnby spoken to me in that manner. As it was, Dr Whitehall's thoughtlessness—'

'Callousness, you mean?' Emma interrupted.

'I fear you are too unkind, Emma,' she replied softly. 'I'm sure the doctor meant nothing by it; certainly, he was not aware of my familial circumstances.' She paused a moment. 'Nonetheless, I was barely able to contain myself until I left the room. I saw you were angered by Mr Carnby's comments, but you continued to stand your ground. How did you manage to control yourself?'

'Oh Jane! You must always remember that a lady's armour are grace and dignity; you must always maintain those. With them you can fend off *almost* anything.'

'But you're not…' Jane began, and trailed off, realising what she was about to say, 'Um…er…' she stammered. She could feel her face turning red, and looked away quickly. What had she done?

Emma patted Jane's knee, laughing, 'Oh, sweet Jane! I'm no lady! I'm far too jaded to be anything close to as virtuous as you!' She took Jane's hands in her own. 'Watch how I act out of doors though; you'll see its quite different to the manner in which I deal with these rogues and scoundrels!'

They laughed together, but Jane was confused. 'Are they, though?' she asked naïvely, glancing quickly at the men engrossed in their cards. 'They seem proper gentlemen to me.'

'All men *seem* proper gentlemen, at first!' Emma snickered, but seeing the perturbed look on Jane's face, she changed her manner. 'You have nothing to fear from these four, I promise. Firstly, I'm certain Mr Wallace has no dishonourable intentions towards you.' She paused a moment, a small smile playing across her lips as she regarded him, across the room. 'Me, on the other hand…' She trailed off.

Jane's eyes widened. 'He wouldn't, would he?'

Emma looked back at her and said, 'Hush dear, don't alarm yourself. In my line of work, one naturally draws the attention of men; most of whom have certain…preconceptions about actresses. One becomes quite skilled at…*managing* those preconceptions.'

'As you say,' Jane replied, nodding uncertainly. 'And the others?'

'Mr Carnby,' Emma continued, '*despite* his coarse exterior, I sense, has what they call a "heart of gold", and would not, I believe, behave in a reproachful manner towards you. I think he regards you highly. In truth and fairness, after his earlier *faux pas*, the look of horror on his face was palpable when he realised you were in the room, and he had spoken in such a manner whilst you were present.'

'I must admit, I find myself feeling fond of Mr Carnby. He seems rough, yet warm and gentle. For some reason, I feel safe in his presence.'

'A woman's intuition is rarely wrong in these matters, dear. An instinctive reaction is a powerful one, and one that is meant to keep you safe from harm. But moving on to the good doctor, I know his type as well. You have no cause for concern from him as he sees women as silly, helpless, flippity-floppity, time-wasting things, whose biggest ambition in life is to ensure their hat and handbag match their dress!' Emma paused. 'I knew a language professor like him once here in London, a very smart man, but what a boorish fellow when it came to dealing with a lady!'

They giggled together conspiratorially.

'And finally, our handsome young Mister Axel,' Emma continued. 'Aside from being far too young and brash, I certainly can see him as a "man of action", as Lord Renfield put it.' She chuckled before continuing. 'I do believe, is quite taken with you, my dear.'

Jane knew she was definitely turning red. For some reason, she found herself having trouble breathing, as the butterflies from her tummy seemed to have filled up her lungs. 'Oh, surely not!' she gasped, looking away. 'I'm sure there are so many other beautiful, worldly women like you that he would find far more fascinating than me. I'm so…plain, and uninteresting that I—'

Emma cut her off. 'Nonsense, Jane! You are a beautiful and charming young lady. Not to mention clearly smart, bright and virtuous! Any young man, such as Axel, should be so lucky as to find himself a young lady like you.'

'You…you really think so?' she asked nervously, even though she didn't really believe a word Emma was saying.

'If the way he was staring at you over dinner is anything to go by.'

'Was he?' Jane half-whispered, the excitement and butterflies overwhelming her again. She shot him a shy peek. 'He is rather dashing and rugged, isn't he?'

Emma rolled her eyes. 'Oh Jane! I've only just met you, and I've already lost you to some handsome young rogue!'

They burst into laughter together.

At that moment, there was a soft knock on the door.

Everyone turned expectantly.

Eight
A Social Outing

The coach rattled down the icy road, making the notorious growling noise for which its lesser cousin, the Clarence, was vulgarly known. Theirs was a larger Hackney six-seater, with Burton, the household coachman steering from the front. Burton was a tall, lean, middle-aged man with greying hair, an unacceptably stubbly face and thick west-country accent. His bloodshot and sunken eyes frowned out at the world over a long nose that had clearly been broken at some point, giving him a grim, almost menacing demeanour. But he was unarguably accomplished at his profession, steering the vehicle masterfully upon the less-than-ideal roads as they made their way south-of-west along Brompton and Cromwell Roads. Their intended route of travel was to eventually turn left and head down Warwick Road, crossing Richmond Road into Finborough, from which

Ifield branched, near the massive Westminster Cemetery. Burton obviously knew the route well, and even though it was a busy Saturday night, they were making good time.

In a break from usual custom, the men were all on the back seat. Axel sat in the back right corner of the cab, with Percy next to him, then Carnby. Opposite him was Jane, next to her Emma, then Whitehall. The passing street lamps threw the occasional stream of light into the cab, illuminating the party momentarily, before vanishing back to dimness.

Axel frowned as he regarded his new associates with trepidation: Emma, Percy and Whitehall were chatting amongst themselves casually, as if they were on their way to a night on the town. They were discussing some matter of politics relating to the empire's plans of expansion in distant South Africa. Were they making light of the circumstances, or had the possibility of real danger simply not dawned on them yet? Being of good birth, it was extremely unlikely for either of the two gentlemen to have any apprehension of violence, nor, naturally, would Emma – whatever her background. But perhaps it was more wilful? Given the disagreeable ending of their afternoon's meeting, it was not uncommon for those of good standing to resort to the banality of mindless civilities to avoid further unpleasantness. Except for Carnby, even their attire was wholly unacceptable. While Axel had suitable rough clothing for engaging in dangerous activities, he could hardly have returned to Belgravia in such an outfit. So their collective mien remained one of a social outing.

Axel interjected into a natural pause in the conversation, 'What do you suppose we will find this evening?'

He was met with a lengthy silence and a collective exchanging of questioning looks. It seemed no one was certain what they would encounter.

'What is it we read about these days? Opium smugglers, perhaps?' Percy offered. 'Or some Hindoos worshipping their curious gods?'

Axel was about to respond that this seemed unlikely when Percy continued, 'What do you say, Miss Halifax? What would Lord Renfield have sent us to resolve?'

'I…' she began quickly before pausing for some time. 'I don't know.' A street lamp illuminated her worried expression as her eyes darted back and forth at everyone watching her.

'I see.' Percy replied. 'Understandable. What of this Mr von Meyerling with whom we are to meet? I trust you know him? What sort of fellow is he?'

'He's German…he…he's nice,' came her thoroughly unhelpful response. She almost sounded exasperated to Axel.

'Ah. Well, that's good, then,' Percy stated with finality.

A street lamp illuminated Jane again, and Axel saw her staring out the window with her face twisted in deep distress.

This was going nowhere fast. For whatever reason, Jane was seemingly going to be of little immediate help. Axel slipped his Winchester out of its bag and placed it barrel down on the floor of the cab, resting between his legs. Recovering a box of bullets, he began to load the magazine.

'I say there, young Axel,' Whitehall called from diagonally opposite, 'What *are* you doing?'

'Just what it appears, Dr Whitehall,' he replied without looking up from his task. 'I'm loading my rifle. That way, when it comes time to fire it, I'll be able to do so.'

'Ifield Road is a row of terraced houses, man, not your Wild West! You can't go about shooting up the place.'

'Dr Whitehall,' Axel retorted, 'I assure you I have no intention to go about "shooting up the place", as you call it.' He put away the box of bullets and retrieved the object from within his coat. Holding the sheath in his left hand, he withdrew the Bowie knife with his right. He held up a blade twelve inches long, and almost two inches wide, curving to a rounded point, turning it to catch the flashing street lamps.

The others stared as he continued. 'That's why I have *this*. I've loaded my rifle in case this is not enough.' He sheathed the knife as he spoke, resting it on his lap.

'Enough?' Whitehall exclaimed incredulously. 'We all have revolvers, as do you, each containing six bullets! That should surely be *enough*!'

'My good Doctor,' Axel said, as he raised the Winchester's barrel sideways across the cab so as not to aim at anyone, and pointed it towards the roof, 'When it comes to firearms and bullets, it's been my long experience that *there is no such thing as enough*.' He cocked the lever of the rifle, as if to drive the point home.

Even in the relatively noisy cab, the sound was loud, and he saw Whitehall and the two ladies start from the sharp report.

''Ear, 'ear!' called Carnby from the other side of the cab. Axel could almost hear him smiling in the darkness.

Axel de-cocked the rifle and slipped it back into its bag, laying it carefully alongside him. 'Aside from Mr Carnby, have any of you had any experience with revolvers?'

'I've fired the odd shot,' Percy quipped. Axel could hear a playful tone in his voice.

'You all have equipment like firearms, lanterns and such. I suggest you check them to be in working order before we arrive at our destination. As you're more familiar with this type of revolver than I am, Percy, can I ask you to demonstrate its operation to everyone else?'

'Naturally, old chap.' There was that playful tone again. Did Percy still think this was all a "lark"?

'For those of you with little experience with firearms,' he continued, looking at Whitehall and Emma, 'mind that you point them at the floor of the cabin while checking them, in case of accidental discharge. I'd rather my evening not end with a short and pointless coach ride.'

Everyone chuckled, easing the momentary tension. They all set about checking equipment.

The earlier knock on the drawing room door had been Hargraves, who before leading them outside to the awaiting Hackney, had led them through the other doorway in the dining room to below stairs. There, in the low-ceilinged hallway with its unfinished brickwork and stonework, he had unlocked a storeroom brimming with arms and equipment. Axel had issued revolvers to everyone but Carnby, who was already armed, and Jane, who balked at the sight of any weapons. He had also distributed some fine-looking kukris, and collected lengths of rope in some canvas bags. There were also what were known as 'bullseye' or 'dark' lanterns, enclosed on all sides bar one, where a glass lens was fitted allowing a beam of light to be shone in a single direction, preventing the user from being blinded whilst in use. The lens also had an aperture to widen or narrow the beam light, or even shut it off entirely. The lanterns had both, handles, and a metal loop of sorts on the side opposite the lens, in order to be attached to perhaps a belt; these too were distributed, as were tins of oil. Finally, there had been a shelf with all manner of ammunition; Axel had searched intently for any suitable to his weapons with no luck. He had only brought a small supply with him, and should its continued use be required, this meant he would have to send away to America for more.

Quickly, and with familiar ease, Axel attached the sheath of his Bowie to the bandolier around his waist, and tied the end to his leg, then set about checking his lantern. He glanced at the group. Percy was demonstrably at ease with his revolver, and he knew Carnby was fine, but he regarded Whitehall with some concern. The doctor had drawn the fine kukri he had been handed, and was studying the blade with a look of doubt and trepidation. He wasn't too sure how the ladies would fare either – this was of course London, not the Frontier.

Percy began to talk Emma through loading and handling her pistol. He saw Whitehall put away the Kukri and actively pay attention.

Axel frowned to himself as he had a sudden insight as to why Renfield had wanted him. Aside – possibly – from Carnby, none of the others seemed like they'd ever taken a life. He had learned that when the matter came down to it, most people froze or panicked. If what they were facing was dangerous, without him, they may not survive. He glanced quickly at Jane, who remained unarmed, and felt a heavy weight of responsibility settle upon his shoulders.

At least they were properly equipped. Being properly equipped was half the battle, and they had already won that part, without a doubt. Axel was far less certain as to whether or not that equipment would be of any use in inexperienced hands. He sat back and considered the volume and quality of the materials he had inspected, and it further proved that this so-called 'Order of the Steel Rose' was indeed well funded.

Nine
Ifield Road

Chelsea

'We're almost there, I believe,' Whitehall said, looking from his window as they slowed at an intersection. Turning back to the cab, he looked to Axel. 'You should see Westminster Cemetery from your window, Axel.'

Axel peered out. Across the street, and to his right, he could see the outline of the stone and iron fence that bordered the cemetery grounds, which lay beyond, mired in darkness.

They began moving again. 'You seem to know the area quite well, Doctor?' Emma asked.

'Yes, I've visited many times. The Smallpox Hospital sits on the western edge of the cemetery.' He paused. 'Rather a convenient placement, when one considers it...'

Axel laughed, turning back to the others. 'That's a rather macabre piece of humour, Doctor!'

Whitehall stared thoughtfully for a moment, before replying. 'I didn't intend it as such, but yes, I suppose it rather was.' And he actually smiled.

The coach slowed about halfway down Ifield road. Axel saw that Burton was pulling the vehicle across to the right side of the empty thoroughfare. He brought them to a smooth and quiet halt in front of the row of three-storey undifferentiated townhouses. Axel looked about the street before alighting. It was dark here on Ifield Road; street lights were few and far between, and only a few surrounding windows were illuminated. It was not pitch-black though, as the collective glow of the city lights reflected from the low overhanging clouds, creating a dim yellow-orange halo. There was ambient enough light to see, but it was still sufficiently dark.

Axel slipped out first and made for the front of the coach.

'That's 'a wun,' Burton said quietly, pointing with his whip 'Nummer wun-hunnerd. Ol' von Meyerlin' lives in that'un.'

Axel moved closer and thanked the coachman. Being that Jane was unable or unwilling to provide any details, he asked, 'What can you tell me about Mr von Meyerling?'

'Oh...'e's an odd wun, that'un, aye. But 'e don' mean no 'arm. A my-tee good fixer-upper o' things, if yoo know whot Oi means.' He paused, thinking. 'An 'invenn'er,' Lord Renfield calls 'im.'

'Very well, Burton. Hopefully we shan't be too long.' Axel lowered his voice and moved closer. 'Keep your wits about you, man. I'm sure everything will be fine, but...be ready to go.'

'Aye,' Burton replied giving an impertinent tip of his weathered hat.

They gathered on the pavement in a tight group. 'What was the saying Lord Renfield gave us?' asked Axel. 'The Steel Rose survives, or some such?'

'No!' hissed Emma. 'It was "Flowers bloom, and flowers die." To which he should then reply, "But the steel abides".'

'Good memory, my dear!' Percy commented.

Emma rolled her eyes. '*I am an actress*. It is my *job* to memorise lines, after all.'

'Yes...' Percy answered, somewhat taken aback. 'Quite.'

'In any case,' Axel muttered. 'Come on.'

They moved up the stairs and Axel rang the bell, but nothing happened. He tried again without success. Percy then tried, with the same result.

'Broken?' Axel asked, though he was beginning to have a sense of apprehension. There was no logical reason for him to feel that way; the bell was probably out of order, but still, there was an uncomfortable sensation he could not ignore.

'Try knocking?' Percy suggested.

'Why does an inventa, 'oo's s'posed t' be good at fixin' things, 'ave a broken doorbell?' Carnby said, keeping his voice low.

They all looked at each other in uncertainty.

Axel felt the urge to draw his Bowie, but resisted. He knocked softly, and strained to hear any response from within. When met with silence, he tried again, a little louder this time. He thought there was a faint sound, like something tipping over. He concentrated, hoping to hear more. But there was nothing. He looked to the others, their skin pale in the yellow-orange halo. 'Did anyone hear that?' he whispered.

Everyone shook their heads except Emma, who was standing towards the back of the group. She nodded with a troubled expression.

He noted again, her seemingly remarkable hearing, but said nothing. Looking over the door and the façade of the building, he murmured, 'We need to get in.'

'Allow me.' Carnby moved to the door. 'Oi can ge'chyew in, no worries. All Oi needs is me *Betties*!' He grinned in the darkness and adjusted his fingerless gloves.

'Betties?' Axel asked.

'Lock-picks.' Percy explained.

Carnby crouched in front of the door and drew a small black pouch from inside his coat. Drawing two slender objects, he inserted them in the lock and went to work.

'And how do *you* know what "Betties" are?' Axel asked Percy, regarding him in the darkness.

Percy merely tapped the side of his nose with his forefinger.

'I see.' Axel frowned.

Within moments they heard a distinct 'click', and Carnby stepped back, smirking as he re-pocketed the tools. 'Done!'

Axel moved to the door. Grasping the handle with his left hand, he took hold of the Bowie with his right, ready to draw. He worked the handle painfully slowly in case it creaked, but got it over without fuss. Gently, ever so gently, he pressed against the door. It opened a fraction, and he applied steady pressure. It opened further, swinging away from the jamb. Darkness and cold air spilled from the gap revealed. He stared at the opening a moment, searching for a flicker of light. But there was only blackness. Also, he realised, something didn't smell good. Quietly, he closed the door again.

He turned to the group, and saw that both Jane and Emma were curling their noses. 'Do you smell that?'

Both ladies nodded disapprovingly. 'It smells like something rotten,' Jane whispered.

Axel went to work lighting his lantern, with the others following suit. Once lit, they closed the apertures and either held or fastened them. Axel affixed his to his belt. Drawing his Bowie, he took hold of the door handle again.

The door swung soundlessly inwards. Axel released the handle as the foul smell from inside washed over him. With his free hand, he turned the lantern's aperture, shining a thin beam of light into von Meyerling's hall.

Ten

The Hunger

Inside was just as cold as outside. The air was still, and the stench hung upon it like a carcass in a slaughterhouse. It felt like a tomb. Dust motes hung heavily in the lantern light, thick like suspended snowflakes. Axel crept with careful, practised steps into the hall. He felt the presence of the others behind him, and momentarily, other lanterns began to shine. He moved forward, allowing room for the rest of the group. Ahead, on the right-hand wall was an open door.

The others had entered, and the door behind was closed without any noise. Axel looked at the Bowie in his hand, and felt a fool. If not for his rifle, he longed at least for his pistol. But Whitehall had the right of it – they could not go shooting around here.

He approached the doorway cautiously, pressed against the wall, light beams playing around behind him. Unfastening his lantern, he held it in front of him. Further ahead he could see the hallway opened to a flight of dim stairs going up. He paused, listening near the door, but was met only with dreadful silence. He moved fast.

Turning, he shone the light into the room, Bowie held at the ready.

The light played over a mess of a living room, where the traditional household furniture did not seem to be present. Instead, the room was dominated by a large workbench covered in what could only be described as *'junk'*. The wallpaper was faded and dirty, the colour leached away by age. In places it was torn away, revealing the pale plaster beneath, like flesh rent away, exposing bone.

Axel played the light left and right as he entered the room, taking it in. The normal furniture *was there*, but it was all covered in sheets, with every free and flat surface seemingly used as storage for more junk. Thick navy curtains, almost black in the darkness, were drawn across the large window that faced the street. He moved to the table as the others entered the room. Circling around it, he searched all areas. He found nothing of interest or concern.

The items piled up were assorted, though mainly they seemed to be dominated by mechanical and engine scrap. Wrought iron hand tools were scattered around the place. On what was clearly an armchair under its covering sheet was piled an immense stack of periodicals. A thick layer of dust lay on the top edition. A coffee table contained a pile of bricks for no clear reason. Empty wooden crates were stacked neatly against the far wall. Bundles of cloth, coiled lengths of rope and wire were strewn about. This looked to him more like a workshop than a house.

On one corner of the workbench, he found an old plate caked with hard, dry gravy, cementing into place what looked like bared lamb rib bones. He sniffed quickly. This was not the source of the stench.

Axel heard whispered gasps and muttering from the others as they took in their surroundings.

Returning to the group, he assessed them in the scattered lights of the lanterns; they all appeared pale and subdued. Everyone was wide-eyed and perturbed. Each – except Jane, and Percy, who was wielding his cane – had a blade drawn, glinting in the moving lights. They seemed to share his unease. He whispered, 'Stay behind me, unless I say otherwise.'

Setting his lantern down a moment, Axel placed his forefinger on his cheek, pointing at his eye. 'This means "look", understand?'

Everyone nodded.

He repeated the action then pointed away. 'This means "look there". Yes?'

They all nodded again.

'The order we walk in: One – me. Two – Carnby. Three – Emma. Four – The Doctor. Five – Miss Halifax. Last – Percy. Okay?'

Again, all agreed silently.

'Carnby, hold a lantern up for me, so I can keep my hand free.'

Carnby gave him a grim nod.

Axel gestured for them to follow.

Out in the hall, the stench was stronger. It seemed to grow as they moved to the back of the house. He heard one of the ladies gasp and wondered a moment if he should suggest they wait outside, but they didn't have time to start fooling about with that.

Creeping forwards, his lantern now back on his belt, with Carnby illuminating his path, Axel prayed the wooden floorboards were in good condition and wouldn't creak dreadfully. So far, they had been lucky.

The hallway opened up here. To his left were the steep stairs, to the right a second door, closed. Directly ahead was another door, open, darkness laying within, and beyond the reach of the lanterns. Moving to the second door, he stopped and turned back. He pointed to Percy, then to his own eye, and then to the stairs.

Percy nodded and pivoted.

Axel pointed to Emma, repeated the action of pointing to his eye, and then to the door at the far end of the hall.

Emma nodded and moved past, her Kukri glinting in his lantern light. He noticed she held it with confidence and ease.

Pointing at Whitehall and Jane, the whites of their eyes radiant in the lights, he indicated they should wait.

They both acknowledged him in silence.

He turned to Carnby and gestured with his head to the door.

Carnby raised the dagger in his other hand in anticipation.

Axel tried the door handle. Locked.

Carnby moved silently into place with his 'Betties' as Axel stepped aside. Even quicker than before, he heard the click, this time deafening in the cold silence. He saw the entire group start at the noise, and he cringed internally at its volume.

Leaning close to Carnby, he murmured, 'Can you do that quietly, at all?'

Carnby frowned and shook his head. He pointed a thick finger at the lock then cupped his hand as if holding something, then moved it up and down, as if judging its weight. He mouthed the word, 'Heavy.'

Axel nodded. He took the handle again, realising as he did that his mouth was very dry. Working his tongue to get some moisture, he swung the door open and raised his weapon, ready. Nothing happened. Axel moved into the room.

As he looked around, he realised that the sitting room had been converted into a highly organised workshop. There were various metal- and wood-working tools – lathes, drills, saws and other equipment he could not name – arranged neatly in stations about the walls of the space. In the centre of the room was another smaller workbench, with clamps affixed, and now-inoperative lighting suspended from above. This surface was clear and tidy, like all the workstations. Unlike the other room, this showed the workings of a highly efficient and organised mind. The other room, then, he thought, must surely be the storeroom for collected goods. A small window in the back corner of the room was firmly closed, with the same type of navy curtain drawn.

He turned to Carnby, who was admiring the equipment with a gleam in his eyes.

After a quick look around netting nothing relevant, they stepped back into the hallway, closing the door behind them.

Two rooms in, with nothing unusual other than a rotten smell, Axel wondered if he was being overly cautious and apprehensive. He hesitated: what should he do?

Unbidden, the faces of the young Lakota Sioux medicine man, Black Elk, and that of the old, dying chief, Spotted Elk, appeared in his mind. The scents and sounds of their meeting on that fateful eve flooded over him. 'If you become still like the deer, and quiet like the mountain, if you silence the noise of the white man, then you will see and hear the truth of the world. You must learn how to use your Sight to pierce the painted lies of the mind.' Black Elk's translation of the Chief's whispered words echoed in his ears.

He had practised a few times since, based on Black Elk's instructions, but the uncanny sensations he experienced had dissuaded him from trying overmuch. Now, he stood still a moment, taking a slow, deep breath. Stilling his mind, he focused on expanding his awareness. He hoped to allay his fears, but almost immediately felt the stab of an overwhelming sensation in his chest and all his hair stood on end. He was freezing in the tomb-like space, and his heart began to race. Something was *very, very* wrong in this house.

Every survival instinct in him screamed: *run*. He gritted his teeth, fighting the urge to obey. He faced down the hall at the open door. The beam from Emma's lantern was so small against the overwhelming darkness he almost expected something nightmarish to march forward from that cold blackness and be upon them before they could even fathom what it was.

His breathing was heavy, and he could feel his heart pounding. Axel fought to calm himself, but every time his goosebumps subsided, they returned almost instantly.

Unsteady, he reached out to support himself against the wall. And it happened. Unexpected, but just as the old chief had described. As soon as his fingers brushed the dirty wallpaper, his world went black. Raging emotions overwhelmed him. Malevolence. Pain. Fury. Urgency. And under it all, an all-encompassing hunger. A raging compulsion to feed. To bite. To repast on the flesh and blood of his prey.

Axel wrenched his hand away, and the world came back, though the feelings remained. As his eyes refocused to the dim light, he saw Emma ahead, with her back to him. For a moment he wished her closer, so he could lunge at her and sink his teeth in to that soft, creamy flesh.

The urge revolted him, and he nearly vomited. Spinning, he was suddenly aware of a strong grip on his arm, and a light shining in his face. Carnby was staring at him, his face close, pale blue eyes stark in the dim light. 'Ak-sul? Are yew all roight?'

Axel blinked in the light, his head still swimming. He felt dizzy, but the other horrific sensations were fading. He never thought they would be *that* strong. He nodded. Focusing on Carnby, he whispered, 'Something is very wrong here!'

Carnby glanced quickly around the cold dark space. 'We ort'a leave.'

Axel shook his head. Righting himself, he replied. 'I'm fine. We must continue.' He turned to the others, who were staring at him in alarm. He paused, taking a deep breath before indicating for them to wait, and began moving forward.

As he passed Emma, he gestured for her to follow. He stared at her a moment in the halo of the lantern beams, her green eyes glittering like emeralds, wondering guiltily what her reaction would be if she knew that he had nearly attacked her.

The foul stench intensified as they approached the doorway. Axel had a clear view of the space ahead. It appeared to be a dining room. Now closer, he could see a shut door at its far end.

Axel recognised that this was the narrower, rear part of the house, common in townhouses like these. Entering the dining room, he saw a large dining table of dark wood dominating the area. Only one chair was placed at the nearby head. Though no proper tablecloth lay on the table, a sheet had been laid on the surface and what appeared to be the disassembled components of some sort of engine were spread out. Grease covered the parts and the sheet. The same navy curtains were drawn against the window on the far-right wall.

At the head of the table, at the solitary, vacant seat, was another plate covered in gravy. As Axel neared, he saw no bones this time, but noticed the gravy glistened in the lantern light. He took a closer look: it was runny. This was fresh, he realised. Cautiously, he dipped a finger in the dark liquid. Cold.

A notebook lay open on the table next to the plate. On the open page were notes scribbled in an atrocious hand, along with a hastily scrawled drawing of some sort of device that made no sense to him. Quietly turning a page or two, he saw similar notes and diagrams. It seemed important, so he picked it up and pocketed it in his coat.

He saw Emma moving out of the corner of his eye and turned to see her watching him, bringing a handkerchief to her face.

He wrinkled his nose, acknowledging the stink and gestured to the next door.

She nodded in reply.

Axel raised the Bowie and approached the door. The awful smell was overbearing now, and he suspected he knew why. He guessed that beyond this lay the kitchen. Horrific images flooded his mind. Images of blood-sprays, severed limbs and broken torsos, *gnawed upon*, raced through his head. He reached for the handle with trepidation, his hand trembling. The door opened outwards into the dining room, and he stepped back apprehensively, expecting to be assaulted with the nightmarish sights that had entered his thoughts.

The stench was almost unbearable. Opening the door unleashed a new wave of stink, and he was forced to control the urge to cough and gag. He heard a muffled gasp as Emma struggled to suppress a cough into her handkerchief. Axel dashed into the room.

He saw the source of the foul odour. Every counter surface was covered with food waste. A large pile of garbage sat on the floor against the opposite wall, blocking what looked like the back door of the house. A mountain of unwashed saucepans and utensils sat on one counter near the washbasin. The piles of decomposing waste made the room warmer than the others, and he saw with disgust that cockroaches appeared to reign supreme here. Then he heard the squeak. Carnby heard it too, for he whipped the lantern across, shining on numerous rats dominating a tipped-over saucepan with some kind of broth spilled on the floor.

Emma whimpered as she struggled to contain a scream and scrambled back out of this rancid playground for vermin. Carnby hissed in disgust and darted from the room. Axel sprang after him, pushing the door shut in one quick motion, lest any rats escape.

He looked at the others and shook his head in disbelief. Their nonplussed expressions showed their agreement. Returning to Percy, Jane and Whitehall, Axel pointed silently at the stairs.

Eleven
Uncle Rudi

Jane slipped into place between the doctor and Mr Wallace as Mr Hastings began to ascend the stairs, the blade of his massive knife gleaming every time a lantern beam played over it. Her mind was a whirlwind of dozens of competing thoughts and feelings, each rising up to take centre stage on the heels of the last. What had just happened to Mr Hastings? Was he alright? What had they found at the back of the house? What was the source of that awful stench? What had happened to Uncle Rudi? Was *he* alright? What had happened here, in his house? It had not been in this state when last she had visited. Had he infuriated and driven off another housekeeper? It hadn't been *that* long since she had visited, had it? It was only…Jane felt a jolt of pain sear through her body. *It was just before father died*, she remembered. That was why she hadn't been back.

Jane alighted the stairs with the others in quiet, practiced steps. 'Breathe, Jane,' her father's words came back to her. 'No matter what, keep your breathing slow and steady. That will slow your heartbeat and make your body relaxed. You *must* be relaxed to be prepared to respond to anything you encounter.' Michael Halifax had had the foresight to prepare his only child for the realities of this world, despite not wanting her to be a part of the goings-on of the Order. Yet, in deference to, and despite his wishes, Jane had studied and practised on her own, going beyond just the things he had taught her – in this case, moving quietly. An overheard discussion in her childhood had stuck with her. And with consternation, she had discovered that it was clearly far more challenging for ladies to achieve silent movement in the heeled boots they were obliged to wear. Listening now to the faintest creaking of the steps below her feet, she was pleased with the results of her efforts.

Was she truly prepared, though? Barely a month ago, Uncle Oscar – who had not disregarded her father's wishes, but rather acquiesced to her insistences – had told her that she was. 'One can only study and practise so much, my dear. No one is ever truly ready to go out in the world and face what we face, until they do.' She had practiced thoroughly over the last two years; she had read her book and memorised what she needed every day, including today. She was, she hoped, as ready as she could be.

Uncle Rudi had written to her at that time, telling her she would overcome all odds. But Uncle Rudi always said things like that to her. Where was he? Had something bad happened to him? An overwhelming dread pressed down on her. 'He's nice.' *Stupid Girl.* Mr Wallace had asked her such a reasonable question; and they had all expected a mature, informative answer. And what had she given them? *Breathe, Jane.*

As they progressed up, Jane came into eyeline with the second floor. Near the top of the stairs, a doorway led to the rear part of the house where the ablutions and a spare bedroom were. Through the landing balustrade, a narrow strip of flickering orange light seeped from below the double doors to Uncle Rudi's bedroom. Everything else lay mired in cold darkness. Jane could have resolved the lack of illumination in an instant, but the inevitable, resultant consternation made her hesitate. It was not at all the time for such a distraction. The landing continued to the right to his small personal library, and to his study at the front of the house, before turning back to the flight of stairs directly above them, leading to the top floor. Uncle Rudi must surely be in his bedroom? Perhaps he had fallen asleep while awaiting them? Why then, was everyone so tense? Why did she feel so apprehensive?

They paused here as Mr Hastings issued silent directions: she and the doctor were to wait; Mr Wallace was to watch the passage to the rear; Mr Carnby the landing and flight up; Emma to the other side of the doors. Mr Hastings approached the double doors, and was reaching for them, when abruptly, he spun towards the front of the house. At the same instant, Mr Wallace and Emma followed suit, and Mr Carnby rapidly played his lantern back and forth. Had they heard something? Jane peered from her position, but could see nothing. However, Mr Hastings now moved in that direction.

He had barely taken two steps when Emma gesticulated wildly at Mr Carnby, who, in turn, grabbed Mr Hastings by the shoulder. Jane saw the young gentleman start, looking back over his shoulder. Mr Carnby indicated to Emma, and when Mr Hastings looked to her, she pointed to her own ear and then to the double doors. Even in limited lantern light, Jane could make out her worried expression.

Mr Hastings took a position to the right of the doors, and indicated Dr Whitehall to the left. He directed Mr Wallace and Mr Carnby back to their initial positions. Jane was to remain where she was. As soon as everyone was in place, he nodded to Emma. *Breathe.*

As the doors swung open, bright warm orange light spilled into the landing, dazzling Jane after the near-absolute darkness and causing her to shield her eyes and look away. When she squinted back, Emma was standing rooted to the spot, and Mr Hastings had sprung into the room, his weapon raised. 'What in all the –?' he roared.

Near to the ground, something large and red was moving, writhing. From where she was, she could make out what looked like a man's pyjamaed leg, protruding from the red mass on the floor. Was that…Uncle Rudi? There was a loud, gurgling, wet hiss, and then another, and then several more. Jane did not have the time to fret.

A great many things seemed to happen at once, and yet everything seemed to be moving slowly, as though the world had turned viscous, like honey flowing from a spoon. Something rose up in the room, and Mr Hastings lashed out with a kick, and she saw a blood-red mass fly backwards through the air, landing in the fireplace, smothering it and the light with it, plunging the space into near-absolute darkness again. Emma crumpled onto the floor, and she saw a viscid red man-like creature scrambling on top of her. Dr Whitehall was similarly tackled by another one as he dashed towards Emma, he and the creature rolling dangerously towards the balusters. Jane instinctively lunged forward to help, dropping her lantern, but at that moment, some unseen objects smashed into both Mr Wallace in front of her, and Mr Carnby across the landing, driving both of them into the floor, and she leapt back against the wall at the top of the stairs. Lantern beams splayed crazily in all directions.

They needed light! Jane raised her hands, but a sudden hissing tore her away from her intentions. She looked towards the sound, up and to her left, into the corner of the ceiling. There, perched upside-down and staring at her, was a translucent man-like creature. Even though illuminated by the beam of a lantern, it was hard to see, its outline unclear, like water in a glass. She recognised these things. She had read about them, seen an illustration in one of the Order's books. But for the life of her, she could not think of their name. It remained, however, that they were now in mortal peril.

It released an inhuman screech and lunged at her.

Jane boldly turned to face the translucent horror as it flew through the air. Forcefully clasping her hands before her, she yelled in Latin, '*Stā!*' The abomination instantly became rigid. Gasping, she flung herself against the wall once more, as the diaphanous monstrosity sailed past her and down the flight of stairs. She heard the thumping of its stiff form crashing into the wooden floor and knew that even if it were still alive, it certainly would not move for quite some time.

Amongst the sounds of inhuman, high-pitched screeching and struggle around her, there was another awful crashing nearby, and she feared the doctor had smashed through the balustrade with his assailant. *Light!* She made a motion like striking a match with her empty hands and whispered, '*Lux sit,*' then flicked her hand towards the stairwell.

A single tiny spark of light, like a faint and distant star, flew from her hand, erupting into a ball of bright white light above the stairwell, casting illumination on the surroundings. It sizzled and spat like one of the hand-held sparklers often lit during celebrations, but much larger, and absolutely silent.

Below it, on the stairs, Dr Whitehall was hacking at the neck of his crimson attacker with his kukri. In the distance, Mr Carnby was furiously doing much the same with a dagger while under another diaphanous creature. In front of her, Mr Wallace, having righted himself onto one knee, with a smooth flourish drew a two-foot blade from within his cane, slashed his translucent attacker twice with lightning speed, before driving the point under the creature's chin, and forcing the blade up and out the top of its skull. '*Die!*' he snarled. '*I insist!*' Jane recoiled in revulsion.

Closer to the doors, Emma, still supine, was shoving aside an inert form that was rapidly draining of its red colour, as she scrambled to free herself. Her face, neck and the top half of her were completely drenched in blood, as was the kukri in her hands.

Hollow Men. That was what these abominations were called, and on the floor of the bedroom, Mr Hastings had just slain one, shoving it aside when the other – the one he had kicked into the fire – had scrabbled out again, burnt and screeching. The fire, given air again, sprang back to life.

Still on the ground at the foot of the bed, Axel lashed out with a kick at the pouncing beast, striking it in the chest, sending it straight back into the fireplace, causing darkness to descend again. He had barely had time to conceptualise the grotesque, blood-red abominations swarming over the supine figure of a man on the floor, before they'd attacked him.

As he had struggled with the one he had just slain, it was clear that it was trying to attach its revolting mouth to him and feed upon him like a monstrous man-shaped leech. When he had severed its head with one powerful downward stroke of his Bowie, tremendous volumes of blood had begun to spurt out onto the bedroom floor.

Axel grunted and pushed himself to his feet. The other monstrosity had clawed its way out of the fire again. With visible burns, and blood seeping from its body, it screeched at him in rage. The creature certainly was tenacious. But then, he knew what drove them. He had felt their all-encompassing hunger. Rage, horror and revulsion still coursing through him, Axel roared and charged. Striking it with his shoulder, he drove it back into the mantle. Before it could recover, he thrust the Bowie into the middle of its chest, snarling like an enraged beast.

It screamed in agony.

He withdrew the blade and swung with all his might, decapitating the foul thing.

Its headless corpse crumpled to the floor, spurting fountains of blood from severed arteries as it went. The head went rolling off to the right, towards a dresser.

Axel spun, ready for the next attack, but save for the bodies, he was alone in the room.

He sank to his knees, gasping for breath. 'Is everyone all right?' He called between breaths. 'Is everyone alive?'

One by one, each answered in the affirmative.

He heard a low, weak groan – barely a whisper – nearby. He looked over at the figure lying on the floor. It was an older man with thinning white hair and an unkempt white beard.

Again, he heard the groan.

The man was alive.

Twelve
The Other Side

Percy Wallace slumped to a sitting position, breathing heavily as he slowly re-sheathed the sword in his cane. Driving it home, he twisted, locking it in place. He was annoyed: that was one little surprise he had not wanted to reveal so soon. However, circumstances had clearly forced his hand otherwise. He looked about him trying to make sense of what had happened. Percy was no stranger to the disorientation that sometimes followed an intense struggle; but this… A ball of silent yet sizzling light hovered in the stairwell, below which he could see Whitehall's head as he sat puffing for breath on the stairs, his face and spectacles spattered with blood. And these…abominations…lay strewn across the floor, transparent like a glass or a cheap window, refracting the light that passed through them. *What the devil is all this*? As blood spread across the floor from the one that had attacked Emma, colour leached from its body, gradually giving it a clear and glass-like appearance as well.

She looked as though she had been bathed in blood as she met his gaze, panting. Her green eyes shone like stars against the near-unmitigated redness. 'Are you hurt?' he asked.

'It's not my blood.' She coughed.

What the devil are these things? He was about ask aloud when, over his shoulder he heard a grunt. He turned to see Carnby lying on his back holding his hand to his neck, just below his jaw, as blood seeped from between and around his fingers.

Grunting with effort as he scrambled over to the burglar, he called, 'Doctor!'

At almost the same instant, Axel mirrored the call from the bedroom.

'Carnby is injured,' Percy said.

'This man is dying!' There was desperation in Axel's voice.

Percy added the pressure of his gloved hand to Carnby's. 'Hold on, man.'

The burglar grunted a pained acknowledgement.

Percy looked to see the doctor staggering to the top stair, wiping the blood from his lenses. He checked on Jane a moment, who appeared to be unharmed, but was pressed against the wall, staring into the bedroom with an expression of near panic. Moving on, he collected his black Gladstone bag, calling, 'Is anyone capable of rendering first aid?'

'Yes,' came the unexpected reply from the young lady behind him.

Donning his spectacles, he regarded her.

'My father taught me when I was younger,' she said, as if to explain.

'Follow me.'

He led her to Carnby, and Percy moved aside as the doctor crouched and quickly examined the man. Rising, he opened his bag, and hastily removed a number of bandages and gauze. 'Stanch the bleeding without removing these,' he instructed, handing her the gauze, 'then fasten firmly in place.' Whitehall piled the bandages into her open hands.

She nodded obediently.

The doctor then hurried into the bedroom.

'Shall I sit him up?' Percy asked Jane as she knelt on the other side of Carnby.

'Thank you, no, Mr Wallace.' She was quickly sorting and folding the gauzes with a practised hand. 'It's better he remains lying.'

There was a cool confidence in her voice, which struck Percy as out of place in this shy young lady, and yet filled him with a sense of relief. As she worked, he grabbed Carnby's lantern and scanned the ceiling, ready for another attack. But for the time being they remained alone in the gore and blood.

'Now Mr Carnby, please remove your hand...' Jane's voice was soft and reassuring.

He watched her quickly press a gauze against the blood flowing from Carnby's jaw. The burglar grunted at the pressure. *Tough old sod,* thought Percy. Immediately the gauze was drenched, but without pause, she had another several in place.

'Can you hold these for me, Mr Carnby?'

Percy turned to the nearby diaphanous monstrosity. As Jane continued to talk to the burglar, he shoved it over onto its back, and its nearly-severed head tilted away from its body at an impossible angle. The ferocity of Carnby's attack on it was not lost on Percy. Drops of blood oozed from the ragged stump of its neck, as did a clear fluid. The mere sight of those who had met violent ends held no horrors for him. He shifted to examine it.

It seemed a naked man, though appearing as if *skinned*, or *flayed*. Beneath moist skin, translucent musculature and arteries were visible, defined by a faint pinkish hue. Its hands ended in thick claws, which he had felt during his struggle with the other one, as they had dug into his clothing. It bore no hair anywhere.

He inspected the head. Its eyes too were translucent, but for pupils and irises, it had only onyx black dots. Where its nose should have been lay two narrow, vertical slits. And its mouth...he felt gorge rising at the sight of its mouth: a thick ring of muscle encircled the opening where a mouth should have been. Percy was thankful for his gloves as he pulled back at the ring of muscle. A row of narrow, filthy teeth like curved needles bordered the inside of the ring. Even worse, numerous fine dark purplish tentacles, the colour of a bruise and slick with blood, hung limply from this nightmarish orifice. If this abomination sucked the blood of its victims, its colourless body and eyes taking on that crimson hue, it must be frightening to behold when satiated. He shuddered in horror and revulsion.

'Is that a bite?' he heard Jane ask in alarm.

Percy looked back to see blood oozing from a circular tear in Carnby's clothing at his chest. Jane had finished neatly wrapping a bandage below the burglar's jaw and around his head.

'Th' bloomin' thing latch'd on good 'n propa,' he grumbled.

Percy was about to ask if that was bad, but from the expression on Jane's face, he already had his answer.

Axel moved aside as Whitehall took his place on the old man's right. Emma had hurried over and was already kneeling on the other side. She held the old man's left hand in both of her bloodstained hands. 'Mr von Meyerling?' she crooned.

The doctor examined the man. 'I fear he's lost a great deal of blood.'

Axel glanced at the pools of blood and despaired. *Blood we have in plentiful supply, could we but get it back into the poor fellow.*

'Mr von Meyerling?' Emma repeated, firmer this time.

The old man groaned, and Axel turned to see his eyes flutter open. Mr von Meyerling looked to Emma, then the doctor, then back to Emma with pale blue eyes. 'Oh, *schöne fräulein*,' he croaked in a German accent, 'You haf blood on your face.' He reached for her feebly with his other hand, but it trembled and gave out, collapsing on his chest.

Axel moved near the old man's head. 'Mr von Meyerling? Lord Renfield sent us. I am sorry we were so very late.' He saw tears welling in Emma's eyes as the man turned his gaze to him.

'Ach! It vas alvays too late!' he whispered. 'Too long I haf liffed in a vorld vere terrible things reign, and yet beauty vill never die. To see such things from the eyes ov an old man!' He closed his eyes. '*That* is to be sorry.' He sighed.

The doctor looked to Axel and gave a slight shake of his head.

'What can we do, sir?' Axel asked.

The old man laughed faintly, his body shuddering with the effort. 'Vot *can* you do? Such a thing only *you* can say, *ja*?' He paused, his breathing ragged and shallow, and looked back to Axel. 'That vhich in the darkness lies, is strong. But you must continue the fight. Continue that vhich ve started.'

Axel felt the hairs on the back of his neck stand up at those words.

Mr von Meyerling paused again, his eyes closing and his breath growing fainter but more ragged.

Whitehall pressed his fingers to the man's neck, feeling for a pulse. Axel saw the look on the doctor's face was grim.

But he opened his eyes. 'Tools you vill need...*im Tresor*...in the safe...*im Keller*.' He turned his pale eyes to Emma again. Tears were running down her cheeks, washing a pallid path through the crimson. Her lips trembled as she struggled to control her emotion. 'Do not cry, *schöne fräulein*. Ve *all* must die *someday*. I go now to The Other Side. I vill find perhaps, such exquisiteness as yours there, *ja*? Vun last time, let me look on such beauty *mit meinen Augen...*'

As he stared at Emma, his faint, shuddering breaths ceased, and the light faded and vanished from his eyes.

'Dash it all!' exclaimed Whitehall. He shifted forward and began thumping the man's chest.

Emma broke down. Lowering her face to von Meyerling's hand, she pressed it to her cheek and wept.

Axel felt his heart breaking for her. Someone so sensitive and compassionate as she, to weep for the passing of a stranger, would never survive this strange and terrible new world on which they verged. He wanted to hold her and tell her it would be okay, but such things were not done.

He got up slowly and staggered away. Steadying himself with the bedpost, he closed his eyes and listened to the sounds of Whitehall's thumping and Emma's sobbing, and held back his own tears. What was this nightmarish reality now revealed to them? Was Spotted Elk, now long with the cold earth, indeed, right?

The thumping stopped, and he heard Whitehall sigh. A moment later he heard the ruffling of paper, and the scratching of a pen, as the doctor stated, clinically, 'Time of death: ten forty-seven p.m.'

Axel sighed in disbelief. *Ten forty-seven*? Not even an hour ago they were climbing into the coach in Belgrave Square as if on a social outing. It seemed a lifetime ago.

A cold waft of air on his sweat-soaked face drew him back from his musings. He looked at the curtained window to the right of the bed. The curtain rustled slightly. Axel drew his revolver. He was taking no chances. Advancing, he drew back the curtain with a swift motion to reveal empty darkness. The window was wide open, and outside billowed the black and endless night. His eye was drawn to a chip in the white paint of the sill. As he looked closer, it seemed to him like a claw mark. *That was how these things entered.* He closed and fastened the panes. Even so, the thought came to him, *There are more windows...*

Axel turned back to the room. He picked up his blood-soaked top hat and examined it: ruined. He flung it aside in disgust. Collecting his gun-bag, he drew his rifle and cocked it. 'Wait here,' he ordered.

Thirteen
Bite

Jane examined the wound on Mr Carnby's chest. 'We must act quickly,' she told Mr Wallace.

'Why?'

'If we delay, he will become one of them.'

'What *are* these things, Jane?'

'We call them "Hollow Men",' she stated matter-of-factly. 'If they have a true name, it is unknown to me.'

He looked around at the translucent corpses. '"Hollow Men" seems apropos. And if they bite one, one becomes...?'

'Yes, Mr Wallace. Their bite contains a venom that corrupts the core of one's being. If one is not bled dry for any reason, and left untreated, the change is rapid.' The import of her words hung in the cold air. 'I have read a record of an entire group being lost when this knowledge was unknown. They merely returned home with the infected man...'

'Oi 'ope there's a bloomin' cure!' grumbled Mr Carnby.

'Silver,' Jane said looking about. 'We need something made of silver.'

Mr Wallace reached for his sword-cane. A sudden apprehension flowed through her. Such an effective weapon, this entire time, hidden in plain sight. What else might Mr Wallace be hiding? Holding its handle up, he showed her the lion's paw. 'Will this do?

She pushed her apprehension aside. 'Is it silver?'

'It's steel, but with a rather expensive silver plate.'

'Yes!' she exclaimed in relief.

'What must we do?'

'You will have to open his shirt, Mr Wallace,' she instructed, 'and apply the metal directly to the skin at the bite.'

'Me? Why must *I*?'

Jane looked at him, taken aback. 'It wouldn't be proper, Mr Wallace, for me to...'

'Ah, of course. At least be so kind as to direct me.'

Jane nodded.

At her instruction, Mr Wallace undid the top part of Mr Carnby's shirt and pulled the left side away, along with his jacket and coat, exposing the circular red welt against pale skin.

Jane looked away to the older man's face. 'I've read it hurts terribly, Mr Carnby. Take my hand if you like.'

'No, luv. Oi wouldn' wan' t' 'urt yew.'

'As you wish.' She smiled, despite the circumstances, and instructed Mr Wallace. 'Press it firmly against the wound until the burning stops.'

'Very well.' He looked to Mr Carnby. 'Ready, old man?'

'Jast get it dun be-fore I turn in'a one 'a those bloomin—' He trailed off into a deep groan of pain through clenched teeth as Mr Wallace jammed the cane handle against his skin.

There was an audible sizzling, like the sound of frying sausages, and a trail of smoke rose from Mr Carnby's flesh. It seemed to burn for ages. The older man's hand flew up and Mr Wallace grimaced as powerful fingers dug into his arm, though he did not relieve the pressure he applied. Mr Carnby was right: he would have crushed her hand with that grip.

The burning eventually ceased, and she saw relief on the supine man's face, and the easing of his grasp. He lay still, gasping.

'All done, old chap!'

'Is he badly injured?' A voice asked from nearby.

Jane started, and turned to see Mr Hastings standing in the doorway. He was brandishing his rifle, his right hand wrapped around the handle and his left around the fore-grip.

She smiled at him despite herself, and immediately felt foolish. She felt herself blushing, but she couldn't help herself. Other than being covered in blood, he was unharmed. And he looked so commanding, standing there with his rifle and that stern look on his face.

Instantly, all her confidence fled her, and she stumbled on her words as she asked, 'Was...was...anyone else bit- bitten?'

He quickly relayed the question to Emma and Whitehall.

Both answered in the negative.

'Only von Meyerling,' he answered. 'But he has passed.'

Jane felt her heart plummet in her chest. Her hands came up involuntarily to her mouth and tears welled up in her eyes. Memories flashed through her mind of the kindly old man with the funny accent who used to play games with her as a child. She sobbed as she remembered how he would tell her strange and fascinating facts about science and history, and show her his outlandish contraptions.

A moment later, Mr Hastings was crouched in front of her, placing his rifle on the floor. After a pause, he gently reached out and squeezed her shoulder. 'Please forgive my thoughtlessness. I should have realised you knew him.'

'It's alright,' she sobbed, looking down and fumbling for her mouchoir. It most definitely was not. *Why lie?*

'There, there...' He comforted her softly. 'Everything will be okay.'

Because women weep and men don't. That's why. It has to 'alright', doesn't it? She dabbed at the tears running from her eyes. After some time, she spoke, her voice heavy. 'I am sorry, Mr Hastings.'

'Please, *Axel*.'

She glanced up at him, immediately feeling embarrassed, looking away again. 'I am sorry...Axel...just the shock of it...you see, I've known Uncle Rudi—, Mr von Meyerling, that is, since I was a little girl.'

'Shhh,' he said soothingly. 'I understand, Miss Halifax.'

After a few more moments, she managed to collect herself. She looked around at the men and said, 'Forgive me. Please, call me Jane.' She took a long breath before adding, 'Mr Carnby should be fine now.'

Axel drew his hand away. He turned to Mr Wallace. 'The bedroom window was open. That's how they got in. The downstairs windows were all shut, but we need to check the others here and upstairs.'

The other man gestured to Mr Carnby. 'Let's move the old chap to the bedroom first.'

'There's also a safe in the cellar that apparently contains what we need,' Axel added.

Jane moved to the bedroom door as the other two men helped the grumbling Mr Carnby to the bed. Despite her show of bravery, her heart was filled with deep, empty sorrow. She stared into the room; the doctor was sitting on the end of the bed, his head in his hands. Poor old Uncle Rudi was lying still on the floor. Tears filled her eyes again. So animated in life, he looked so small and frail in death. Emma was kneeling next to him, holding his hand in hers, looking down at him, crying.

Jane wiped away her tears even though more were coming. She remembered when she was a little girl, he used to tell her, 'People will alvays say to you, you cannot do this, or you cannot do that, because you are just a girl!' Then he would smile and say, 'Do not listen to them, my child. You can do anything you vant! Because you haf two arms, two legs, a heart, a brain and most of all – because you are you!'

This was her world: the only life she had known. The Order of the Steel Rose had been her family for as long as she could remember, and it was growing ever smaller. First, her mother, though she had been too young to remember her; then her father; now Uncle Rudi. Only Uncle Oscar remained from the circle of loved ones she had had since childhood.

Yes. The cold and silent voice said inside her head. *That's right. They all die, don't they*? It almost sounded perverse in its sadistic malice. *Despite all your power, there's nothing you can do to save them, is there*?

Jane started. The world seemed to spin with a sense of nightmarish *déjà-vu*. She was sure she had never heard the voice before, but it seemed ever so familiar. And that frightened her.

She looked about into the empty landing and felt terribly alone.

Someone was calling out to her from the immeasurable reaches of the beyond...

'Jane!' Axel called out again. He had already called out twice and was about to go to her when she turned, wiping tears from her eyes.

'Yes...Axel?'

'Percy tells us these things are called "Hollow Men"?'

'Yes, that's correct.'

'What are they?'

She glanced at the two translucent forms in the bedroom. 'Abominations. Cruel mockeries of what were once men, diminished in thought and reason, corrupted by...' she trailed off.

'Corrupted by what?' Percy asked.

She stared at Percy a moment before answering cryptically, 'That...*that which lies in the darkness...*'

Axel felt the hair on the back of his neck stand on end again. Jane was reciting almost word for word what both von Meyerling and Spotted Elk had said. *Uncanny*, he thought.

'And what lies in the darkness, Jane?' Percy persisted.

Her eyes darted about the place, taking in the ceilings as she searched, before regarding him again. 'It is not always wise to speak of such things, Mr Wallace.'

Given what he had felt touching the wall, Axel shared her unease, but could not ignore the potential danger. 'There may be more.'

'Jolly good,' Percy muttered, wiping blood from his face with a handkerchief.

'There's one that's probably still alive,' Jane said in a straightforward manner.

'What?' Axel grabbed his rifle, alarmed. 'Where?'

'It's helpless.' Jane folded her arms, holding herself. 'I promise it's not going anywhere.'

Fourteen
The Sight

Axel, Jane and Percy stood near the top of the stair.

They had left Carnby, Emma and Whitehall in the bedroom with the door closed. As the doctor had tended to the burglar's wound, Axel had given Carnby his cut-down shotgun and clear instructions not to hesitate if anything came through the door that wasn't them.

Emma was of more concern. Even as they left, she sat staring at the dead von Meyerling, weeping silently. Axel feared she may have suffered some kind of mental collapse at the sight of a man dying before her eyes. Ladies here in London were not exposed to such things, so these events came as a terrible shock.

Out on the landing, pointing at the ball of silent, spitting light, Axel asked, *'What exactly is that?'*

'Light,' Jane replied, as if it were obvious.

'Yes...' Axel rubbed his eyes and grimaced. 'But how? Where did it come from?'

'I made it!' Jane beamed, with her hands on her hips.

Axel and Percy stared at her.

'Did you now?' Percy asked with an expression of incredulity.

Axel was not sure he believed her, either. 'Could you do it again?'

'Of course!'

He watched her make a staccato gesture with her hands as she whispered something. She then motioned as if casting something down the stairs. A tiny seed of light, like the smallest, faintest star in the night sky flew from her open hand down the stairwell, before bursting into light at the bottom. It, too, looked like a sparkler, and aside from the dead Hollow Man halfway down the bloody stairs, it illuminated another one on the lower landing.

Percy's jaw dropped.

Axel blinked repeatedly. 'Amazing!' He was in awe. 'And you can just do that?'

'Yes.'

'And you can keep on doing that?'

'That?' She pointed, nodding, 'Yes. That's quite easy. Other things are harder. They require more effort.'

'How long will it last?'

'The light? Hours. Or until I dispel it.'

'How extraordinary!' Percy exclaimed, regarding Jane.

They now stood over the rigid, motionless and awkwardly splayed Hollow Man. Its clawed hands were outstretched, grasping, and its legs were partially bent. Axel examined it. He didn't know if one could say it was 'alive', but it appeared to be breathing. Though the satiated ones with their crimson rage-filled eyes and grotesque waving-mouth tentacles, which he had found feeding on Mr von Meyerling were far more horrific, this *thing* was still nightmarish enough.

'And you did this too?' he asked Jane.

She nodded, her ebony eyes sparkling with both fear and excitement in the new sizzling light.

Axel looked about him. 'Percy, would you keep an eye out?'

'Of course, old chap.' He cocked his now-drawn pistol.

Axel crouched and studied the monstrous face. In its diaphanous state, it was hard to make out the details, but he could see the onyx dots in its eyes. And he could feel the malevolence radiating off it. Axel reached out tentatively.

'I say, man! What are you doing?' Percy exclaimed, alarmed.

Axel ignored him. He took a deep breath and touched the abomination on the shoulder. Blackness, rage, malevolence and the all-encompassing hunger flooded into him, filling him up. But this time, he was ready. Closing his eyes, he concentrated, breathing slowly and deeply. He was above this. He was a man, not a beast. He could resist the animal urges.

The world changed. Axel became the beast, seeing the world through its eyes, with its mean and stunted intellect. It did not so much think, as have *thought-feelings*. As he experienced the creature's memories, he had to maintain enough of his own awareness to assign words and meanings to the things it could not comprehend.

They were in the field of stones...the cemetery. He and his pack-brothers...the other Hollow Men. He and the other Hollow Men were so very hungry. The graves marked the locations of cold-men...corpses...in the ground, but they did not feed on corpses. Others fed on corpses, but they did not. The corpses were dry, with no blood for them to feed.

The Dark Master was there too. The Dark Master was a man. The Dark Master was commanding them, but he did not understand the words. The Dark Master gave them visions in their heads, making clear what he wished: across the grounds of the cemetery, at the row of man-lairs...houses, there was one specific house in the vision they were to scale the wall of, and enter. Inside was an old man with white hair, and they were to feed on him.

The visions stopped. There was only one man. He would have to hurry. He would have to get to the old man before the other Hollow Men, so he could feed.

The Dark Master was angry. He wanted them to feed on the old man. If they did not feed on the old man, the Dark Master would become the Pain Master again. The Hollow Men did not like the Pain Master. They hated and feared the Dark Master. But they feared the Pain Master even more. It was time to run.

The gravestones were a blur. The cold air was alive. Low down, racing between the graves, he could see and hear the other Hollow Men racing beside him. The thrill of the hunt rushed through him. Soon, he knew, he would feed.

The house grew closer. They all went over a wall, up the side of the house, and inside two open windows. Some inside one, some inside the other.

He could not find the old man. But there were more men here! A whole man-pack...a group! They were on the ground floor, moving around. He was going to go down to them, but he heard the group of men coming up to him and the other Hollow Men.

They moved quietly now, moving to the right places on the ceiling, looking down at the men. They were moving to leap down and attack.

Axel had a dizzying, disconcerting moment as he watched himself and the rest of their party through the Hollow Man's eyes. *He saw there were she-men...women...in the group. He liked the women: their blood tasted better.*

Axel watched Emma open the door, and himself dashing into the room. Then the fight began. *The other Hollow Men leapt at the group.*

The other woman was by herself. She was only small, but there would be enough for him to feed. He leapt at her. But she waved her claws…hands, and he couldn't move! He went past her, and he wanted to grab her, but he couldn't move. He wanted to scream in rage, but no sound happened. And he was falling down to the ground floor. It was coming. The pain was coming. He hit the ground and felt the pain. Not as bad as the Pain Master. But there was pain. He heard the other Hollow Men fighting the group above. But he couldn't move. He couldn't fight with them. Rage filled him. Rage and unsatisfied hunger…

Axel started, coming back to reality, pulling his hand away from the monstrosity. Jane was regarding him carefully, amazement and intense interest on her face.

'You have the *Sight*!' she whispered in excitement. 'What did you see?'

Percy looked at her, then at him. 'The Sight? Whatever do you mean?'

Axel glanced from one to the other. He couldn't speak. He had but a single thought in his mind. No…a *thought-feeling*. He knew only one thing: *The Dark Master would be angry…*

Axel sprang to his feet, jumped over the Hollow Man and was dashing up the stairs two at time.

Carnby looked at the old man lying still on the floor.

At least the doctor had finally stopped fussing over him. Whitehall had said the bleeding had slowed, and that he would 'sew up the wound' when they returned to the house. Finally, the doctor had given him an injection. Carnby had never been 'sewed up' by a proper physician. He felt *privileged*. It was a strange, uncomfortable feeling. But then, that might just have been whatever the doctor had stuck into him. He realised that most of his pain had gone, and he felt a little light-headed. And a little happy. It felt a bit like being drunk.

It wasn't right, he decided, to just leave von Meyerling lying there like that.

'Docta.' His voice sounded thick and heavy, and it was hard to speak with the bandage wrapped around his jaw.

'Hmmm?' Whitehall looked up at him. He had been kneeling over one of the Hollow Men doing something with the instruments in his black bag.

'We can' jast leave 'im layin' there loike that.' He pointed at the inert figure.

'No, you're quite right. We should move him.' His gaze settled on the bed. 'Let's put him on the bed.'

'Roight-o.' Carnby struggled to his feet, his body screaming with a moment of sharp pain. He grunted and felt the world spinning about him.

The doctor moved quickly and was supporting him by the arm in a flash, scrutinising his face. 'Are you all right there, Carnby?'

Carnby said breathlessly, 'Jast a li'le dizzy, ay Docta.'

'That's an effect of the morphia.'

'Bluddy good stuff, that!'

'Really, Mr Carnby! Do at least *try* to contain your vulgarity! But yes, it does the trick, doesn't it? I'd wager your pain has greatly reduced?'

Carnby nodded. They were about to move to the body when they heard the unmistakable thumping of footsteps ascending the stairs at speed. He reached for his weapon, the world swimming as he grabbed hold of it, and he nearly toppled over. But the footsteps went racing past on the landing, towards the rear of the house.

A moment later came another set of thudding steps, and they heard Percy's muffled voice calling with urgency, 'Axel! Wait, confound it! Axel!'

Finally, another set of steps, softer and slower than the others. *Miss Halifax?* Carnby wondered.

The two men regarded each other uncertainly. They both looked at Emma, motionless on the floor.

'We can't leave her in this state,' Whitehall said.

'No, we can',' he agreed. 'We get th' old fella on th' bed, an' then we'll see, ay?'

'Miss Westover?' Whitehall said. He crouched near the old man's head. Carnby was at his feet. When she did not respond, he called again.

Her eyes, red from tears, moved to his.

'We're going to move Mr von Meyerling to the bed, Miss Westover.'

She blinked.

'You'll have to let go of his hand.'

Without a word, she dropped his hand and stared off towards the closed doors.

They grasped the body and lifted, moving to the bed in unison. Shifting around, they positioned von Meyerling's corpse. Placing him as respectfully as they could, the doctor then gestured Carnby over. Whitehall spoke quietly. 'I should like to examine Miss Westover. Depending on what occurs, I may need your assistance to restrain her, or I may require you to excuse yourself. In any case, I may have to strongly medicate her.'

Carnby regarded him and nodded. 'Roight-o, Docta.'

They turned back to the room. She was no longer where she had been seated. The door to the landing was open, and Emma Westover was gone.

Fifteen

The Dark Master

Axel was in such a rush he had even forgotten his rifle. 'Confound it!' Percy cursed, as he grabbed the weapon and raced after the young man. Why had he gone and touched that abomination? Had it infected him in some way? Behind him, he could hear Jane's boots clomping up the steps.

Percy halted abruptly at the entry to the rear of the house. It was dark here and his lantern was smashed from the fight. The light behind him threw his elongated shadow on the floor before him. And Axel had dashed in recklessly.

He felt Jane press her hand against him for support as she also came to a sudden stop, panting.

'I say, my dear, are you able to do your light trick again?'

'I can do better.' She held out her hand. 'May I see your cane, Mr Wallace?'

He presented it to her.

'Please, hold out the end. Not the handle.'

He spun it, pointing the end towards, but not directly at her. She repeated her earlier actions, but this time, as the tiny spark of light formed, she ran her hands in a spherical motion around the space at the end of the cane. Immediately a smaller, though identical bright ball of light sprang into existence, hovering about three inches from the end of the cane.

'I say, you really are quite remarkable aren't you!' he exclaimed. 'I shudder to think what manner of trouble we would be in without you here.'

Jane smiled and looked away, blushing at his compliment.

Percy, amused at her naïve sweetness, moved to take on the darkness, pistol at the ready.

Ahead, there were two open doors on the right.

'Those are the ablutions,' Jane whispered.

Indeed they were, and they were empty. He checked the ceiling as he went, wary of another ambush from above. There was just one doorway directly ahead, and it was open. He felt a cold rush of air wash over him. The breeze had a distinct bite, chilling against his sweaty brow: it would likely start snowing again. He could feel Jane close to him, staying safely hidden behind his form as he approached the door.

A voice hissed, 'No light! No light!' He recognised it as Axel.

He lowered the light, but still uncertain, he murmured, 'Axel?'

'Yes!' came the quiet reply. 'In here, but no light!'

Jane placed her thumb and forefinger close to her lips and blew, as if dousing a match. The light went out abruptly, and they were adrift on a sea of infinite darkness.

Percy crept forward. Slowly, but surely, as his eyes adjusted to the stark blackness and the dim light entering from the landing, he could see the shadowy outline of the door ahead. He felt Jane grab on to his coat firmly as he moved, which, despite the danger, he found rather amusing.

He had the sensation of moving into a larger space. Ahead he could see the clear-cut outline of the window. The blue-black of the night contrasted sharply against the unmitigated blackness of the room around him. And silhouetted against the night was the distinctly powerful form of Axel. Around him billowed dark, towering, amorphous shapes, undulating in the wind. After a moment of near panic, Percy realised with relief that these were only the curtains.

Axel couldn't see them, so much as sense them. He gestured them over, and felt Percy and Jane approach.

'I say, what *are* you doing, Axel?' Percy murmured, as cold air buffeted them.

'I'm looking for a man.'

'A man?' he peered out into the night. 'What man? Where?'

'Jane?' Axel said, ignoring Percy's question.

'Yes?'

'Does "the Dark Master" mean anything to you?' He had realised that the man in his vision – the Dark Master of the Hollow Men – was likely standing out there somewhere in Westminster Cemetery. Axel was trying to retrace the abomination's movements back to the dark, shadowy being that had unleashed it.

'No...' came Jane's reply after a short time. 'Is that what you saw, Axel? This "Dark Master"?'

'Yes...' Distracted by his search, he explained, 'He looked to be a man, dressed in black, with a cloak and hood, and he seemed to direct these Hollow Men to come here and attack Mr von Meyerling.'

'Directed them?' The surprise in her voice was unmistakable. 'How did he direct them?'

But Axel barely heard her question. 'There!' he hissed, pointing. Standing between two gravestones was the dark silhouette of a man.

'Where?' Percy moved closer.

Axel directed the two as best he could, but after a moment Percy replied, 'Sorry, old boy. I see nothing but gravestones and shadows.'

The lone figure was standing quite still, and if not carefully searching, Axel thought, one could easily mistake the man for a statue such as those of angels scattered across the great cemetery.

Jane was so close to him on his right, he could feel the presence of her body almost touching his; he could smell her delicate perfume. He wanted to turn to her, but forced himself not to look away, lest he lose sight of the dark figure.

'I see him,' she whispered, so close. 'There! Up from that mausoleum. Near the gravestone with the large cross.'

'Yes,' Axel replied grimly. 'Indeed. If I had only thought to bring my rifle.'

He felt Percy pressing the weapon into his hand. 'Here. Lucky one of us has his wits about him, what?'

A wry smirk spread across Axel's face in the dark. Taking the weapon, he pressed the butt against his shoulder, and adjusting his grip, took aim.

'Can you make that shot?' Jane wanted to know.

Axel did not reply. He was concentrating on judging the correct aim in the almost non-existent light, and into this strong breeze. 'No,' he admitted defeat. The distance was seemingly less than about two hundred yards, but in these conditions... He wanted a single shot only. That would be bad enough given their surroundings; he certainly wouldn't have the luxury of several. In any case, he doubted the mysterious figure would simply remain stationary and allow him repeated attempts.

Axel frowned and lowered his weapon. At the same time, the figure began to move, heading south-west and away from them. It paused a moment, as though waiting, before continuing. Axel's initial urge was to give chase. This Dark Master had been responsible for the Hollow Men attacking them and slaying von Meyerling, and he needed to answer for that. But then he remembered the near-impassable disaster in the kitchen below. Exiting on to Ifield Road, then venturing north or south, to skirt around the ends of the cemetery was impractical; the figure would long since have departed. In a moment of madness, Axel considered climbing out the window and somehow scaling down the side of the house, and then over the brick wall that separated the property from the narrow, muddy lane that was meant to pass for a mews, and then the fence of the graveyard.

'*Others fed on the corpses...*' The thought-feeling pushed itself into his mind. The hair on the back of his neck stood up. What other monstrosities lurked in the murky gloom of Westminster Cemetery? Creatures that fed on corpses. And perhaps attacked lone men rushing foolishly through the darkness? *No*, he decided. They were, as a group, too scattered, unsteady and unprepared to face whatever other things lay out there. Besides, they already had a task to accomplish this evening, for which they were now very likely late.

As Axel watched in helpless frustration, the figure melted into the night.

'Blast,' he swore through gritted teeth. 'I'll have you yet, Dark Master,' he promised.

As they returned to the landing, a soft sound came to Axel's ears. He paused. 'Shh. Do you hear it?' he asked the others. It was a steady, wet, thudding noise coming from ahead. And it seemed to be accompanied by a low chanting.

The other two whispered their agreement in the darkness.

What now? he thought in exasperation. Axel raised his rifle, and moved forward, towards the light.

They came out into the hallway to see Emma Westover standing over one of the motionless Hollow Men, kicking it, and making the wet, thudding noise they had heard. Though it was clearly dead, she continued to attack it, driving the toe of her boot into its translucent flesh. With every kick, she spoke a word, the rage in her voice unmistakable. '…This. Was. One. Of. My. Favourite. Coats.'

Carnby and Whitehall were standing in the doorway of the bedroom, open-mouthed.

'Emma!' Axel called, 'It's dead! Let it be!'

She turned from the monstrosity, her eyes afire in the bright light; her earlier tears had caused her dark *kohl*, or – to use the popular new word – *mascara* – to run down her cheeks in vertical streaks.

She looked to him like some fierce tribal warrior woman, her face a melange of red, black and white, her sea-green eyes burning with fury.

'I know!' she snapped. 'But look at this!' She gestured to her coat, heavily soaked with blood. 'Do you know how hard it is to get blood out of a garment?'

Axel cocked his head at her. 'Yes, I do. But what do you know of getting blood out of garments?' he asked, wondering when last she had been drenched in blood.

She glared at him reproachfully, as if he were a child. The look spoke volumes, and he almost heard her voice in his head saying, *'Think, Axel!'*

A moment passed before realisation dawned on him. He rolled his eyes back in his head as he shut them from embarrassment and let out a sigh of exasperation. There were some things it was absolutely forbidden in society to draw attention to, and he had just done exactly that. There was an extremely vulgar four-letter word the Americans liked to use that described intimate relations. That word pushed itself into his mind now. He forcefully pushed it away. *Gods*, he thought. *You oaf! What the hell did you just say?*

An uncomfortable silence fell on the group. Someone coughed.

He opened his eyes as Emma's voice cut through the awkward quiet. 'We need to get to the safe, Axel.'

'He could feel the fire in his cheeks. 'Th-the safe?' he fumbled, mortified at his own crassness.

'Yes, Axel. Mr von Meyerling's safe with the tools we need.' She paused, sniffing. 'I suggest we do so post-haste. I wish to leave this accursed house of death as soon as possible, and never return!'

Sixteen

The Quality of Silver

Jane, Percy and Axel had finished their sweep of the study, library and upstairs two rooms – which turned out to be storerooms with more junk – finding nothing. In the meantime, the others were to have collected their scattered lanterns, ruined hats, and other items, and doused the fire in the bedroom. In practice, this fell to the two men, while Emma had stood at the top of the stairs in silence, arms crossed, tapping her foot impatiently.

With only the most cursory explanation having been provided to these three regarding Jane's creation of the strange floating light, much consternation and discussion took place between the two men. 'Poppycock' was one word used by the doctor regarding the possibility that she had just 'created' the light from nothing. Emma ignored them.

The group now formed a loose circle around the paralysed Hollow Man. They had all watched Jane douse the light on the first floor as they descended, their illumination coming from the sparkling ball above them.

'What shall we do with it?' Axel asked the others.

'Kill th' bloomin' thing.' Carnby was unequivocal.

'I say finish it, old boy,' Percy added.

'There...' Jane began hesitantly, 'there may be benefit in capturing it.' She looked up at everyone. 'We could learn things, such as what corrupts them.'

'She may just have a valid point.' Whitehall looked at the group over his lenses. 'The benefit to science could be immeasurable from study and dissection.'

Axel caught Jane scowling at Whitehall out of the corner of his eye.

'Emma?' Axel regarded her. 'Your vote decides.'

'Suffrage at its best!' Percy said, but the joke fell flat. Percy shrugged to Carnby, who shrugged back even though he had not laughed.

Emma stared down at the creature with all the cold contempt of a triumphant empress. She spoke with finality, the chilling malevolence in her voice hanging in the air, 'Kill it.'

Axel nodded. Drawing his Bowie again, he knelt beside the creature's head.

'What about your vote, Axel?' Whitehall interjected.

The young man paused and looked to the doctor. 'There are benefits to both choices. But were I to vote, it would only support the majority decision,' he said grimly.

Whitehall sighed in quiet surrender to the group's choice.

Axel addressed the ladies, 'Jane, Emma, you should turn away.'

Jane quickly complied, but Emma didn't budge. She turned her steely gaze to him. 'Not a chance, Axel.'

'As you wish.' Focusing on the monstrosity, he brought his blade up, and with a swift, powerful chop down on its neck, he ended it.

The door to the cellar was built into the wall panelling making up the bottom of the stairwell. It was covered in the same wallpaper as the walls around it, which was how Axel had not spotted it on their original sweep of the ground floor.

Axel had cursed himself. If he had missed this, what else had he missed as they'd made their way through the house? Given what they had just experienced, such carelessness could get them all killed. He shuddered to think of the consequence had something emerged from within and set upon them unawares. Particularly when they had fought the Hollow Men. Or when he had run off and left Percy and Jane alone. He chided himself on his carelessness.

As Carnby was rather pale and unsteady on his feet from the morphia, Axel had asked him not to risk the uneven stairs, and wait on the ground floor. The doctor had earlier found von Meyerling's keys on the dresser and had given them to Axel. Emma had volunteered to remain with the burglar, declaring, 'I've had it with stairs and monsters.'

Jane had fired off another of her lights before they had descended, and now, in a cellar largely given over to the storage of even more junk, against the middle of the north wall, Axel and the other three saw the unmistakable safe.

It was massive, almost five feet across and deep, and nearly six feet tall, with an imposing solid door. The entire thing had once been painted blue-green, but the colour was fading and the paint chipping, revealing the dull metal below. In the middle of the door was a keyhole and handle.

Axel began to try the keys one by one. He succeeded on the third. There was the heavy 'clank' of the mechanism turning. He turned the handle next, to a resounding 'thunk' of metal against metal. Standing back, he braced and pulled. The immense, thick door moved grudgingly, resisting the urge to be displaced from its rest. Axel grunted from the effort, and quickly, Percy was next to him assisting.

'I say! Jolly heavy, what!' he gasped as he pulled.

It seemed to Axel to be the type of safe that belonged in the Bank of England.

As the door swung the last few feet under its own momentum, Axel regarded the contents within in astonishment.

The safe was full of *weapons*. Stacks upon stacks of weapons: sabres, daggers, kukris, clubs of a sort; and on shelves, *ammunition*, boxes and boxes of ammunition.

Percy pulled out one of the sabres.

Axel picked a box of ammunition. Opening it and drawing a bullet, he saw that while the casing was quite ordinary, the projectile was not made of lead, but rather a much shinier metal that seemed to be silver.

'This is not steel.'

Axel regarded Percy, who was holding the drawn sabre at length, turning it in the light and hefting the weight of the blade.

'It feels the right weight, but the sheen of the blade...it appears to be something else...'

'Nor is this lead.' Axel held up the bullet for all to see. 'It looks almost like silver.' Peering into the safe, he said, 'In fact, all of the weapons here seem to be made of silver.'

Percy turned to Jane, lowering the sabre. 'Is it silver?'

Jane nodded. 'That would make sense.'

'Why silver, Jane?' Percy asked. 'Upstairs you said we needed silver to treat Carnby's wounds, and when I struck that creature, that Hollow Man, with the silver handle of my cane, it seemed to inflict tremendous pain.'

Jane took a deep breath before answering. 'The reasons are unclear. In myths around the world, silver is held to have special properties. It is said to be associated with purity and healing. In the texts I've read, the commonly held supposition is that this cleansing aspect of silver renders it harmful to these beasts, as they are tainted by a foul corruption. Silver then, is the natural antidote to the poison that aflicts them, if you will.'

Whitehall snorted in derision. 'Next, you'll expect me to believe that we have silver weapons to hunt *werewolves*!' He laughed. 'These things are fantasy! The creations of ignorant, superstitious minds!'

'There may well be some scientific rationale of which I am not aware, Doctor,' she answered with the faintest trace of defiance, 'but, as Mr Wallace asked *me*, I can only answer with what I know. Perhaps you may be able to shed some scientific light on the truth of the matter.'

'Speaking of light,' Percy said kindly, 'and as we're having answers: how exactly do you do that?' He pointed at the ball of light near the foot of the stairs.

Jane glanced at Whitehall before turning back to Percy. 'I'm sure Dr Whitehall will find this a most unsatisfactory answer, but—'

'Oh, please! Do go on, Miss Halifax! I do love a good fairy tale.' His tone was caustic.

Axel and Percy both glared at the doctor. Percy spoke, 'I think that's quite enough, Doctor. As I asked the young lady, I would like her answer.'

Axel could see that Jane was now apprehensive, her confidence having fled her under Whitehall's derision. 'Please tell us, Jane,' he soothed. '*Percy and I* would like to know.' He scowled past her at Whitehall and continued, 'And if the doctor can kindly refrain from interrupting...'

It took her a moment to collect herself. 'In...in my research, I came across some texts that addressed certain ancient...rituals...a combination of actions, words, symbols and intent of will that can create...*changes*...in the world around us. Some of those written of are simple, some quite difficult, and some highly dangerous.

'There are no codified rules, you understand,' she continued with growing confidence. 'There were only descriptions as to how one brings about these...events. I had to formulate my own words and gestures through trial and error, while thinking on the thing I wished to occur. I had to create my own *lexicon*, if you will, using Classical Latin, Sanskrit and even a little English.'

'That's quite remarkable!' Percy exclaimed.

'Are you saying that what you do is, in effect, *cast a spell*?' Axel asked. 'Is this...*magic*?'

Whitehall snorted loudly and derisively, but kept otherwise silent.

Jane glanced at the doctor again before answering. 'I suppose there are those who would refer to it as such, Axel.' She paused, slowly wringing her hands and biting her lip. 'But I like to think that it is some way of knowing and interacting with the world that we, as human beings, don't yet fully understand.' She again peeked at Whitehall, before adding, 'Much like science...'

Apparently, the doctor could take no more. 'Oh, I protest! This is too much! One cannot seriously profess this *mumbo-jumbo* to be on an equal standing with *science*! Science is the rational explanation of the world, and all that lies within. This is *superstition*!'

Jane reacted to his words as if she had been struck. Axel could see the emotion in her eyes and her lips trembling, before she clenched her jaw tight. 'Thank you, Doctor. *That is quite enough.*

If you would be so kind as to check on Emma and Carnby, we will be leaving shortly.

Whitehall was clearly about to argue, but reconsidered when he glanced from man to man. 'Outrageous!' he cried, storming off towards the stairs. They could hear his continuing tirade as he ascended. 'Put a pretty lady in front of a man, and he becomes a simpering idiot!'

Percy put down the weapon in his hands and moved to Jane. She had her eyes downcast, and was breathing slowly and deeply; her jaw was still clenched, and she was trembling. He offered her his handkerchief. 'Pay him no mind, my dear. *I* believe you.'

'As do I, Jane,' Axel seconded.

Jane politely waved away Percy's offered handkerchief and drew her own. She took a deep breath and dabbed at her eyes. 'Thank you. Thank you both. I can't tell these things to most people, they would think me quite mad...'

Percy playfully gave a slight bow. '*Seeing is believing*, my dear.'

'I promise, I've seen enough strange things to not disbelieve you!' Axel laughed.

Jane laughed as well. Blinking again she took another deep breath and shook the tension from her hands.

'Now, shall we continue?' Axel turned his attention back to the safe, stroking his chin.

'What do you have in mind, old chap?' Percy came and stood next to him, as did Jane.

'Ideally, I'd like to take whatever we—' He paused, noticing a distinct box on one of the lower shelves.

'What?'

Axel reached for it. The box was large and heavy. 'Help me here.'

They placed the box on a nearby surface. Unlike most other containers they were familiar with, this one was made of a shiny, thin, but apparently extremely strong, metal. It bore no paint or labels, but in the centre of the lid was embossed the unmistakable logo of the Steel Rose.

Opening it, Axel saw it was full of ammunition, but he was drawn immediately to the folded piece of paper. It was a note that read:

My Dear Mr Hastings,

Lord Renfield has to me advised that you are returning from America, and that American firearms you are carrying are of the Colt and Winchester makes.

It is apparent to all that you will have not the sufficient quantity of ammunition to suit your purpose.

Please accept these as a gift of the Order of The Steel Rose.

Yours Truly,
R.V.M.

There must have been dozens of silver bullets packed within, including shotgun, pistol and rifle rounds. And he could plainly see that *half* of that number were of the .44–40 calibre required for both his weapons.

Axel began to laugh.

Seventeen

The Man in Black

The man in the black cloak and hood strolled through the gloomy darkness, unhurried, towards the fence, not far from the southwestern corner of Westminster Cemetery. The biting wind striking him in the face did not bother him. Nor did the hungry and opportunistic predators lurking in the shadows of the gravestones, eyeing him, trying to ascertain whether he was easy prey, or not. They had much more to fear from him than he did from them, and clearly they knew it as they shrank away at his approach.

He stopped now at the tall fence, where the end of a narrow lane abutted it. The bald, hulking coachman with his thick, grizzled beard approached from the other side, watching him in silence. Inside the nearby large, covered wagon, the cages would return empty.

'Go,' the man in black ordered. 'We are done 'ere.'

Surprise crossed the hard face of the coachman, and his cruel blue eyes narrowed in suspicion.

'*Les bêtes sont—*' he stopped himself. Releasing an exasperated sigh, he snarled, 'The beasts are dead. Go! Report this.'

The coachman snorted out a smirk of self-satisfaction, a disdainful sneer tugging one side of his mouth upwards as he glared contemptuously at the man in black through the metal bars. Without a word, he about-faced and stalked off into the gloom. A moment later came the sounds of him mounting the wagon, followed by a harsh and deep '*Harh*!' before the wagon began to move.

The coachman had no loyalty to him, he knew, and would only too happily report the destruction of the creatures upon his return. An anger started to well within the man in black at the driver's insolence. Were it not more trouble than it was worth, he would have slowly and exquisitely sliced open the barbarous serf's throat then and there, ensuring that the *plouc* looked only into *his* eyes as his life slipped away, so he would at last understand respect.

His hand wrapped around the hilt of the large dagger at his side, and he clenched with all his might as rage washed over him. He forced himself to let it pass. *It is of no consequence*, he told himself, as he turned and continued towards the very corner of the cemetery. Snow was beginning to fall again, as he considered what had occurred. Yes, the wretched beasts had been slaughtered, for which he would have to account, but not before they had fulfilled their task of slaying that meddlesome *boche*. But, more importantly, he had learned much, and with this new knowledge came leverage.

Removed from the furious action, he had observed a great deal, studying this new group – their faces and features, and of course, their capabilities. There was more than one surprise to be had; the greatest of which for him, perhaps, being when the handsome young man with the moustache had reached out through the beast's mind.

This, more than anything in a long time, had excited the man dressed in black. At first, he had expected a reaction of some sort: a pursuit or even shooting. But nothing had come of it, and when it was clear that the beasts were lost, he had departed. However, as he had made his way back, he had found himself intrigued at the possibility of coming face-to-face with someone else who had the Sight. In all his experiences, he had yet to meet another who could perceive the world as he did. These thoughts he would save for himself, though.

He stopped at the corner, where a parallel lane also abutted the cemetery, aware of a malicious intent towards him. Turning back, he glared at the hungering shape creeping forward from behind a large gravestone. He did not shout, he did not wave his arms, charge, or attack. He did not need to. He simply glared at it, channelling all the violence his contempt would unleash, towards it.

It cowered and slunk back behind the gravestone.

Effortlessly, he mantled the fence and its spiked posts.

Further down this lane was the Clarence carriage he had arranged to meet him.

As he neared, he saw the coachman sitting completely still atop it, staring straight ahead. Good. He was still under control.

Entering, the man in black drew back his hood and slipped into the back seat. He realised immediately that aside from the other man, his associate – who was expected here – others were present as well. Opposite him, his associate sat back, his head resting against the wall of the cabin, an expression of pleasure on his face. Next to him, a young woman was leant over, her head in the man's lap, working rhythmically up and down.

'Oh my!' came a lascivious purr from next to him on the back seat, followed by an intoxicated giggle. The other young woman who had been waiting there was upon him in an instant. 'Wot 'ave we 'ere? Your friend didn' say yew was so 'andsome!'

He regarded her as she pressed against him. Blonde hair, massive, dilated pupils and a lewd smile filled his vision. At once, her hand was working its way up between his legs as she glanced over at the other woman, giggling again, then back at him. 'Reckon *Oi'm* th' lucky one!'

As she leant in to kiss him, sudden, contemptuous rage exploded within him. *This was not the time for this!* He pulled his head away from her face. 'What is this?' he barked at the other man.

'Ple-zhure, my friend. Pure ple-zhure.' The other man moaned without opening his eyes.

'This is not the time! We 'ave other—' The young woman was becoming more vigorous with her ministrations between his legs and was kissing his face and stroking his hair with increasing intensity.

He shoved her away with considerable strength.

She splayed back across the seat, banging into the side of the cabin, laying there laughing in hysterics.

'Laudanum?' he snapped.

'Hmmm…' came the useless reply.

He became even more enraged. He did not need *intoxicants* to make women desire him.

As the woman flailed and struggled to gather herself and assail him again, he reached out and pressed two fingers against her forehead. '*Dors!*' he commanded.

At once, she fell backwards, unconscious.

Without hesitation, he repeated this with the back of the other woman's bobbing head. She, too, slumped in an instant.

The other man swore, enraged. He unceremoniously shoved her off him, and she crumpled onto the cabin floor. Neither man moved to help her.

'Oi was en-joyin' that!' his associate complained, struggling to arrange his trousers.

'*Angliche stupide*! Your impatience will be the end of you.' Fury and contempt radiated from him.

The other man grumbled under his breath.

'*Alors*. We 'ave an important matter to accomplish tonight.' He gestured to the women. 'I *should* have killed them. But we will play with your toys later, *ouais*?' A sardonic smirk twisted across his handsome face. After all, who was he to deny himself pleasure? *When the time was right.*

Lounging back, the man in black barked, '*Allez*!'

Instantly, the carriage jerked into motion.

Eighteen
South Lambeth

Axel huffed as he and Percy carried the heavy box out to the street. The cold air struck him like a slap in the face, causing him to gasp. Snow was falling again as they hurried towards the coach.

They found Burton tending to the horses. 'Ah! There y'are m'lords. We was startin' t' get a mite cold! All go well?' He moved to them to assist.

A sombre shadow passed over Axel's face as he shook his head. 'No. von Meyerling is dead. And we were attacked.'

'Dead, m'lord?' Burton paused. 'May 'e res' in peace! 'Oo attacked yoo m'lord?' He now saw the state of their clothes, and of the others emerging behind him.

'Hollow Men.'

Burton spat on the pavement and cursed. 'Is...is e'rry wun all roight?'

'Some injuries, but nothing serious,' Percy reassured.

'Praise be t' th' stars, then m'lord!' Burton grunted as they shoved and hefted the box onto the floor of the cabin. 'Them 'Ollow Mens is danger-us!'

'What do you know of the Hollow Men, Burton?' Axel asked, intrigued.

'Nowt, but whot Oi 'erd from Lord Renfield, an' 'em. Enough t' know they be moighty danger-us, m'lord.'

Axel frowned. *What other dangers await us?* he mused. 'Where to from here? South Lambeth?'

'Aye, m'lord. 'Cross th' Batt'rsea Bridge, past th' park, then down t' Wan'swurth Road. There's a small road called 'Amilton Street, comes off'a that wun, m'lord, jus' near th' Suthern Railway Wurks. Small fact'ry there – nummer 10, it is. But we be runnin' late m'lords. We best be off.'

'Indeed.' Percy agreed.

As they set off, Axel had several competing thoughts. First and foremost, he wanted to stop the coach, and for them to have a detailed discussion of what had transpired, and what they might encounter at their next destination. However, they were indeed running late. Their stop at Mr von Meyerling's house should have only taken ten or so minutes; he had checked his pocket watch before they left, and it was then almost a *quarter-past eleven.* They would have to make do with whatever discussion they could manage during the transit. The rest would have to wait until they returned to Belgrave Square.

Second, he regarded the group: everyone seemed somewhat shaken to varying degrees, but by no means displayed the hysteria or shock the ordinary person would have, being confronted by such enormity. In his own case, the two prominent Lakota men had told Axel that strange things existed in the world. And he had himself experienced…*unsettling* sensations in certain places throughout his life, though he had not truly *believed* any of it, thus far. He was still struggling to comprehend the ramifications of the words of Black Elk and Spotted Elk being true.

Could it be that his new colleagues, too – Jane aside – were not so unfamiliar with the *supernatural*? They had certainly acquitted themselves well enough in the face of those alien dangers. Even Emma had not screamed and been merely a 'helpless woman'. Perhaps there was a compelling reason that these individuals had been chosen by the Order? Perhaps they were not as incapable as he had first assumed.

Of course, it was thoroughly improper to just ask, 'Who are you all, really?' Instead, he posed the question to them, 'Have any of you encountered one these Hollow Men before?'

No one professed any prior knowledge.

Jane explained, 'I've read of them, and seen an illustration, but I've never encountered one personally.'

'What are they?'

Jane opened her mouth to answer, but she was cut off.

Whitehall had drawn his pipe and was filling it, though his hands were shaking, 'The evidence indicates that they were men, though reduced to their lowest, and most degenerate form.' He tapped the pipe on the narrow window ledge, settling the tobacco within.

Axel realised he desperately wanted a cigarette to calm himself, and dug into his jacket pocket. Thankfully, the packet did not seem completely crushed.

The doctor continued, 'Affected by some sort of corruption, perhaps chemical, perhaps through infection. The symptoms of which would include certain *mutations*, such as a destruction of the *pigmentation* – the colouring, that is – of the skin, and a need to take nourishment from blood, rather than normal fare.

'In any case, I have taken some samples from one specimen. If I have the opportunity, I shall be most interested to see what other facts I am able to ascertain, and what conclusions I can draw.'

Axel glanced around the cabin. No one seemed satisfied with the doctor's answer. It really was a scientist's way of saying, 'I don't know,' he mused. He looked to Jane, but she was sitting with her arms crossed, clearly annoyed. Pursuing this particular line of questioning right now was going to cause problems. 'What might we expect in South Lambeth?' he asked her, instead.

'I don't know.' Where her earlier reply with the same answer to Percy had suggested uncertainty or hesitation, this time, her voice bore an air of authority. 'We could face any number of situations. I confess, this is my very first time truly engaging in activities on behalf of the Order. Other than the facts I've studied and learned, these are new experiences for me as well.' She regarded the others. 'And, *no*, Lord Renfield *did not* provide me with any information beforehand.'

Emma, who was sitting next to her, leant in and patted her arm. 'Of course, dear. No one here is questioning your character or motivations.' She gave Jane a warm and reassuring smile, which seemed to have the intended effect. 'But what we encountered in Mr von Meyerling's house was a shocking and frightening experience that I'm sure none of us were expecting. And I imagine that Axel was only asking in order for us to not be caught unawares again.' She looked to him and flashed the same smile. 'Isn't that right?'

'Emma is absolutely correct, Jane,' Axel agreed, as he was passing a cigarette across Percy to Carnby. 'I assure you, I did not mean to suggest any deceitfulness on your part, whatsoever.' She was clearly and understandably already upset, and he did not wish for her grief to worsen.

'I- I'm sorry…Of course you didn't…' She bit her lip, looking out of the window before turning back to the group, her eyes wet with emotion. 'Uncle Ru-…that is, Mr von Meyerling *wanted* us to have silver weapons. Which means we should expect something…*unnatural.*' She quickly resumed staring through the glass as her eyes welled up.

Axel let her be. He lit his cigarette and cracked open his window. By rights, he should not be smoking in this proximity to the ladies, but…*convention can wait on need*! he thought, as he drew back and savoured the acrid flavour.

Emma purred at him. 'Oh, Axel. Would you be a dear?'

He lit another and passed it to her.

Carnby, having lit his cigarette, spoke. "Oi said be-fore, Oi was told in that there let'er that this was a job. This 'ere's danger-us work.' He waived his hand, 'Oi don' moind me sum 'ard graft, but the re-ward's got t' be roight.' He rubbed his fingers together in the familiar gesture indicating lucre.

'Oi'm not jast beein' greedy, neither,' he continued. 'Not meanin' t' be rude t' any 'a yew folks, bat, that blummin' 'Ollow Man would'a 'ad me.' He regarded all the faces in the cabin, turned to him. 'See, if somethin' bad 'appens t' wun 'a yew, yew'll be roight, not meenin' no dis-re-spec'. Bat wot 'appens t' ol' Carnby if Oi can' work no more? Oi got no family. Oi got no 'igh-up sta'us.'

There was a silence within the cabin. Axel realised he had never considered the consequences to someone in Carnby's circumstances. Perhaps no one else had, either. Should he, himself, be maimed or crippled, his family would support him. It was very likely that the same was true for the others. Or at the least, they had the means to provide for themselves. But what, indeed, would a burglar face? Destitution and starvation on the streets? He leant forward a little to speak to the other man. 'So, what is it you're asking, Mr Carnby?'

'Is it wurth it?' The bluntness of the question drove the point home. No one seemed to have an answer.

'Miss 'Alifax,' Carnby called in a gentle voice, 'Oi don' reckon yew know 'ow much 'is Lordship is off'rin' t' pay us, neither?'

'I'm sorry, Mr Carnby, but no, I don't.' Jane frowned as she gave her quiet response. 'However, I will say that I have never known Uncle- Lord Renfield, that is, to be anything but generous. More than anyone, he knows the risks involved, and I can't imagine that he would not offer commensurate compensation.'

'Ay?' Carnby pulled a puzzled expression.

Axel was about to explain, but Percy spoke first, 'Miss Halifax means that it will, indeed, be "worth it".'

'Ah.' The burglar appeared relieved.

'Let's ensure we all make it through *whatever* is coming next, together,' Percy addressed everyone. 'And we can then get a clear answer from Lord Renfield tomorrow, as he promised.'

There was a general consensus of agreement.

'Have a short rest,' Axel suggested, 'Then we should all change our ammunition for the silver bullets.'

'By the way, what happened to you, old chap, when you touched that abomination?' Percy asked him. 'I saw your eyes *change.*'

Axel smoked while unloading and reloading his weapons, as he recounted seeing through the Hollow Man's eyes, and of what he had observed of this so-called Dark Master.

Everyone listened attentively – even – he noted, Whitehall. The doctor's brow furrowed in contemplation from time to time during Axel's exposition, as he alternated between his weapon and his pipe.

'Quite remarkable, Axel!' The doctor exclaimed when Axel was finished. 'We must discuss this ability of yours further at a more suitable time.'

Axel saw that the others were also surprised at Whitehall's apparently open reaction.

'How does it come about, Doctor,' Percy asked, 'That you can accept Axel's claims of seeing the creature's thoughts, and yet you can't accept that Jane created the lights in the house?'

'Simple.' Whitehall's manner was that of a haughty professor condescending to explain matters to a fresher, 'The mind is a vast and as yet not fully understood instrument. Phenomena such as *mesmerism*, *telekinesis*, *clairvoyance* are all unexplained creations of the *mind*. Such events are frequently recorded in detail. I know of no such recounting of methods akin to those described by Miss Halifax, other than in fairy tales.'

'Yes, but couldn't such abilities also be a function of the mind?' Axel argued.

'They could,' Whitehall answered. 'But by her own admission, Miss Halifax denies these as such. Rather, she claims that they are "ancient rituals" that she has...appropriated and utilised. That does not suggest to me in the least that this is a phenomenon of the mind.' He paused and drew more steadily on his pipe. Apparently, the opportunity to engage in scientific debate was sufficient for him to regain his composure. 'Finally, I have observed Axel to be a level-headed young man, and hence, I am far more inclined to believe his statements than the claims of some hysterical young lady.'

'Doctor!' Emma snapped at him. 'That is most uncalled for! I think you forget Lord Renfield's mandates about equality.'

'Equality aside, glare at me as much as you wish, Miss Westover. You only reinforce the generally held consensus that women are, at the heart of it, reactionary, hysterical, emotional and prone to flights of fancy.'

Emma turned to Jane. 'Pay him no mind, dear.' She spoke with comforting reassurance.

Jane, who had silently attended the conversation, had tears streaming down face. She fumbled in her purse for her handkerchief. Drawing it, she dabbed at her tears with her jaw clenched, and ignored everyone by staring out the window again.

How could I even begin to comfort her? Axel wondered. On her very first outing for the Order – while still mourning her father – her 'uncle' had been slain, and then she had witnessed such carnage, something he was certain she had never seen before. And this obnoxious doctor insisted on belittling her. How could she *not* cry? His instinct was to tell her that 'everything would be all right', but then he realised he had done just that at von Meyerling's house, and in hindsight, it sounded utterly foolish. For her, at least, everything *would not* be all right.

With barely contained irritation, he asked, 'So, Doctor, what do *you* think the lights were?'

Whitehall puffed on his pipe for a moment, looking out at the passing cityscape. 'Some sort of electromagnetic phenomenon, I imagine. It would seem that without realising it, Miss Halifax is able to manipulate electrical and magnetic conditions to create a small burst of energy. Perhaps her hand gestures, combined with some other factor manipulates *static electricity* to the point of ignition.' Whitehall sat back with finality.

Axel could see it was pointless trying to reason with the man. 'Load your weapons, everyone.' He sighed, and put out his cigarette.

Percy stared at Emma sitting opposite him as the coach rattled along. She stared back. Her green eyes glittered like jewels, and even with her face a mess of colours, she still looked breathtakingly beautiful. Everyone else had at least made efforts to remove the blood off their face and hands. 'I say, my dear,' he began, 'Aren't you going to clean all that muck off your face?'

She regarded him a moment longer before digging into her purse and drawing out a small hand mirror. Turning it to catch the fleeting lights, she examined herself a time before replacing it. 'No!' she answered.

'No?'

'I look far more fearsome like this, don't you think, my dear?' She flashed him a mischievous grin.

Percy smirked, drew out a hip flask and drank from it. The burn of aged scotch in his mouth and throat was an immediate relief from the preceding tension. It was a miracle they had emerged from that assault essentially unscathed, he mused.

Emma never took her eyes from him. She drew on her cigarette and blew the smoke upwards.

Percy offered her the flask, more out of gall than sincerity. He was surprised when she brazenly took it, and throwing her head back, gulped it down. The liquid spilled down her chin and long, slim neck in a most vulgar manner.

Lowering the flask from her enticing mouth, she sensually licked her lips, savouring the flavour, never removing her eyes from his. She held it out to him. 'I even left you some!'

'How kind.'

She giggled. 'It wouldn't be ladylike of me to finish it all, now, would it?' she fired back, wiping her chin with the back of her hand, smudging the dried blood.

Apparently, he thought, *a dose of decent scotch makes her quite liberal.* He would have to remember that.

Even though they were crowded into the coach, it felt to him as if they were the only two people in the world. Lewd and indecent thoughts raced through his mind, as he pictured her naked body against his, writhing in pleasure, a look of ecstasy on her face. He felt his heart racing, his breath quickening. As Percy knew all too well, desire and good judgement made poor bedfellows. Messy and sweaty as they were, were they but alone in this carriage, he would have leapt across at her and had his way with her then and there. And from the look in her eyes, he knew she would not have objected.

Then Axel was speaking, the young man's words intruding on his thoughts, bringing him back from their licentious isolation. '...change your ammunition, Percy.'

Percy was suddenly conscious of the presence of others. He took a final swig of scotch, for she had indeed left him at least a mouthful, and put away the flask.

He drew out his revolver to exchange the rounds.

'Oh, Percy?' Emma called. He looked up to see her gingerly holding out her weapon by the handle. 'Would you be so kind? I'm so terribly awkward with these things, and I know I can trust you to do it for me properly.' She batted her eyelashes, and an inviting smile crossed her lips.

He gave her his most rakish grin and took her firearm.

It took longer to reach their second destination than their first. Even though there was much less traffic in this part of the city, it was also much further from Ifield Road than Belgrave Square. It was also much darker here, as this was a more industrial area. A number of factories, small and large, serviced the nearby rail yards. Farther south, east and back west, Percy knew, were neighbourhoods filled with poorer residences. Much of the working class lived in these areas.

While faint light drifted from across the Thames, reflected by the low clouds, Hamilton Street, before them, lay mired in pitch blackness. Burton slowly moved the coach off to the side of Wandsworth Road.

'No lights,' Axel said.

Though only two of the lanterns – those belonging to the ladies – had survived their earlier altercation, and were primed for use, he stated he was not willing to make their presence known.

Percy studied the – except for Emma – pale faces around him. Nonsense like hats had been done away with by everyone, including the ladies. Carnby had, much to Whitehall's chagrin, taken the ash from his cigarette and smeared it about the bandage around his face. As he had explained, to mitigate the stark whiteness. It had proven largely ineffective.

'No more foolishness,' Axel commanded. 'This time, there are no neighbouring houses. Shoot to kill.'

Percy approved of Axel's authority and confidence: he had the natural talent to become an exceptional commander one day. There was always a great need for someone like Axel, and Percy resolved to observe the young man's progress.

Number 10 was at the far end of Hamilton Road, on the right. They all regarded the unexceptional two-storey brick façade, dark from soot in colour. On the right of the building were large double doors, broad enough for two medium carriages side by side. These were shut and seemingly locked from the inside. Starting in the middle of the building, wrought iron stairs ascended across the front face to a tiny landing at the left edge, where they doubled back up to a single door, clearly accessing the upper level. Above the door, in unostentatious lettering, was written:

TOD SCHWARZ BROS.

FABRICATION

They ascended the stairs, treading lightly, in single file. The door was of course, locked, but Carnby made short work of that.

Crouching on one side of the entrance, Percy watched as Axel, on the other, swung the door inwards, revealing an inky well of black. After a moment, he saw that somewhere within the building, a pale light flickered and glowed.

Nineteen
Howling at the Moon

South Lambeth

Axel crept into what was unquestionably an office. It was small, dirty and sparse, inhabited only by a desk on each side of the room, and what seemed a bureau and cabinet. The wooden floor creaked beneath his feet, and he heard and felt the texture of dirt between his shoes and the floor. The ubiquitous smell of soot – so common all throughout London – was multiplied in this space, mingled with scent of iron filings, acrid yet oddly pleasant, like the aroma after the discharge of a modern bullet. The wall directly ahead contained a door in the middle with a dirty glass panel. Similarly, the walls on either side of the door contained windows – also dirty – overlooking the factory floor. The flickering glow of what was apparently a fire somewhere within the building, provided the modicum of lighting by which he moved.

He approached the desk on his left and pressed himself against the bulky side. Turning to his right he looked to the door from which they had entered. He saw the squat, heavy outline of Carnby silhouetted against the indigo-black night sky. He gestured, and the other man entered without making a noise; despite his bulk, Carnby moved like a cat and in seconds was against the other table, opposite Axel. The others entered less gracefully, save for Percy, whom Axel noted again moved with the same fluidity as Carnby. The ladies of course struggled by virtue of their costume, and the doctor, Axel surmised, was simply unfamiliar with such activity.

Axel considered for a moment the interesting contradiction in terms that was Percy Wallace. The man had the air and manner of a marquess or a duke, whilst possessing knowledge pertaining to the nefarious side of life and moving with the skill and grace of the foremost burglars. He was seemingly quite capable in a fight, demonstrably familiar with pistols and swords; and of course, Axel had caught a glimpse of that blade hidden within Percy's cane as he sheathed it. At some point in the near future, he would have to solve that particular mystery.

Percy shut the door as he entered, and all remained still and quiet as they adjusted to the darkness, and the sights and smells of this unfamiliar locale.

After a few moments in the silence, the faint sounds of chanting permeated the thin walls and came to Axel's ears. He could not make out any specific words, but the rhythmic and repetitive nature was unmistakable. He looked to Emma for her preternatural confirmation, but could make out no details in the gloom.

Axel crept forward, painfully aware of the soft creaking of the floorboards as he moved. He prayed that there was no one stationed in darkness below the office. Edging to the wall, he raised himself slowly and peered into the open space of the factory proper.

Like so many buildings in London, the factory of Tod Schwarz Fabrication was narrow and long. On the other side of this wall lay a wrought-iron, railed walkway that trailed away left and right. At each end, he saw a stairwell descending into the darkness of the factory floor. Within that cavernous space, the tops of machines rose from the gloom, hulking like behemoths at rest. At the distant end of the building was another raised area, larger and apparently given over to storage. It was illuminated from below by a fire, hidden behind one of the far machines – the flickering glow casting fleeting and dancing shadows on the rear and side walls, including those that seemed of men, towering, gaunt and ghoulish in the pale light. Stairs also descended from both sides of that far storage area, and at the centre of its railing was a device resembling a small crane. Most of its space was given over to large wooden crates, likely lifted by said device. The length of the building was punctuated evenly by two rows of brick support columns, closer to the sides, leaving the central floor open.

Along the tops of the three walls ran a row of windows, no doubt providing the only daylight those indentured to labour here had the privilege of experiencing. Some of the windows he saw were open. *It must be freezing in there,* he thought.

Behind him, he heard a whimpering, and turned to peer at his companions. Jane was shuffling uncomfortably. Hardly surprising, given that young ladies of good standing were not wont to go crouching and skulking through darkened factories at night. Before returning to the others, he tried the door. It was, of course, locked.

'It's okay, Jane,' he whispered once he had closed with his companions. 'Stand up, there's no one near.'

Jane stood then leaned on the desk. 'I am sorry everyone. I'm afraid I'm quite unused to this.'

'I'm sure *most* of us are quite unused to this!' Axel quipped. He noticed that Emma seemed not in the least inconvenienced, though Whitehall took the opportunity to stand as well.

'Carnby?' Axel gestured towards the door. 'Would you be so kind?'

Like a cat, Carnby moved there, but after a moment of examination, returned with equal stealth. 'Nah. They barred or bolted it from th' otha soide,' he whispered.

'So, how do we pass?'

'Oi'll cat it.'

'Cut the door?' Axel queried, perplexed.

'No! Th' glass. Oi'll cat th' glass. Bat Oi need sum 'elp.'

'I'm with you, man,' Percy volunteered. He had taken a sabre from von Meyerling's safe, which he had traded for his cane on the coach, and handed it to Axel.

Axel observed as the two men moved in unison. Percy's actions almost mirrored Carnby's. The burglar fished a tool out of his coat somewhere. As he pressed one end to the glass panel, Axel saw that it resembled a mathematical compass. Carnby then 'drew' a small circle on the glass in the bottom left corner of the pane, near the handle. He carefully pulled and the small disc came away silently. *How exactly does that help?* Axel was wondering, as Carnby moved to the other side of the door. He repeated the action in the bottom right corner, and then again in the top two corners of the pane.

Axel watched in silent curiosity as the silhouette of Carnby nodded to that of Percy. The other man moved forward and grasped the pane where the circles had been cut out.

Working around Percy, Carnby then drew the tool, like a pencil, along the edges of the pane, where they met the door. In this manner, he followed the perimeter of the pane.

Once complete, the men positioned themselves on either side of the door, and each grasped one side of the pane, top and bottom. They nodded before gently pulling inwards. The sheet of glass came noiselessly away from its resting place. Moving to a corner, the men lowered the glass to rest and returned to the door. They motioned the others over.

Axel and the group crept over to the two. Crouching, he looked to the two men. 'I say! Jolly good work, chaps!' he murmured.

'Yew sound jast loike 'im!' Carnby pointed at Percy.

'Good work, indeed!' Emma whispered. 'Most impressive!' Her perfect teeth were stark white against the dark shades of her face as she grinned.

'You look like a murderous chimney sweep!' Percy joked.

She stuck out her tongue in a most unladylike manner.

'Jast be care-ful a' th' edge,' Carnby whispered as he folded what appeared to be thick canvas. He placed it along the bottom edge of the frame. 'There's still glass, an' it'll ca'chya.'

'Ready, all?' Percy asked. 'One by one.' Without waiting for confirmation, he stood and deftly passed through the open space.

Carnby followed next, just as nimble.

Axel directed Whitehall to collect a chair from one desk, while he retrieved the other. He passed Whitehall's chair through to the other men. He then placed his with the back against the door. Carnby and Percy mirrored his placement, creating an improvised set of stairs.

'Emma,' he said, offering his hand.

'So chivalrous!' Taking it, she stepped onto the chair, ducked and stepped through, as Percy took her other hand and helped her exit.

They repeated the actions with Jane. She took his hand but quickly looked away from him. Axel felt like one of the gallants of old, holding her dainty hand and assisting her ascent. 'My lady,' he almost whispered, but held his tongue.

Finally, Whitehall climbed through. Axel passed his rifle and the sabre to Percy and, taking advantage of the makeshift stairs, he, too, climbed quickly through.

It was indeed freezing out on the catwalk. The scent of wood smoke drifted across the space to them. The sound of voices chanting, though still faint, was much clearer in the crisp air. Crouching in the cold, Axel felt the same sense of apprehension he had felt outside von Meyerling's house. Something here was quite wrong.

From his new vantage point, he could make out that the floorspace around the machines was clear and open; however, to both sides, where the columns stood, crates and equipment had been neatly stacked, and he could just make out the outlines of shelves against the walls. There appeared to be an unobstructed, if narrow, passage between the stacked crates and shelves.

He swiftly assessed the situation. Pointing to Percy, Whitehall and Carnby, he directed them to go left and follow that wall towards the rear of the building. He indicated that he and the two ladies would go right. 'Wait for my signal,' he instructed.

'What will that be?' Whitehall whispered.

'When I make a clear gesture for you to reveal yourselves,' he made a beckoning motion.

Whitehall and Carnby nodded, but Percy stopped him. 'One moment, old chap. Why do I get these two, and you get both the ladies to yourself?'

'Oh, Percy!' Emma whispered.

Axel shook his head and waved them away in ire.

Percy winked at them before turning away.

He looked to Jane and Emma, seeking their readiness, then began to move. The reason he wanted the ladies with him was to keep them safe and out of harm's way. The narrow space of the passage meant he could easily block it from either direction by himself, keeping them from any hostile threat. Or he could direct them away from danger, as required. Furthermore, he felt he may need to call on Jane's expertise.

The office of Tod Schwarz Fabrication did not take up the entire width of the front of the building. Between it and the outside wall they found a darkened area, apparently given over to more storage. There were shelves in here, and what appeared to be rather large machine parts. Looking to the left of the building, he saw the three men also examining a similar space.

Satisfied that no one and nothing lurked within, they began their descent.

On the floor, he led the ladies directly to the narrow passage, and found to his satisfaction that it was indeed well covered by the items stored alongside the columns. As they drew closer, the shadows playing on the walls became more defined. He counted at least three figures, and they appeared to be moving in a rhythmic, ritualistic fashion, bowing and gesturing. The chanting, too, became more audible. He listened intently as he crept forward. It sounded like German. Each part was spoken by one voice, then repeated by numerous others. Although he had studied *Hochdeutsch* at school, without practice his comprehension was sorely lacking. He paused and gave an enquiring expression to Emma. 'Do you understand what they're saying, at all?'

She huddled closer and whispered:

'O Great Malevolence, grant us a small part of your power
Accept that which we have sacrificed in your name
Show us the way from the light
Show us that which lies in the Darkness.'

Axel's hair stood on end. Again, that expression: *that which lies in the Darkness*. Resisting the shudder of revulsion rippling through him, he gestured the ladies onward.

Approaching the north end of the factory, the scene finally came into view as they rounded a column. They crouched, peering over some crates. In the space between the last of the machines and the rear storage mezzanine, a fire had been lit in a shallow metal drum or tub; to the right of the fire, and dominating the area, lay a large ring of cheap candles, illuminated. Within the candles was drawn – perhaps with chalk – a five-pointed star. The entire thing was about ten or twelve feet across.

Outside the circle, at each point of the star, knelt a dark-robed, hooded figure. Another robed figure was standing in the centre of the star, holding a book.

The standing figure spoke again, seemingly reading from the book, with the kneeling supplicants repeating every line. Once more, Emma whispered a translation:

'Look upon us favourably as we do your work
Look upon us as we bring forth the shadows
Look upon us as we use your gift to serve your greater glory
Look upon us as we bring your corruption into the world!'

Axel peered across the floor to the opposite columns. After a moment, Percy's face appeared, pale in the firelight, before ducking back out of sight. *Good*, he thought, *they are in place.*

'This is all wrong...' Jane whispered.

Axel looked to the young lady; she was watching the scene intently. 'In what way, Jane?'

'The circle is not complete. A ring of candles simply won't do. One must have an *unbroken* line. And the *pentangle* is...is *just wrong*. It's not used like that. It serves no purpose here.'

The standing figure began a chant that Axel couldn't understand. Again, the others followed.

Sha-na-ka-cha-naka-ma-la
Na-ra-gana-sha-ka-sha-ba
Na-ja-na-ja-kamahala
Ka-ra-ko-ra-ko-ra-ka-ta-na!

'What is that, Jane?'

She shook her head. 'I don't know. It's nonsense.'

He turned to Emma. 'Does it mean anything in German?'

She shook her head too, fixed on the ritual, her green eyes radiant in the pale light, her face indeed fearsome in the encroaching darkness. She turned her gaze to him. 'No. It's not German.'

Across the factory, Percy was watching him. Axel shrugged, and the other man nodded almost imperceptibly. He again addressed the ladies. 'What the devil is this business?'

'See their robes, Axel?' Emma pointed.

'What about them?'

'Their robes are tatty, and full of holes. The material is cheap and thin.'

Axel peered into the dim light. After a moment he could see she was right.

'So, what does that mean?'

'I think these people are misguided amateurs,' Jane offered. 'Everything is wrong. Everything is of a poor quality. I think they are trying to engage in *Occultism* as they understand it.'

Axel laid his rifle across the box. 'So, we were sent here in error?'

'I don't know,' Jane replied.

'Are these people a threat?'

'I don't think so.' She shook her head. 'I don't know.'

The chant returned to the first verse they had heard. Thanks to Emma, he could now follow it better. *"O Great Malevolence..."*

Axel felt an icy cold finger of dread run along his spine as he observed the ceremony. *Malevolence.* There was talk about darkness and corruption also. He frowned as he watched on. *No matter how much one howls at the moon,* he thought, *one will not become a wolf.* Was there something unnatural actually occurring here? Not to his knowledge. Were these people misguided, as Jane claimed? Perhaps. The fact that they used words such as 'malevolence' and 'corruption' suggested ill-intent and, possibly, malice on their part. But this, then, was clearly a matter for the authorities. Like a man howling at the moon in hopes of becoming a wolf, these people were surely misguided. *Or insane.*

Axel was about to signal to the other three for a retreat when the chanting stopped. He paused and watched. The chant leader spoke to the figures on his right, nearer the back wall. 'Bring it here,' Emma translated.

The two figures bowed, then rose, and made their way into the shadows. They hefted something large between them, and returned. The leader moved away from the centre of the star. Axel saw the other two carried at each end, a long object that sagged in the middle, wrapped in a dark cloth. Without actually seeing it, he had the awful realisation of what it was. He had seen that kind of motion before; he knew exactly what the two men lugged across the floor, and a sickening chill of horror worked its way up his spine at the memory of it. They laid it silently along one axis of the star, part of it in one arm, part jutting between the opposite two. The two figures quickly unwrapped it. It was a corpse.

Axel was transfixed by the pallid figure. Its pale skin was smeared dark in places with what he guessed was fresh grave-dirt. Which meant that this body had not come from a hospital or morgue, but from a cemetery. This was at the least then, *grave-robbing.* The man – for it was a man, apparent by its nakedness – had dark hair, and was clearly of an impressive stature in life – at least as tall as Axel himself.

Axel had the sudden sense of embarrassment at the ladies viewing a man in a state of undress, but he realised there was little he could do now. 'I am sorry you had to see this,' he whispered. He glanced at them, but both were gripped by the scene, expressions of horror on their faces.

The two that had carried it over had resumed their places, and the chant began again from the second verse, stopping at its end.

Axel realised he had to make a decision. Matter for the authorities or not, he disliked the idea of grave-robbing. He disliked even more intensely the idea of the desecration of a corpse. It was instinctively unnatural. And that was enough for him. It was time to put a stop to this. He reached for his rifle.

Axel was shocked by the intensity of Jane's grip on his wrist. 'Wait!' she whispered, the alarm apparent in her voice.

He saw her eyes were wide with fear. 'Jane? What is it?'

'No! It can't be. I don't believe it...'

'Jane?' he repeated. But the leader had begun to chant again.

Axel turned back and saw that the leader was kneeling over the corpse, with his hand in the air above it. Something small and dark dangled from his hand as he moved it back and forth along the supine figure. He alone made the nonsense chant:

Sha-na-ka-cha-naka-ma-la
Na-ra-gana-sha-ka-sha-ba
Na-ja-na-ja-kamahala
Ka-ra-ko-ra-ko-ra-ka-ta-na!

Axel gaped in disbelief. It appeared as if the left hand of the corpse *twitched*. *Surely not,* he thought. It must be a trick of the flickering light.

The leader repeated the verse with greater volume and intensity:

Sha-na-ka-cha-naka-ma-la
Na-ra-gana-sha-ka-sha-ba
Na-ja-na-ja-kamahala
Ka-ra-ko-ra-ko-ra-ka-ta-na!

The left hand – no – the arm twitched. *No!* Axel thought. *This cannot be!*

The leader chanted the verse again, near shouting it this time:

Sha-na-ka-cha-naka-ma-la
Na-ra-gana-sha-ka-sha-ba
Na-ja-na-ja-kamahala
Ka-ra-ko-ra-ko-ra-ka-ta-na!

The eyes opened.

A wave of ineffable horror crashed down on Axel's soul, and his hair stood on end. *No!* he thought again. *What am I seeing? Such things are not possible!*

A victorious, wordless shout erupted from the participants, drowning out the muffled cry from Jane.

The group began chanting two words now, over and over. '*Stehe auf.*' *Stand up*. The body began to move. Awkwardly, it rose to its feet, as if it lacked full control of its limbs. The leader rose as well. Dangling the small dark object before the animated corpse's blank, staring eyes, he spoke, '*Gehorche mir.*'

'*Obey me.*' He heard Emma's voice in his ear.

The cadaver grunted a hoarse, raspy groan.

Across the room, Axel saw the pale, stony faces of Percy, Whitehall and Carnby, wide-eyed in silent horror.

The leader was talking again, followed an instant later by Emma, 'Now the time has come! Now is our time! Now they shall see what power is! What they have will belong to us!'

Revulsion washed over Axel. He wrenched his hand free of Jane, and in a smooth motion collected his rifle and brought it to bear. This...this *insanity* had gone far enough. Axel aimed his weapon at the chest of the walking dead man, and fired.

Twenty
Nzambi

Percy had been translating the German in whispers for the benefit of Carnby, and somewhat for the doctor as well, who had occasionally nodded his understanding. All the while, he had been trying to keep his growing apprehension in check. Now, he couldn't believe what he was seeing. What he was watching was an…*impossibility*. What did one even call such a thing? It was not alive; but no longer dead. *Un-living? Un-dead?*

Even though he had been coiled and ready to act, transfixed as he was the sudden shot caught him off guard.

The…un-dead stumbled at the hit, falling to the ground, smoke pouring from the on-target wound in its chest. Then, just as suddenly, Axel burst from the darkness, leaping over a low crate, his rifle raised, now pointed at the leader of this profane congregation, as he advanced on them with speed and aggression. *No!* Percy thought. *Don't be such a—*

'*Nicht bewegen! Don't move!*' Axel roared. "*Machen Sie deine Hände auf!*'

The group of occultists were frozen in place, clearly stunned, their hooded heads all turned to Axel.

'*Hände auf!*' the young man repeated, nearing the leader.

Percy had an odd moment of jarring incongruity: the situation was now even more dangerous thanks to Axel's hot-headed actions, yet the other man's hopeless German almost made him want to laugh. '*Hände hoch!*' was all he had needed to say.

However, it was foolhardy for Axel to expose himself all alone. 'Stay here, chaps,' he whispered. Effortlessly, he mantled the crate in front of him and brought his pistol to bear on the group. '*Gehorcht ihm! Hände hoch!*' he barked.

The hooded figures started at his voice, most turning to the new command. Momentarily, they slowly raised their hands, though the leader appeared fixed on Axel, unmoving. The small pendulum-like object still dangled from his outstretched hand, violently swinging to-and-fro.

How odd, was all the thought Percy had time for.

The un-dead at Axel's feet lunged up and grabbed him, dragging him off balance, and Axel tipped backwards, crashing to the ground.

Percy barely had the time to register this when the occultist directly in front of him spun and leapt at him, a large blade in his hand.

Percy fired reflexively, hitting his mark, and the figure collapsed.

He raised to fire at the leader, but another shot went off from his right, whizzing past him, forcing him to leap backwards and scramble for cover. Immediately, another shot followed, with an accompanying scream of pain.

Was that Axel? Alarm spread through him. The young man was now alone and exposed.

Jane's ears were still ringing, and she had been dazed from Axel's shot when he had leapt over the crate and dashed out onto the factory floor. She had never heard a gunshot so close, nor within an enclosed space, and it had shocked her enough to prevent her from stopping him.

She watched in helpless horror as the *Nzambi* – *what else could it be?* – dragged Axel to the ground. Other shots were ringing out, and she forced herself not to rush out into the open to help him.

Of course a wound to the chest was not going to be enough. In order to stop a Nzambi, one needed to—

The shot next to her startled her afresh, and she jumped. Emma had fired, and surely hit one of the robed figures, judging from the cry of pain. Jane was awed by the expression of stony determination on the other lady's face as she pointed the pistol into the room. A returning shot forced Emma to duck for cover. These men were armed too!

Out on the floor, the leader had drawn a large dagger and was lunging at Axel.

Jane's hands flew up, palms out in a defensive gesture, the habit of much-repeated practice taking hold. '*Scūtum*!' she yelled.

Not more than a foot from Axel's chest, the tip of the dagger struck something intangible. The air around it vibrated and shimmered, and the leader was driven backwards, staggering to maintain balance.

Jane fought down her panic as nervous energy coursed through her. *Breathe*, she told herself. She needed to be able to react to protect him, but she very much doubted she could stop a bullet as they were just too fast. They needed to save Axel! 'Emma!' she cried in desperation.

'Yes, dear!' Came the breathless reply, and the other lady leant out and fired again.

The leader had recovered, and lunged once more.

Jane was ready, but Axel had regained himself and fired into the other man's chest at close range, toppling him the floor. A distant, logical part of Jane's mind told her that she should be horrified, as for the first time, she was seeing a man killed before her very eyes. But at the same time, her overwhelming concern was saving Axel.

Now, for the Nzambi… She needed a clean line of sight. She scurried past Emma, 'I need to— Don't let them shoot me!'

Without a word, Emma sprang up and moved out in front of her, the pistol raised.

Jane darted close to the nearest machine. She could now clearly see the Nzambi struggling with Axel. She swiftly brought her hands together in a forceful clasp, '*Stā!*'

The Nzambi locked rigid.

Good, she breathed a sigh of relief. *That would be sufficient. Now—* She froze. All thoughts fell away into oblivion as she stared past the scene, straight at the…*nightmare* creeping through the window at the rear of the building.

No! She thought. *No! Never in my life should I have dreamt to see one.* That it was here, was terrible in ways she could not define. Terror – pure, unmitigated terror – filled her soul, and she screamed.

Jane turned and fled. She ran as fast as she could. She ran from what was creeping in the window. She ran from Emma, Axel and everyone else. As terror overwhelmed her, her presence of mind shattered like glass, and she felt her hold on the Nzambi collapse.

Twenty-one
The Things That Should Not Be

Dr Whitehall ducked behind the column as bullets whizzed in their direction. As a gentleman, he had fired a pistol from time to time – at *targets* – and he was a rather good shot. He had never fired at another human being. And, more importantly, he had certainly *never* had people shooting at *him*. It was a singularly unpleasant sensation.

Thankfully, the other two men seemed to be more than adept in this regard. He had to even acknowledge Mr Carnby's courage and capability in returning fire against their attackers.

Of most concern, right now, was that his new young associate had gotten himself into great danger as he wrestled with this awful desecration. What the desecration actually *was*, was a matter for later deliberation: no doubt Miss Halifax would make foolish claims of the *supernatural*; however, there *had* to be a rational explanation for its apparent animation. Nevertheless, the doctor needed to aid the young man in the middle of the floor without being able to run out there and drag the animated corpse from him.

Steeling against the incoming fire, he pressed himself against the far side of the column and observed the dead man. As a surgeon and physician, Whitehall was all too familiar with the need to solve problems under great pressure. When all else failed in such situations, he returned to logic. Logical thought was the process by which all problems were solved, and mankind had achieved such sophistication, even when a problem seemingly defied logic.

All evidence suggested it was a corpse: the lividity; the absence of breathing; the glassy, sightless eyes; the absence of blood issuing from the wound where the bullet had passed through. And yet, it was *animated*, as though by some outside force.

Presuming an outside force compelled its action, then no known means of ceasing the processes of life would surely work. Suffocation, exsanguination, paralysis, tranquilisation, were all irrelevant. Dismemberment? Perhaps effective, but lengthy and dangerous.

Axel might be injured, Whitehall observed, as the young man was struggling greatly to overcome his attacker.

Decapitation? Why would it work? Presuming these things were animated, ending the natural processes of the brain should not affect them. Yet, all thought, all action performed by the body, originated in the brain.

Whitehall was out of time, and out of options. His young colleague would die presently. 'When all else fails...' he muttered softly. He raised his pistol and aimed. He was very aware that the ladies were somewhere opposite him, and that he needed a clear shot in order to not hit Axel.

Axel had crashed hard into the ground, hitting his head, and had had the breath knocked out of him. The world had reeled around him and he had been dimly aware of the constriction of the corpse around his waist. Then, his head had cleared just in time to see the leader about to attack, and he had managed to bring his rifle up and fire, downing the man. Another dead at his hands.

However, the animated corpse was unrelenting. Though it had gone rigid for just a moment, it now resumed its assault on Axel. Smoke issued from the wound in its chest, and the flesh there had blackened, but its blank, unseeing eyes betrayed no sense or emotion. Axel's skin crawled at the sight of a lifeless face trying to murder him.

Somewhere in the distance Axel heard a bloodcurdling scream from one of the ladies, and nearly panicked. *Has one of them been taken? Or injured?* His struggle suddenly became all the more urgent.

Relieved of the fetters of human decency, or pain, or consequence, the living dead man struck a terrible blow to the side of Axel's head with its open hand.

The hit burned like fire and shook Axel. But his own hands were free, and he still retained his rifle. Though he could not bring it to bear in these quarters, he returned in kind, using his substantial strength to strike it in the jaw with the butt of the weapon.

The unnatural creature reeled back from the impact, and at that moment a shot rang out, and the front of its head exploded outwards as a bullet passed through it.

Bits of skull and dried brain-matter erupted onto him as the now truly-dead corpse slammed down on him, driving the breath from him again.

Without pause and still gasping for air, Axel shoved at the corpse. He needed to—

In a sudden moment of clarity, he realised the factory was completely silent.

'*Was ist das*?' A voice came from his left. Two of the hooded supplicants were standing in the middle of the circle, heads tilted upwards, fear on their now-illuminated faces as they stared at the back wall. He followed their gaze, and the hair on the back of his neck stood on end. Some…*thing* was crawling through the open window.

How did he comprehend something for which no words existed to describe? It looked like a man, but yet it did not. There was a head, a body and limbs, but thereafter the similarities became scarce. It was creeping down the wall like some monstrous spider, its arms out at its sides, much like a lizard. From either side of its chest extended another arm, the hands twisting at unnatural angles as they pressed to the wall. Its legs, though the proportion and shape of a man's legs, moved and twisted in ways that no man's leg should. The legs splayed out to the sides, and then curled inwards, as if disjointed at the hips, knees and ankles. The feet rotated around as it moved, shifting to find purchase against the wall. Worst of all was the head. Instead of pointing downwards – as it should in someone climbing down head first – it was tilted back. So far back, it was almost parallel to the body. The face had long and wild black hair and a ragged beard of the same colour. Its mouth was open in a perpetual grimace of excruciation, and a long, disgusting tongue lashed out from time to time. Its eyes were wide and watery, glistening in the flickering fire light, and they burned with pain and malicious intelligence. Its skin had an unhealthy grey tinge. It was difficult to guess its size, but it seemed to be that of a large man. Certainly, larger than him. It was dressed in ripped, tatty, soiled rags that appeared to be the remnants of clothing.

Axel was paralysed with terror. Of all the things he had seen this night, this was the most impossible and horrific. He felt terribly exposed, and that he should dare not move or utter a sound, lest it notice and come for him.

As it approached a large crate against the wall, it *twisted*. Pivoting on the limbs of one side of its body, it lifted its body and swung over, touching the other side's limbs back to the wall. As it did, everything contorted. Arms turned at the shoulder and chest, legs at the hip, and knees buckled and warped in ways that were impossible for a normal body. He saw from the powerful muscles that the chest was now 'outwards'. It was almost too much when the head rotated upwards and twisted around to take the same position it held a moment ago.

Oh God, he thought. He gritted his teeth. *No. No God would allow such a thing to exist. No good, sane, just God would permit such a thing to walk the Earth.*

He felt the hair stand on the back of his neck anew as he saw *another one* entering through the window. *We're going to die tonight.*

Suddenly, and silently, the first one sprang with frightening speed and landed on the crane-like device at the front of the mezzanine with a resounding clang, splaying its limbs and grasping on like some nightmarish bird roosting on its perch. The machine screeched and groaned under its weight as it swept its gaze over the factory floor, even as the other one climbed down the wall.

The supplicants spoke in hushed German, but Axel gathered the gist of their conversation:

'Did you make them come?'

'No.'

'Did Klaus?'

'I don't know...'

Axel forced his gaze to them as the one who did not know limped forward and collected the small dark object that the felled leader had held. He stepped out of the circle, standing over Axel and brandished it, dangling, at arm's length. 'We serve...' He didn't quite follow the next part, but it seemed, 'that which lies in the darkness,' much as they had spoken of earlier. 'Do you serve that which lies in the darkness?'

The nightmare on the perch jerked its head up and down and opened its mouth in a hideous, toothless rictus of a smile.

'Do you come to aid us?'

It jerked its head in semblance of a nod again. The smile was most chilling.

The second creature landed on the railing next to the first with a ringing clang that was deafening in the silence. It looked much the same, except its hair was lighter.

Axel was filled with a plummeting sensation, as though he were falling into a black abyss. Beyond the obvious reasons for apprehension, this...*aberration* was emanating an air of *treachery*. Was this his 'Sight' Black Elk had told him of, now warning him?

The man with the object began to laugh, slowly at first, then with increasing confidence. The other one nervously joined in.

Axel kicked at the corpse in desperation, and cocked his weapon, every fibre of his being screaming at him to flee.

Relaxed, the German now held up the object again. 'Kill our enemies!'

The monstrous mockery of a man smiled again. But this time it shook its head, never taking its gleaming, malicious eyes off the supplicant.

'What?' he shouted. 'If you serve the darkness, kill our—'

The black-haired abomination leaped at him, and his words trailed off in a horrific scream.

Axel scrambled to escape but was too slow.

A force like he had never felt struck him in the back, and he went sprawling. In unreal, slow time, he saw Emma's red and black face illuminated in the firelight, the pupils of her green eyes huge, as she reached for him. As he slammed into the ground, he discharged his weapon in her direction, and there was an instant of shock on her face, followed by a scream as she fell backwards! *No! Gods no! I*—

His thought was cut off as he smashed into the column rushing to meet him.

There was a resounding *clang*! behind him, and the room went dark. For an awful moment, Axel was crippled with stinging pain. He groaned as he struggled to right himself into a sitting position. The tub with the fire had been upended and still-burning logs were rolling across the floor, casting fleeting, wildly dancing lights. *Emma*—

Before he could reach for his weapon, the figure was looming over him. Axel scrambled back against the column.

The black-haired monstrosity closed on him on all fours. In close proximity, it was indeed very much larger than him. It studied his face, as though curious, its wide, watery eyes still burning with rage and pain. Its long, revolting tongue protruded, lashing about like a reptile's from a mouth fixed in a toothless cry of anguish. Below its face, in the gloom, Axel could make out the German, pressed to its body with the extra pair of twisted, grey arms holding him firmly in place, and yet another disgusting hand covering his mouth. Axel could see the unmitigated terror in his eyes. They pleaded to him for aid.

Before he could reach for the man, Percy's panicked scream echoed in the darkened space, 'Kill them!'

Immediately gunshots rang out, and the monstrosity darted away. In one powerful leap it regained the crane device, which shuddered and bent on its landing.

In front of him, in the middle of the floor, the other aberration was crouched, indifferent to the bullets striking it.

Emma suddenly appeared, grunting with effort, leaning over the crate next to him, with her arm outstretched. She shot at the monstrosity as well. Axel was dimly aware of her handling the weapon with ease.

Though she, too, struck it, the light-haired horror remained focused solely on stalking the last supplicant, who was within the circle, like a mountain lion about to pounce.

The German shouted, 'No! You cannot enter the circle!'

It tilted its head to the side, much like a dog might at a new sight or sound.

'You must obey the rules! I am inside and you are outside!'

It nodded now, in the same slow, jerking manner. Once more, a sense of treachery washed over Axel.

'Yes! Leave now. In the morning people will come. I will stay here, and you will not kill me! You cannot harm me in the circle.'

Something about that bothered Axel.

It leapt at the man.

The German screamed and ducked, and the monstrosity sailed over his head. Landing smoothly within the circle on all six limbs, it raised the upper part of its body. Axel saw in the dim, flickering candlelight that its face contorted into the visage of a hideous scream. Arms... *another* pair of sinewy arms...erupted from the middle of its chest and grew outwards at terrifying speed, with clawing, yearning hands at the end. They latched on to the man's feet or ankles before he could react. As soon as it had hold, the thing dashed back through the circle, upending the man, and dragging him behind it.

Axel could see the terror on the man's face as he released a wordless scream. '*Hilfe*! *Hilfe*!' he cried, as he reached and clawed desperately for purchase on the dirty floor.

As Axel drew his Colt and cocked it, heart thundering in his chest, the light-haired aberration leapt up with nightmarish ease, and perched on the rear railing, the man dangling in mid-air behind it.

Instinctively, he knew those men faced a horrific fate. 'Don't let them be taken!' he screamed, and fired again and again.

❧

Whitehall fumbled to reload his weapon; he was dropping bullets on the floor. Nearby, Mr Carnby was imprecating in vivid fashion, as he was shooting and reloading. Shots were surely hitting, but these things moved impossibly fast, and there was some fear – at least in his mind – that the men would be hit.

Successfully reloaded at last, the doctor stepped out into the open. He was fixed on the one dragging the man below it: that was the most likely shot to succeed. He aimed carefully, judging. Fast as it was, as it neared the window, he fired. He saw the shot strike true in the back of its head, causing it to flinch at the blow.

It stopped. Slowly jerking, the head swivelled impossibly around. It scanned the floor, and fixed its glimmering eyes on him. Whitehall felt a stab of terror in his heart at the savage intensity of its gaze.

So. The words pushed themselves into his mind. *I see you now. Good. I know you now. I will find you, afterwards.* Whitehall was transfixed with horror as its mouth twisted in what could only be silent laughter.

The two nightmares crawled out through the windows, taking their victims with them.

And like that, they were gone.

A cold, terrible silence settled on the building.

Twenty-two
Cold and Dark

Axel had already called to the others across the factory, 'Is everyone alive?' cringing as his voice boomed and echoed in the empty space.

The three men across the factory had given their shaken confirmations.

'If one could call it that,' Emma muttered, next to him.

Puffing and gasping for breath, his heart still pounding, he scrambled up around the crate now, to help her as she slumped back to the ground. 'Are you hurt? Did I shoot you?'

She winced. 'Yes, you shot me, you ass!' She slapped him, hard.

Axel must have blanched as he felt the blood drain away from his face in mortification. 'I'll get Doctor—'

She grabbed his arm, looking at him, alarmed. 'It's nothing serious!' You only grazed me!'

'Are you sure you're not badly hurt?' He looked at her closely.

'Yes! I told you, I'm fine!' She shoved him away.

'I heard a scream.' His head whipped back and forth as another wave of panic swept over him. 'Jane…is she…?'

'She ran.' Emma pointed to the front of the factory, grunting as she struggled to her feet with Axel's help. 'I think those awful…*creatures*,' she waved towards the back wall, 'Terrified her, and she fled.'

'*What the devil were those things?*' Percy demanded, his face a mix of fear and anger. The other three men had come to them, casting fearful glances at the surrounding windows. 'Where's Jane?' he asked without pause.

Axel felt a deep sense of burning shame: he had utterly failed to protect both ladies.

Emma repeated her explanation.

'What?' Percy exclaimed, as alarm spread through the three men.

'I—I need to find her.' Axel cast his eyes down and looked away.

'Go. Find her.' Percy's voice was reassuring. 'But don't go alone. Take Carnby with you. He's well-armed.'

'No.' Axel shook his head. 'There may still be Germans here. I lost track in all the chaos. You should all stay together.'

'Listen—'

'No!' Axel snapped. It was his fault she had fled. 'I'll be fine. I— I'll go.' He looked at the other men. 'I *will* call for Carnby, should I run into any problems.'

'Go then, man. We'll hold down the fort, as it were.'

'Are you injured?' The doctor cut in quickly, addressing Axel. 'Miss Westover?'

Axel examined himself. 'No. Nothing serious.' He looked to Emma, who was holding her left hip with a pained expression.

She moved her hand away and stretched out the side of her already-bloody coat, showing a clear bullet hole passing through. 'I got shot,' she said matter-of-factly.

Axel was engulfed by guilt.

Whitehall's eyes bulged. He started forward. 'What! I must attend to it!'

But Emma raised her hand, stopping him. 'It's fine, Doctor. It merely grazed me.'

'Nonetheless, I should examine—'

'Yes, Doctor, but I hardly think this is the most appropriate setting.'

Whitehall glanced quickly about at the men. 'Yes, quite right. As long as there is no bleeding. But you must allow me to check the wound at the first possible instance. And you must let me know, at once, if the pain increases significantly.'

Emma nodded, her eyes flicking to Axel's a moment.

Daggers of guilt stabbed at his heart. 'I...I...I must find Jane,' he stammered. Turning quickly, he collected his rifle and strode towards the front of the factory.

Percy watched the young man hurry off. 'What was that about?'

Emma's expression became solemn. 'I think he feels guilty. That...he...failed to protect me...' She paused a moment. 'You know how it is with you men!' she gave him a blithe and dismissive smile.

'Ah.' Percy nodded. 'And I imagine Jane having run off somewhere doesn't help.'

There were murmurs of affirmation.

'When he returns with her, I'd jolly well love to know *what the devil those dashed horrors were*!'

He was met with subdued murmurs and troubled glances at the windows. A moment of uneasy silence fell over the group before Carnby spoke, 'Do... Do we go af'r'em?'

The unease continued. At last, Percy decided, 'No.'

'So, we le' 'em tayke 'em?'

Percy regarded Carnby. He admired the man's courage, and the thought *had* crossed his own mind, but practicality forbade them this course of action. 'I imagine you or I could get up there easy enough, old chap,' he gestured at the windows of the back wall, 'but what about Emma and the doctor? Should we leave them, or Axel and Jane? I know I struck the blighters more than once, but our bullets seemed to have no effect on them, whatsoever. Could either of us – or even both of us together – defeat one of those things?'

The other man pondered his words. 'No...' he said at last. 'No, s'pose you're roight.' He adjusted his grip on his shotgun with a grim expression. 'Bat one 'a us ort'a keep wotch on th' windows.'

Percy nodded. 'Do it, man. We'll see to the fire and round up any of those wretches that may be lurking about.'

'Oi don' speak th' Sossidge lingo any-way.'

'Right you are, old man. Anything at all untoward, shout, man. No matter how trivial.'

'Roight yew are.' Carnby broke open his weapon to reload.

'Doctor,' Percy indicated to the bodies of the Germans, 'Perhaps some of these wretched fellows are still alive?'

'Hmm,' Whitehall was pocketing his pistol. 'I shall examine them.' He surveyed the dark space. 'Though, I should require light.'

'Very well. Let's to it, shall we? Emma, I take it your *Deutsche* is up to par?'

'*Natürlich*!' She gave him a dazzling smile and readied her revolver in her gloved hand.

Axel was a cauldron of conflicting emotions. As he advanced through the darkness with his rifle raised, wave after wave of fear washed over him. The preceding events played one after the other in his mind. At every step, he almost expected one of those *abominations* to descend upon him from above. His apprehension was so palpable, it was almost paralysing. Percy had the right of it: *what the devil were those things*? They were impossible. No creature could move in such a way; no man's body could contort and twist in that manner and stay whole. It was sickening to behold. He shuddered violently. *Something like that could only be born of Hell*, he mused. *But that would mean Hell is real…* The thought was, again, almost paralysing, but he shook it off. He *had* to find Jane, and ensure she was safe and sound.

Guilt welled up within him. He had – even accidentally – shot Emma. Unbidden, images flooded back to him of that cold hillside in South Dakota. He heard the gunshots and the cries of fear and pain. Shame flooded through him. Shame at his incapability both on that day, and to protect Jane tonight. She had run off, and was perhaps in great danger. And he had not been able to stop her.

Finally, pain wracked his body. Physically, the struggle with the walking corpse had been no worse than any other similar fight, but the blow from that…nightmare…was *staggering*. Every step; just keeping his rifle up, hurt.

All this turmoil raged through his mind and body as he impelled himself forward, driven to find her. *I've let you down, Jane.*

Axel forced his fatigued body up the stairs, and he peered into the storage area. Now, without the benefit of the firelight, it was all shadows and darkness. His mind recoiled at the thought of what may lie in wait within. 'Jane?' he called softly. Oh, for some blasted light! *Perhaps I should have brought Carnby?*

He was met with silence.

Axel moved past the storage area without daring to turn his back to it. He pressed himself against the office wall. Crouching with aching legs, he advanced.

His plan was to check the opposite storage area next, but as he passed the office door, he bumped into the chair that was placed there. As he did, he started and almost cried out in the darkness, as something soft brushed his face.

For an instant of chilling horror, he imagined it was Jane's hair, and that her dead body laid draped in the gap of the door, with her head hanging through.

Axel almost scrambled back and cried out in fear and grief.

Composing himself, he reached out and grasped a piece of fabric in his hand. It had snagged on a small, sharp angle of glass remaining from Carnby's cuts. He pulled it away carefully and examined it in the dark. Of course, it looked black. But it felt like the fabric from a dress.

He peered up at the dark opening. Had Jane gone through? If so, had she fled outside? How would he find her then?

The place smelled of smoke and blood and death. The familiar, mingled scents brought a rush of memories back to Percy. An array of locales, buildings – houses, flats, offices, barns, cellars – even town squares, beaches and fields flashed through his mind. But regardless of the beauty or ugliness of the scenery, the result was always the same: he always walked away with his goal achieved, blood and death behind him. Then, as though second nature, he swept those useless thoughts aside. They were replaced with an overwhelming sense of fatigue and a desperate desire for a drink.

He yearned to turn back and glance at the windows above him, but he knew Carnby was there. Outside the nearer side of circle was the dark shape of the body of the German leader, motionless, and on the other, the upturned tub that had held the fire. Nearby, dully glowing logs lay on the factory floor. He barely spared a passing thought for how cheaply life was so often bought.

Percy circled around the candles, and with the assistance of Whitehall, they righted the tub. It was heavy, even with the two of them, and that aberration had flipped it just by crashing down on it, indicating its substantial mass. And yet, it moved *so fast*.

Emma was scanning the area with her pistol at the ready. He noticed with some surprise, that despite her earlier protestations of helplessness, she now held the weapon with ease. The striking incongruity piqued his interest.

Near the tub were some kindling, narrow timbers and a poker. Percy collected the nearest glowing log, holding it with his gloved fingertips. His gloves were ruined as it was; the additional scorching was of little consequence. Hurrying back, he dropped it in the tub. He repeated this action with two more logs. Crouching in front of the tub, he basked in the merciful heat radiating from it. Taking the poker, he jabbed at them until they started to break apart. The small dark red flames that danced across glowing embers licked across the surfaces of the smouldering wood. He collected some kindling and added it to the logs, blowing on it. Immediately, they ignited. Quickly, he added some smaller pieces to the fire.

Collecting one more large log, shortly, he had an adequate fire burning, thankful for the heat. And more importantly, the light.

Percy and Emma fanned out cautiously, away from the light, their weapons at the ready. Though limping, she seemed capable enough of movement. Whitehall had remained to check the bodies.

As Percy was making his way between the narrow passage on his right and a machine on his left, he had that inexplicable sensation of being watched, and felt the hair rise on the back of his neck. Ahead, he spotted a dark object on the ground between two crates. He realised he was looking at a crouched figure. Quick as a whip, Percy raised his pistol. '*Halt*!' he shouted in German.

The figure bolted, dashing between the machines.

Percy sprang after it, at the same time hearing Emma shout, '*Halt*!' Dodging around the machine, he heard Emma yelling again, '*Halt, oder ich schieße*!'

A moment later, a desperate male voice pleaded, '*Schießen Sie nicht*! *Schießen Sie nicht*!'

Percy rounded the machine to see a dark-robed figure on its knees, hands in the air. Several feet away stood Emma, her pistol levelled at the figure, an expression of fiery intensity in her eyes.

He aimed his pistol and approached. 'Don't be foolish!' he said in German.

The figure turned his head slightly at the sound of Percy's voice. 'Please! Don't kill me!' he begged in Hochdeutsche. That suggested this fellow was educated.

'Keep your hands up,' Percy cautioned as he approached.

Emma had not taken her eyes from the figure. It seemed to him that she could shoot at any moment, though he saw none of the nerves or uncertainty so common in those unused to combat or firearms. That perhaps was most chilling: that she knew what she was doing. She gave the impression that she held this man's life in her hands, and it was hers for the taking, should she choose.

Percy yanked back the hood, revealing a lean, youthful face with messy black hair and frightened blue eyes. *Gods*, he thought, *this fellow can't be any older than Jane! He's still so young.*

The terrified young man begged him, still speaking German, 'Please don't kill me! It was their idea. I went along because they told me we'd get rich! I didn't know!'

'Stand slowly,' Percy commanded. 'Keep your hands up.'

The young man struggled to his feet.

'Have you any weapons?' Percy asked.

'No! I threw it away!'

Percy patted the young man down, and indeed, he was unarmed.

'Please! Please, sir!' The young man continued to plead, 'Don't kill me!'

It was Emma who answered him. 'Give us no cause, and we will not harm you. However, try anything, and you will die before your body falls to the ground!'

The menace in her voice was palpable. Percy felt chills of dread as he heard her threat. Even he did not doubt she meant it.

'Walk!' Percy commanded. 'You need to answer some questions about what took place here.'

Emma moved back, not lowering her weapon. As they passed, she fell in beside Percy.

They approached Whitehall, who was kneeling beside the leader, doing something. Further along, Carnby was watching them.

The doctor looked up as Percy and Emma approached. 'Caught one, did you? I think that accounts for all of them, yes?'

'Indeed.' Percy prodded the young German forward. 'What's the diagnosis, Doctor?' He asked.

'Those two poor fellows are dead.' Whitehall pointed at the other two bodies. 'This one's still alive!'

The young man gasped, '*Klaus lebt?*'

Axel stared about the dark space with a growing sense of futility. In the distance behind him, dim light flickered into existence. They must have started the fire. But the remaining darkness that had aided them earlier, now hindered him. And, alone in that mire, he still felt more than uncomfortable. Again, he wished he had brought Carnby with him.

Seeing little choice, he placed his rifle on a desk and struck a match. The little sun that burst to life in his hands drove away the night. Immediately, and thankfully, Axel spied a lamp on the desk in front of him. Making use of the existing match, he lit the lamp and placed it back on the desk, then retrieved his rifle.

He squinted around the drab and dirty office. Even with light, there was little apparent to see. A neat stack of bills sat on the desk in front of him under a paperweight, next to a ledger.

Axel looked to the door. Jane must have fled outside. He moved to it and was about to open it when he heard a faint whimper. Axel turned back and scanned the room.

He saw her. She was curled up beneath the other desk, her hands covering her face. She was quietly sobbing, seemingly oblivious to his presence.

Axel collected the lamp. He moved back to the desk and crouched, placing the lamp on the floor. 'Jane?'

She started and pulled her hands away. Her eyes were wide with fear, and red from crying. 'Axel?' she gasped, then glanced at the lamp. 'Put out the light!'

'What? Why?'

She stared at him as though unable to comprehend the situation. 'Is it just us?'

'What?' He struggled to understand her.

'Are we the only two left? Are…are the others…dead?'

'What? No! Apart from some minor injuries, everyone is alive and well!'

'But...but...*the Broken Ones*! They came. I felt sure we would all...' she trailed off, tilting her head, as if thinking.

'Those *abominations*?' He thumbed towards the rear of the factory. 'They didn't attack us. They carried off two of the Germans.'

'They...?' Surprise spread across her face. 'Did they, really?'

'Yes!' He held out his hand, 'Everyone's okay. Come and see.'

She reached out, but hesitated, before grasping it. He helped her out, and to her feet.

Her large ebony eyes met his. He stared into those eyes, wet from tears, and wanted to embrace her, tell her she was safe and not to worry. But such behaviour was most inappropriate.

A moment of silence passed between them. She looked down at their hands and back at him, pleased, before quickly turning away from his gaze.

Axel realised he was still holding her hand. He pulled his hand away with a jerk. 'Oh! Do forgive me, please! I...er...I...' he stumbled, feeling colour rising to his cheeks.

'Oh, no! No...not at all...' she stammered, then turned away and drew her handkerchief to dab at her eyes.

Axel felt a right fool. He had clearly offended her. Of course he shouldn't have held her hand! That was a thorough transgression of propriety.

He felt compelled to break the silence. 'We...we should join the others...'

She nodded her assent without looking back at him.

Twenty-three
The Focus

'We should burn it,' Jane said. She was clutching the book Emma had handed her, and glancing about apprehensively.

'What's that?' Mr Wallace asked. He was crouched a few feet away near the edge of the circle, cautiously examining the Nzambi with a firm grip on the sabre as though ready to draw.

She was standing near the middle of the circle, and had been flicking through the small book when the thought occurred to her. 'The Nzambi,' she explained. 'And the candles, and robes…and scrub this away.' She motioned to the pentagram.

'The "what"?' Emma asked from near Dr Whitehall and the two Germans. The leader was still unconscious on the floor, with the doctor attending him, but the other one – the young one with the black hair, thin, hard face and blue eyes – had been made to kneel nearby with his hands on his head. The young one kept staring at Jane, and it made her nervous.

Jane gestured to now truly-dead corpse. 'The walking dead. The Nzambi.'

'Is that what they're called?' Mr Wallace asked.

'It's one of their names, yes. The original, perhaps.'

He prodded it with the end of the scabbard. 'Will it rise again?'

'I hope not. But I'm not sure. I'd rather not take the chance.'

'Quite.' He prodded it once more. 'Very well. Once the other two return, we'll attend to it.'

Jane bit her lip as she did her utmost to maintain her composure. She forced herself not to turn her eyes or thoughts to the two dead Germans. Lying there, they looked so much like Uncle Ru— *Stop*! Her emotions were in complete turmoil. It took almost all her effort to not break down in front of everyone.

After her dizzying flight from the Broken Ones, she had somehow managed to climb through to the darkened office and, near hysteria, had almost fled out of the front of the factory. When she had opened the door and scrambled onto the landing, however, she had caught sight of the black silhouettes of the surrounding buildings against the grey-black clouds. Jane had stared down the dark lane at Wandsworth Road in the distance. Nightmarish images had raced through her mind of Broken Ones scrambling in their horrific spider-like crawl over the edges of roofs, and leaping down to seize her. Panicked, she had fled back into the building and scrambled under the table in sheer desperation. There, she had all but given up: in a world where the things that people believed were myths were in fact reality, these things were still thought to be myths. Nothing she knew armed her to fight one. All that she had learned were unreliable rumours, which told her that when the Broken Ones came, death inexorably followed on their monstrous and multitudinous heels.

And in that awful hollow under the desk, the terrible voice had returned. *So, you've left them to their doom? Good-for-nothing, spineless girl. One such as you, who could have spared them their fate, whimpering here like a mewling wretch. Those profanities were nothing before you! Pathetic.*

Jane had wept at her craven actions, and how her flight had now condemned the others.

And then, somehow, as though a miracle, Axel had found her and told her that everything was alright. That everyone was alive. Though she would have been happy to have seen any of the group, the fact that it was Axel who had come for her was somehow more meaningful. Immediately he had smiled at her, told her everything would be okay and had offered his hand, she'd felt safe again. And when he had been holding her hand and looking at her, she'd felt so nervous and excited. Despite everything, at that moment, she'd wondered if he would kiss her, like the heroes did in the books she had read. It made her feel a little giddy, and her heart had raced. But then he had pulled his hand away, and she'd panicked: she'd thought she had done something wrong, and turned away to hide her embarrassment. After that he had barely spoken to her, and it had been terribly uncomfortable. Surely, he must have been angry at her.

Once they had returned to the others, seeing them indeed alive and well, Jane had felt embarrassed and foolish for running away. She had anticipated derision and contempt, especially from the doctor, for being 'a hysterical woman'. But other than Emma, who'd made a fuss over Jane's well-being, no one had said much, other than to ask if she was all right. Dr Whitehall had even approached and inquired – in that manner of all doctors – if she had been injured, or required any medical attention.

It had then been agreed that Axel and Mr Carnby would go for Burton, to bring the carriage to the factory. Mr Carnby could pick the lock on the double-doors, and Axel could keep watch with his rifle. Before they had left, though, Mr Wallace had pulled everyone close together and whispered a warning, 'Mind what you all say to each other. This young fellow understands English.

He claims to be an unwilling participant, but we don't know for certain where his loyalties lie.' He had paused. 'And one more thing. Should we have to address each other, use nothing more than Christian names, understood?'

Now that he was not here, all of a sudden, she wanted Axel back. And despite the book in her hands, she'd found herself surreptitiously glancing back towards the front of the building, anticipating his return.

Jane returned to the book; Emma had explained it was the one from which the leader – Klaus – had been reading. She'd thought Jane could make some sense of it. Examining it, she suspected she knew what this was. She suspected because she had her own version. Though hers was far better than this. The handwriting was appalling, and it was in German anyway, which she couldn't comprehend. But the symbols were the clue.

Mindful of Mr Wallace's caution, Jane hesitated a moment before calling, 'Emma?'

The other lady turned to her, 'Yes, Jane?' As she approached, the young German stared at Jane again.

Jane shivered, uncomfortable, aware of his eyes on her. She leaned close to Emma. 'That...that man...the German. He keeps staring at me. Please tell him to stop.'

'Oh?' She seemed half-amused. Emma looked back at the young man, then spoke to him tersely in German.

The young man's eyes widened, then he ducked his head, staring down at the ground. Mr Wallace began to laugh. Dr Whitehall whipped his head up and stared at Emma with an expression of shock on his face.

Jane was perplexed. 'What did you tell him?'

'Oh, just that it was rude to stare,' she gave an airy shrug. 'You should learn to accept it, my dear. You are a pretty young thing, and men have no shame whatsoever!'

'I say!' Mr Wallace interjected, approaching the two. 'That's rather uncalled for.'

Emma raised an eyebrow. 'Really?'

He stopped. 'Well...er...that is to say...'

'Ha!' Emma grinned.

Jane frowned at Emma; she was sure that that was not at all what Emma had said to the young German, and she did not appreciate being condescended to. Yes, she was younger than everyone else, but there was no reason to treat her like a child. Jane did not argue though. Instead, she passed the book to Emma, and asked, 'Can you read this?'

Emma took the book and squinted at the scrawl. 'Good gracious!'

'What?' Jane started to bring her hand up, ready to swat the book away from Emma.

'This handwriting is utterly atrocious!'

Jane sighed in relief. 'Are you able to translate it, though?'

Emma squinted at the text again, reading it aloud. 'To draw the vitality from an enemy, form the hand into a claw. Think on the image of your enemy's essence escaping their body and entering your fingers, and then utter the following—'

Jane grabbed Emma's arm. 'Wait!'

Emma started and looked at her, an eyebrow raised in question.

'Don't read it aloud.'

'Why not?'

'In the ancient Vedic texts, they say that once something is spoken, it becomes reality, and...I've found some truth to the idea.'

'So, you think if I...?' Emma trailed off.

How did one easily explain such esoteric concepts? It wasn't just a matter of uttering the words; it was far more complex. Having read the sentence, the idea was now implanted in Emma's mind. Not that that guaranteed success – much depended on the individual. Then there were the specific words, the language of transmission: in Jane's experience, both of these were fundamentally important. And this had been prepared to work in German by whatever means, rather than in the ancient tongues of the world. There was no telling what would take place if spoken in English.

Instead, Jane merely shrugged. 'Power, when unguided, tends towards chaos. Why take the chance? Especially with that one.'

Emma smiled at her. 'I think that's quite a wise approach, my dear.' She closed the book and handed it back. 'Keep it safe, and later we'll translate it together. Carefully!'

Jane tucked the book into her coat for safekeeping.

'I say...'

Jane turned to Mr Wallace, who had crouched nearby, reaching for something on the ground. 'Might this be of some interest—'

Too late, she realised with alarm what it was. Before she could speak, Mr Wallace flailed, his whole body spasming. He cried out in shock and dropped the small black object as he toppled backwards.

'Wait! Don't touch it!' It was the adumbration that had been used to raise and control the Nzambi. Now that she made the connection, she suspected that this was how the abilities in the book worked when spoken in German. This was a Focus.

Emma dashed forwards and knelt by Mr Wallace. 'Are you okay?' she supported him.

Sitting on the ground, stunned, he stared at Emma, then at Jane. 'I say! That was rather frightful!' He looked back at the object. 'The dashed thing gave me quite a shock!'

'You mean it was electric?' Emma asked, putting her hand on his arm.

'No...no...it was...' He paused, searching for words. 'It was like an assault upon my very soul!'

Jane moved closer. 'It is a thing of the Darkness,' She fished out her mouchoir, carefully collected the object, and began wrapping it up. It was surprisingly heavy for its size. 'That's why it affected you so. It is tainted and radiates malice.'

Mr Wallace looked at her. 'Have you ever seen one?'

'No.' She shook her head. 'I've only ever read about—'

'Here! You!' Dr Whitehall's shout interrupted her. 'Come back here at once!'

Jane spun to see the young German racing at top speed away from the group, and towards the front of the factory.

She heard Mr Wallace behind her exclaim, 'Blast!'

The young man suddenly skidded to a halt. In front of him stood Axel and Mr Carnby. Axel had his pistol raised, and Mr Carnby, his shotgun.

Axel gave a wry smile and said something in German.

'That's roight! Wot 'e said, Sossidge!' Mr Carnby added.

The young man's shoulders slumped in defeat.

Jane smiled broadly, despite herself. She did not know what Axel said, but she guessed it was dashing and witty! And exciting!

Twenty-four
Cleansing

Axel leaped nimbly back as the conflagration took hold. On Jane's advice, they had scrubbed the chalk circle away using what they had at hand – the robes of the two dead supplicants – before piling the robes and candles on the Nzambi in the centre. He and Percy had then doused the pile with the spare oil they had brought. The two dead men were excluded from the flames. As Jane had explained, they had been participants, but seemingly they had not used the dark object – the *Focus*; they had not been corrupted. At Axel's insistence, the men had laid the two dead Germans side-by-side with some small semblance of dignity. As they finished, Jane had turned away, her petite frame shaking from hidden tears.

As the flames and dark smoke licked upwards, Axel watched the dead flesh sear and crack and curl. He turned away from the scene and saw the others watching in silence, their faces golden in the firelight, including Jane, almost as though she were forcing herself to watch, tears streaming down her face. *Poor thing,* he thought. He wondered what it was like to read about something for years, only to finally face it, and then learn that the reality was far more horrific than anything one could gather from words on a page. He imagined it must be like *reading* about war, and then having to actually stare across a battlefield at an enemy. Axel remembered the first time he had taken a life. A trio of nameless, and ultimately faceless bandits, who no doubt believed they had found easy targets in him and his travelling companion. He again felt the fear he had experienced that day. And the knot of panic and guilt and shame at having taken a life formed once more in his stomach.

His eyes went to the leader, Klaus, now on his back, bandaged and under the careful attention of the doctor. Whitehall had exclaimed repeatedly that it was a miracle the man was alive: Axel's shot had struck above the man's heart and to the side, but still in his chest, and there were wounds demarcating the entrance and exit of the bullet. The man had lost a frightful amount of blood, and yet – the doctor informed them – despite all logic, his heart was still beating.

Where along the way had it become so easy, he thought? So easy to squeeze a trigger with the intention of robbing another of that only thing that anyone could truly say belonged solely to themselves? Inadvertently, he stared back at the burning flesh. Was this thing truly the monster here, or was he?

He looked to the young man. He had confessed his name to them. Mathias. His face was blank and his eyes dull, staring at the flames as he sat on the floor, helpless, and without uttering a sound. A part of Axel felt pity for the young man – there was, he felt, almost a similarity to Jane. Here he was staring at his terrible reality, so far from whatever he might have imagined.

After they had thwarted his escape and returned him back to the group, Carnby had suddenly walloped him in the back of the head with his weapon. Even as the young man cried out and stumbled forwards, a swift kick to his back from the burglar had sent him sprawling to the ground. Quick as a whip, Carnby was upon him. In moments, he had him trussed up like a chicken with a rope they had brought from the coach. He had then gagged him with a piece of fabric. Axel had been taken aback at his ruthlessness. But then he himself had shot their leader, Klaus. Did that make him a hypocrite?

Axel turned away from the heat and light, and moved almost aimlessly towards Burton and the waiting carriage, where he had parked it inside the entrance to the factory.

The coachman regarded him expectantly. 'Whot 'bout dem two, m'lord?'

Axel studied him for a moment, not comprehending. 'What about them? We take them with us.'

'Oh, no, no m'lord! We carn't do that!' The man waved his hands rapidly. 'Lord Renfield said 'e wants all as is 'ere, taken care of!'

Axel was fed up and heartsick. 'I don't care what Lord Renfield said—'

'M'lord, please! You ourt'ta finish 'em now. Lord Renfield will be roight cross if we brings 'em back aloive.'

Axel had had enough. 'I don't care what Lord Renfield *will be*!' he snapped. 'I say we're not doing anything to them but taking them with us! He ground his teeth. 'If you feel that's wholly unacceptable, you're welcome to do something about it!'

Panic spread across Burton's face as Axel reached for his Colt and gripped the handle. 'Oh, no, no m'lord—' The other man sputtered, retreating, his hands up in submission.

Axel was yelling now. 'Then you'll bally well take us – *all of us* – back on the coach, or you can bally well return by yourself and tell Lord Renfield he's bally well welcome to find himself another bunch of thugs more willing to murder on his command!'

Burton shrank back in deference and compliance. Having overstepped his mark, he was apologetic to a fault. 'Sorry, m'lord. Please for-give me. Oi meant no dis-respect. As yoo say, m'lord, we takes 'em as well.' He scurried away.

Axel let out a deep sigh of exasperation.

The sombre mood continued through the coach ride back to Belgrave Square. Klaus had been laid on the floor. Percy and Axel sat in the back with Mathias between them; trussed and gagged as he was, he had had the further indignity of Carnby securing one of the canvas bags over his head. Whitehall sat opposite Percy, closest to Klaus' head, in order to monitor the supine man. Carnby volunteered to ride up front with Burton to make room as Emma and Jane filled the remaining two seats next to the doctor. Once the coach drove out, Carnby shut and re-locked the double doors, while Axel, with his rifle raised, scanned the surrounding roofs, apprehensive of another attack by these so-called, 'Broken Ones'.

The coach turned east onto Wandsworth Road, in the opposite direction from which they had arrived. Barely had it begun to rattle up to speed when Jane, who had been observing the unconscious man on the floor, turned and buried her face in her hands.

Emma regarded her with an expression of compassion, and then moved closer and began to gently stroke her hair.

Axel wished that he could soothe Jane himself, but again, he found himself constrained by propriety. Regardless of whatever Emma felt *she* was free to do, *he* certainly *could not* embrace Jane, nor comfort her. In America, far from the cities, people were far more liberal in their physical expressions; but so too, in turn, were they with all aspects of their behaviour. Civility and dignity came with their own inhibitions, he mused as he stared out of the window.

He had a vague idea of the route they were taking. He suspected Burton would take the Vauxhall bridge back across the Thames, and then most likely veer left and join Belgrave Road, and whichever road that led into, leading directly to Belgrave Square. The name of the latter escaped him, but he knew it well enough.

Axel had not been in this part of London for a long time, and certainly not at this hour on a Saturday night, so he couldn't say what traffic they would encounter, but even as they turned onto Vauxhall Bridge, as he correctly surmised, he noticed a definite increase in other traffic.

A flash of light to his left drew his attention. He noticed Whitehall's hands shaking furiously as he attempted to light his pipe. Eventually, the doctor succeeded, and the man's body slumped in relaxation as he drew on the tobacco. Axel, for his part, was so worn out he couldn't even bring himself to light a cigarette. He was about to speak about the events that had just transpired, but he remembered Percy's warning regarding the young German, and so bit his tongue.

Across from him, Emma murmured to Jane, who turned towards her. Emma wrapped her arms around her and stroked her hair. She began to sing softly.

Axel couldn't hear the words, but Emma's voice was undeniably beautiful and soothing. The melody was bittersweet and comforting, and within moments, he felt himself relax. Listening to the mellifluous tones along with the rocking of the moving vehicle, he felt his eyelids growing heavy, and wanted nothing more than to close them and lose himself in the merciful tranquillity of the sound. But he forced himself awake. He dared not rest in the unlikely circumstance that the young man next to him should try something foolish.

Axel woke with a start as the coach stopped. They were in a dark lane, with buildings on both sides. Next to him, the young man's head was slumped forward, and Axel could hear soft snoring. Everyone other than Emma was fast asleep. She was no longer singing, but was still holding Jane. There was something deeply maternal evident about Emma at that moment, that Axel would never have considered earlier in the day or evening.

He heard the sound of footsteps, and a moment later Burton appeared at his window. Off to his left, he heard the sound of a large door being swung open.

'Where are we?' he asked, his voice thick from sleep.

'Th' myooz, m'lord. At th' back o' th' square.'

'Yes, good thinking.' He yawned. The mews was a better option than entering the house from the front of Belgrave Square in the state they were in.

'Jus...jus...wun thing, m'lord?' Burton rubbed his gloved hands together as though pleading.

'Yes?'

'Wen we goes in, will yoo please wait with th' carrij 'til Oi goes an' gets ol 'Aar-graves?'

'Will this be a problem?' Axel asked, his voice taking on a hard edge.

'No, no m'lord!' Burton was quick to reassure. 'Ol' 'Aar-graves is all roight. It be that Missus Manner-in' yoo ourt'ta look out fer! But 'Aar-graves...'e'll 'elp.'

Axel nodded. 'Do it, man.'

Burton gave a deferential bow and retreated.

Twenty-five
Below Stairs

Belgravia, 15 February, 1891

No sooner had Percy, Axel and Carnby disembarked inside the coach-house behind number 30, than a young boy around twelve or thirteen appeared at the door from the stable proper. He was dressed in bed-clothes, his brown hair tousled from a pillow, and his brown eyes filled with excitement.

Dismounting from the driver's seat, Burton spotted him instantly. 'Will'yem! Why are yoo outta bed? We got a roight early start in th' mornin'.'

The boy ducked behind the door jamb. 'Sorry, Mista Bur'on!' he chirped in a young Cockney drawl. His voice was at that odd stage where it was changing – it broke as he spoke, some parts sounding like a child, some almost like a man.

Percy smiled to himself. *Ah, yes,* he thought, *and you haven't even discovered the horrors of women yet, boy.*

'Well, make yer-self yooseful then! Go get sum propa clothes on – y' carn't show yer-self in fron' 'a lords an' ladies loike that! Then come down an' tend t' these 'orses!'

The young boy dashed away.

Burton addressed Axel, 'Oi'll be roight back wit' 'Aar-graves, m'lord.'

With the young man's assent, the coachman departed. Percy moved to the doorway into the stable and watched Burton leave from the door at the front of the coach house, which led to the garden. Across the garden, the lights in the dining room where they had dined earlier were still lit.

A moment later, the boy reappeared in a rush. Percy heard him bounding, taking the wooden stairs two or three at a time. He had attired himself in a dirty white shirt, brown trousers with suspenders, and bare feet. He had clearly given over entire seconds of time to straightening his hair.

The boy, of course – in the way of all boys – did not tend to the horses. Instead, he approached in that brazen manner of all youths from the East End, and began questioning them without so much as a 'How do you do?' or 'By your leave'.

'Are yew really lords?' he asked of Axel and Percy.

Percy forced a smile. 'No.'

'Cor! Bat yew been in a propa foight t'noight, ay?'

'Well...there was...' he trailed off. Why was he bothering to explain himself to the *stableboy*?

'It's nothing for you to worry about, William,' Emma called from the coach.

The boy saw her now, for the first time. He ran over, mouth agape, and grabbed the coach window sill. 'Cor!' he exclaimed again, 'Are yew awl roight, Miss West-ova? Is that blud? Didj'yew ge' 'ert? Is Miss 'Alifax all roight?! Did she ge' 'ert?' He rattled off, without pause.

'It's fine, William.' Emma's tone was soothing. 'It's not our blood. There was an accident, but none of us got hurt. Miss Halifax is fine; she's just exhausted and is sleeping, so please keep your voice down.'

'Yes, Miss.' The boy lowered his voice. He peered into the coach at the two Germans and the doctor before whipping back around to Percy and Axel. 'Are they your pris-er-ners? Is 'e a docta?'

Without waiting for a response, he dashed around to the other side of the carriage. ''Ere, Docta! Didj'yew—'

Whitehall's snarl cut him off, 'Begone, you wretched whelp! Let me work!'

The boy came dashing back, sliding in the hay, a look of panic on his face. Recovering himself in an instant, he approached the two men again, saying, 'Yew did 'ave a foight, din' yew? An' yew wun, an' awl!'

'Why do you say that?' Axel asked.

The boy looked him up and down. 'Well, look at th' soize 'a yew. A big'un loike yew must'a smashed 'em all!'

'Is that what it takes to win a fight? Just be bigger? What if someone was bigger than me?'

'Then 'e'd win, an' yew'd lose!' William answered matter-of-factly.

'What about me and him?' Percy asked, gesturing to himself and Axel.

'You're both th' same 'oight, but 'e's bigga,' William said, thumbing at Axel and puffing his chest and arms out, 'So, 'e'd win, Oi reck'n.'

Percy gave a derisive snort as he began to walk off. He caught Axel glaring at him and he smirked. No doubt Axel was strong and tough. And though he had been caught off-guard by the Nzambi, the young man could probably fight well enough. But there was *no chance*! He moved to a wooden post to lean against it, ignoring the rest of the conversation as his young colleague continued to humour the boy.

It almost felt to Percy like the first time ever that he had been warm. The weather outside had been progressively worsening, and even though the carriage house doors were still open to accommodate the horses, he was thankful for the tranquil warmth of the stables. As they waited for Burton's return, he leaned against the post, closed his eyes and half-listened to the boy's prattle as he now went to bother Carnby.

Here, indoors, it felt like the boudoir of a pretty young dowager: warm, dark, safe and filled with...pleasantries. And all with no need for quiet, nor any concerns of an unexpected husband. Percy was still drowsy from the deep sleep he had fallen into on the coach ride. Only half-trying to rouse himself into full wakefulness, he mused that it was odd for him to have slept so deeply – something he rarely did, and certainly never in situations such as that. However, the scent of hay seemed so comforting and familiar that he thought he could have happily taken to one of the piles and slept like a babe.

Abruptly, he was reminded of a particular bit of business one summer a few years ago, in the south of France. It was jarring to be confronted with this memory: it was almost as though it had always been there, but he had simply chosen to ignore it, like a neglected book, forgotten on a shelf. Nor could he seem to recall when or where he might have purchased such a book. The memory washed over him, fragmented images appearing in his mind, telling a fractured, disjointed story.

Something had gone wrong. In his line of work, affairs sometimes did. Not for the first time, he was bleeding, exhausted and wracked with pain. Caught in a rare, violent summer storm while on the run from...someone, he had come across a lone farm in the countryside, in the middle of the night. Accessing the barn had, of course, not been an issue. He remembered undressing from soaking clothes, crawling into a pile of hay, shivering, and thankful for the warmth. And then...

He felt a terrible chill of dread run through his very soul.

'Ay!' Carnby barked, bringing him back to the present, and he opened his eyes. The burglar was pointing a finger at the boy and mouthing off in rhyming slang that even Percy could barely follow. Inadvertently, Percy's eyes darted about, looking for the source of his terror. Thankfully the barn remained warm and welcoming. Though as he looked upon Axel, Carnby and Emma's tired faces, an unsettling feeling tickled at the edge of his consciousness.

William retreated from Carnby's verbal assault, barely containing a smirk and pleading, 'Sorry, Guv'na!' with no sincerity whatsoever, only to barrel into the returning Burton, and the accompanying Hargraves.

Although Percy had never given any meaningful thought to children, and was indifferent to them at best, he did feel a little sorry for the lad as Burton then unleashed a torrent of unintelligible abuse at the boy, who fled at top speed and began to tend to the horses as he should have.

Immediately outside the coach-house were stairs that led below ground. Axel and Carnby carried the unconscious Klaus down, whilst Percy and Whitehall escorted the still bound, gagged and bagged Mathias. Emma assisted the now woken, bleary-eyed and sullen Jane.

They emerged in a narrow corridor that stretched off to their left. Axel surmised that this was the far end of the same corridor as earlier, when they had accessed the equipment store. It was cold below stairs, and the unfinished brickwork and stonework was illuminated by periodic lanterns fixed to the wall. Several doorways led off to both sides. To their right, the corridor ended in another three doors. Hargraves led them to the left, stopping at the first door on their left, before departing himself.

Here, Burton, who had gone ahead, and another young man, had moved a large table and several chairs aside, and were setting up rude cots. This young fellow was introduced to them as Edward, one of Emma's staff. That struck Axel as unusual: while ladies generally had a maid – well, not that Emma was *technically* a lady, in Axel's opinion – who would accompany them on their travels and their stays as guests, it was irregular for them to have a young man as staff. Unless, as scandalous as that was, she employed him for more *personal* reasons. But Axel regarded him now, and he was no older than the young German, Mathias, with a similar, naïve look to him.

William stood a few inches shorter than Axel, and had short, thin sandy brown hair, blue eyes, a snub nose and a broad, freckled face. He did not speak, but complied with any instruction. Axel noticed the young man eyeing the men in the group with suspicion as they moved into the room and laid Klaus on the finished cot, under the doctor's supervision, placing Mathias on the other one.

Edward only reacted when he set eyes on Emma limping into the doorway with her arm around Jane, alarm bordering on panic spreading across his face. Immediately dropping what he was doing, he hurried to Emma, shoving past Percy – much to *his* visible chagrin – as he went.

'Yew all roight, Miss—'

Emma raised her hand, stopping him. She pointed to Mathias.

Axel turned to Burton. 'Please be so kind as to watch these two.' He motioned the others out of the room.

'Aye, m'lord. Roight yoo are.' He crossed his wiry arms and glowered at Mathias.

Pulling the door shut, they all crowded into the passageway and spoke softly.

'Are yew 'ert, Miss Westova?' Edward asked, his voice tight.

Emma shook her head. 'No, no, it's not my blood. I just have a minor scratch. Has Irene retired for the night?'

'No, Miss. Yew know wot she's loike. She won' go t' bed 'til she knows you're back sayfe'n'sound.'

Emma nodded. 'Be a dear and fetch her then, would you, Edward? I shall need a hand with Miss Halifax.'

'Yes, Miss. Roight a-way, Miss.' The young man raced off immediately.

Alone now, Axel addressed the group. 'We ought to have a conversation about this evening. The things we've seen, Lord Renfield…What he told us this afternoon…I can't even think where to begin…And we should question this fellow, Mathias.'

Whitehall had taken off his spectacles and was rubbing his eyes. 'I agree. However, I must attend to our group's injuries, and that other fellow as a priority.' He waved towards the room.

'I don't think the ladies are in much of a state for that sort of thing, old boy.' Percy gave him an easy smile. 'Though, I for one, would also like to ascertain what these chaps know.' He gestured to the door behind him. 'And if it's grave risk to have them here, bound or not.'

Carnby slumped back against the wall. 'Oi reckon, leave it, Ak-sul. Oi wan' 'ta know too, bat…toie 'em up an' mayke 'em tawk in th' mornin'.' He sighed and waved his hand in dismissal. 'Roigh' now, Oi wan' a blummin' drink!'

'Discussing exactly *what* those monstrosities were, in my view,' Percy offered, 'would be more practical tomorrow, with Lord Renfield.' He paused, looking to the ladies. 'Unless Jane feels up to providing an explanation?'

Jane seemed to not be listening to any of their conversation.

Percy's logic was sound to Axel: the discussion could wait. Their prisoners should be the primary—

Emma, stooped and appearing exhausted, declared, 'I think it best if I see Jane to her rooms, and into bed.' She glanced at the other lady. 'I'd love to have Jane's input, but I don't think she's in much state for it.'

At Emma's voice, Jane started and regarded them, silent and listless, leaning on the wall for additional support.

The others murmured their assents. Axel sighed. Emma was right too. This had been far too much for Jane as an initial outing – for all of them, really. He, himself, was struggling to focus on any one of the evening's events, let alone put his thoughts in any meaningful order. Clearly, nothing had gone to plan this evening, and yet they were all extremely lucky to be largely unharmed. Rest and recovery should be the priority. Any conversation could wait until the morning.

Whitehall spoke, 'Of course, Miss Westover. See to Miss Halifax as you must, but return to me at once. I must examine that wound.'

Emma regarded him. 'As you say, Doctor.'

A moment later, Edward returned puffing. He was accompanied by a young woman in a plain maid's dress. She was of a height with Emma and Jane, and she shared Edward's sandy hair, though hers was longer and tied in a simple bun, as well as his snub nose and broad freckled face. It was impossible to ignore the blatant eye-patch she wore over her right eye. A large scar was visible over her eyebrow, descending below the patch, and emerging underneath on her cheek. Whatever had caused it, it had clearly been a nasty wound. Her left eye was the same shape and colour as Edward's. *They must be siblings*, Axel thought; they appeared to be about the same age, so possibly even twins, which might explain Edward's employment.

She gasped as she drew near, wearing the same expression of alarm as Edward had. She focused solely on Emma, pushing through to her. 'Miss West-ova! Wot 'appened?'

'It's fine, Irene,' Emma reassured her. 'It's just a scratch on my hip.'

Irene wheeled and glowered about at the men before returning to Emma. 'Well, we'll soon tayke care 'a that!'

She moved to help, but Emma cut in. 'I'm fine, dear. But help me with Miss Halifax.'

'Yes, Miss West-ova.' She moved to the other side of Jane and put her arm around her. 'Ca'mon, luv! We'll soon 'ave yew in a noice 'ot bath!'

The men quickly bade her a good night before she was led away by Emma and Irene.

As the trio departed, Hargraves returned, passing them. He addressed the men in his measured, dry tone, 'Forgive me, sirs, but Lord Renfield anticipated you may have concerns after this evening's experiences. He instructed me to convey his regrets at not being able to receive you in person upon your return.'

Axel spoke, 'Why did Lord Renfield not tell us what to expect this evening, Hargraves?'

For a fleeting moment, the butler broke his poise as he glanced at Edward, before answering. 'In anticipation of a…challenging outing, I have taken some small liberties.' He addressed Emma's young servant, 'Edward, be so kind as to prepare the bath on the third floor. The gentlemen will clearly need to bathe after the evening's activities.'

Edward nodded to the butler and departed in silence.

'Forgive me again, sirs, but I believe it would be best for you all to discuss the matter with Lord Renfield in the morning. Despite my years in the employ of Lord Renfield, my knowledge is limited to the expectation of required facilities upon return from an outing such as yours.'

'I see.' Axel rubbed his forehead, suddenly fatigued. There were no ready answers to be had here.

'As such,' Hargraves continued, 'I have also arranged for the preparation of the staff bath on the top floor. Once Miss Halifax has bathed, I shall see to the availability of the bath on the second floor, as well.' He paused. 'There are four rooms on the third floor. I have had the fires lit and the beds turned down in preparation, my lords.'

'Very well,' Percy said.

Hargraves bowed slightly. 'I have also taken the liberty of gathering some bed clothes for sirs.'

'Inform me in the morning what time Lord Renfield intends to visit tomorrow, Hargraves,' Axel instructed. Despite his independence and self-reliance of the last two years, he found himself startled at his ease with old habits: issuing orders to household staff felt uncomfortably like second nature.

Hargraves bowed again. 'As you wish, sir. If sirs do not require me for the moment, I shall take my leave to attend to these matters, before returning.' The butler bowed a final time, and departed.

Twenty-six
Coercion

Carnby unleashed a litany of profanities, and Whitehall pulled away. 'Really! I've only just begun!'

'That bluddy 'ert, Docta!'

Axel watched from against the wall, drawing on a cigarette, as Carnby sat up despite the former's protestations. The doctor had made him lie on the large table against the opposite wall of the room. Additional lamps had been brought so the doctor could see to work.

Now that the tension and danger of their encounters this evening had passed, Axel was starting to feel exhausted and wracked with pain: his side and back where that Broken One had slammed into him ached incessantly. He wondered if he had broken any bones in his shoulder or ribcage.

On the other side of the room, Percy was getting up from crouching next to Mathias, whom he had bound to the cot. Percy had been questioning the young man, and he returned to Axel.

Whitehall was speaking as he prepared a syringe. 'Very well, I'll provide you a further dose of *cocaine*, but *no more* as it shows itself to be terribly addictive.'

Carnby grumbled.

'Well?' Axel leant close to Percy.

Percy answered in a matching, hushed voice, 'The same business: he doesn't know anything. He says he was forced into it against his will…doesn't know anything about the ceremony or how this other chap went and resurrected the bloody *dead*! Just that he was terrified out of his wits. Oh, and he doesn't want us to kill him.'

'Kill him?' Axel exclaimed, without raising his voice. 'We're not going to kill him!'

'Yes, but *he* doesn't know that.'

In the corner of his eye, Axel was aware of the doctor inserting the needle with the *anaesthetic* under Carnby's jaw. Instead, he studied the helpless figure on the cot over Percy's shoulder, and drew on his cigarette. 'Do you believe him?'

In the distance, Carnby grunted in discomfort.

'If he's a liar, he's a dashed good one. That being said, I've met a few good liars in my time.'

Have you, indeed?' Axel turned his attention to the other man.

The side of Percy's mouth pulled up in a wry smirk. 'You, my young friend, have no experience with women!'

Axel rolled his eyes and let out an exasperated sigh. He drew on his cigarette again.

Percy turned serious, 'Right now, however, there are two different ways I could make him talk.'

'Oh?' Axel eyed Percy critically. He did not like the sound of that.

'There's the long way: I talk to the chap, convince him that I'm a friend who's here to help him, get him to trust me, and then he'll tell me.' Percy dug out his pocket watch and checked it. 'But that takes hours. Or days, at worst.' He repocketed the watch and looked Axel in the eye. 'Or…there's the *quick* way.' He pressed the fingers of one hand into a fist with the palm of the other, cracking his knuckles.

Axel clenched his jaw. He most definitely did not like the second suggestion. 'And I suppose that makes this poor wretch Edward the Second?'

'You *do* know that's a myth?' Percy retorted.

Axel ground his teeth. *Of course it's a bloody myth*! *That's not the point*! He wanted to yell. He almost couldn't believe the other man was seriously suggesting *torture*! Axel would be *damned* if he were to allow that. He stood upright and glowered at Percy, his eyes boring into the other man's. After everything this evening, were they really about to have a confrontation, now?

Percy squared off against him, staring straight back without hesitation. '*Don't get righteous with me*, my friend. *You* wanted answers, and you wanted them *immediately*.' He let that sink in a moment. 'In fact, I have a much better solution than either of those two options, if you'd care to hear it.'

Axel released a slow breath, relenting. Percy was right: *he*, himself, had wanted all the answers right now, regardless of reason or practicality. 'What do you suggest?'

'You didn't see the way this chap was admiring Emma and Jane, did you?' He leant against the wall. 'Emma *clearly* has some sort of ability to charm people into cooperation, as you, yourself, experienced today. As he's already taken with her, turn *her* loose on him.'

'Hmmm…' Axel drew on his nearly-finished cigarette. As an option, it was not violent, nor torture.

'One catches more flies with honey than vinegar…'

With the men present, Emma would be at no great risk. Though he couldn't remember a word she had said to him, at that moment during the afternoon, he had wanted nothing more with every fibre of his being than to help her with her urgent difficulty, no matter what it was. He exhaled, 'Why not?'

Percy raised an eyebrow. 'Why not, indeed?' He smirked again, slapping Axel painfully on the shoulder. 'In the meantime, *be as nice as you want* – butter him up all you like, so he thinks we're a decent lot!'

Percy had gone off for his bath, leaving Axel with much to ponder, little of it good. The man was a complex set of contradictions: cultured and criminal at the same time; joking one moment, ready to dole out violence the next. Axel did not know what to make of it.

Percy had initially hesitated, pointing at the two Germans laid on the cots. 'What about these two?'

'There are three of us here. One of these chaps is unconscious, and both are bound. I'm sure it will be fine.'

'Go on,' he'd insisted. 'If we're not done by the time you're finished, come back and check on us, if you like.'

Percy had relented. 'Very well then, old chap.'

On the left of the room, the doctor was still sewing up Carnby, but it appeared as though he was almost finished.

Axel had had his fill of blood for the night; he did not want to watch the proceedings any further. Instead, he considered the two Germans. The doctor had explained that normally, he would have attended to Klaus first, but there seemed little point, as the bleeding had all but stopped and his breathing and heartbeat were strong. It was terribly peculiar, they had all agreed, but the doctor could offer no explanation as to why this should be the case.

He eyed young Mathias, who lay on the other cot. Though bound, the bag and gag had been removed. The young man stared at him with blank eyes. He looked across the room to a jug of water and glasses, which Hargraves had brought, and licked his lips. '*Wasser. Bitte*,' he pleaded to Axel, his voice little more than a whisper.

'*Wasser*?' Axel asked.

The young man nodded.

Axel was not certain that his German was up to scratch. 'How's your German, Doctor?'

'Middling at best. But please do not distract me right now.'

While pouring a glass, he asked Carnby, 'If I undo this chap, can you bind him again?'

Carnby grunted and nodded his assent.

'Do keep still!' Whitehall snapped.

Carnby grunted again.

Axel returned to the young man with the jug and glass. Crouching next to the cot, he asked, '*Verstehst du Englisch*?'

'*Ich verstehe Englisch, aber ich kann es nicht sprechen.*'

Axel was mindful of Percy's warnings. They did not know what this man's intentions truly were. Nonetheless, it was cruel to deny a man water, and Axel certainly did not need Percy's permission to show compassion, even to a prisoner. 'I will untie you. Do nothing stupid and I will not harm you. Understand?' he instructed in English.

Mathias nodded.

It took a few moments to work out Percy's secure bindings, but they finally came away. Axel moved back a little and handed the young man the glass as he sat up. He gulped thirstily, and held the glass up to ask for more. Axel poured him some more. He finished that glass without gulping this time.

'Good?' Axel asked.

Mathias nodded.

Axel asked the young man if he wanted to use the amenities.

Mathias nodded again.

Axel addressed Carnby and the doctor. 'If we're not back shortly, do send the cavalry.'

'Yes, yes!' muttered Whitehall.

They stepped out into the hall and almost ran into Edward hurrying towards the front of the house with a pailful of coal.

Axel stopped him. 'I say there, where are the facilities?'

Edward stared at him blankly a moment, before Axel saw understanding dawn upon him. He pointed at the next door across and to their right, opposite where they had descended from the garden.

'Ah! Thank you, man.' Edward turned to leave, but Axel stopped him again. 'Would you be so kind as find some chairs for us here? Two should do, I think.'

Edward nodded before rushing off.

Odd fellow, Axel thought, as he led Mathias by the arm to the bathroom. He can clearly speak, but he won't. Why? And why glare at him and the other men so intensely? Perhaps it was resentment arising from class distinction? It was possible.

As they were returning from the bathroom, Axel heard a woman's voice nearby call out to him softly: '*Axel...*'

Axel spun on his heel, yanking the young man around with him. He looked up and down the hall, and at the nearby doors. They were all shut, and they appeared to be alone.

'*Was?*' Mathias asked.

'Shhh!' Axel whispered, looking about. 'Did you hear anything?' he asked in English.

Mathias' head whipped back and forth as he tried to look in all directions at once, then back at him. 'Those things are here!' he hissed in German. 'They've come to take us away!'

Axel felt a wave of terror rush through him, and all his hair stood on end. He almost panicked, but fought to control the urge.

'No,' he said firmly, after gathering himself. 'You're quite safe here. They're not coming to take you or Klaus away.'

The young man cowered. The fear was palpable in his eyes.

'I promise.' Axel said. 'You're safe here.' He hoped it was true.

There was a soft rap at the door. Axel turned away from Carnby tying Mathias back to the cot. Opening the door, Edward was looking at him expectantly with a chair on each arm. He slid out into the hall. 'Ah, yes. Thank you, Edward. I think here will be fine.'

Edward placed the chairs side by side against the opposite wall.

'You're employed by Miss Westover, yes?' Axel asked.

The young man's eyes narrowed in suspicion.

'It's quite all right, man. I just wanted to thank you for assisting us, regardless.'

Though he saw the suspicion leave his face, Edward still didn't answer him.

'Yes...well...thank you, Edward.' Axel waved a dismissal. 'That will be all.'

Edward nodded wordlessly, and raced off.

Axel watched him go for a moment, further puzzled, before Carnby exited into the passageway, supported by the doctor. The burglar was reeling a little from the second dose of morphia the doctor had given him.

'You should go and bathe, and lie down.' Axel said to him.

'N'Oi'mmm'roigh',' the other man slurred.

Axel shook his head. 'Go on. We'll be fine here. Percy will be back shortly. It'll do you a world of good.'

Carnby looked about as though in a dream. 'Wellll...'

Axel squeezed his shoulder and said, 'Go on.'

Carnby nodded and mumbled something, and shuffled in the wrong direction. Axel and Whitehall quickly righted him.

Watching him go, Axel wondered if he shouldn't accompany him, but Hargraves was upstairs, and he was not keen on leaving the doctor alone, even though the two Germans were secured.

Then Whitehall was speaking to him. 'I gave the young fellow a shot of something that should keep him asleep through the morning.'

Again, Axel wasn't sure how he felt about that. 'Against his will?'

'Come now, the poor fellow seems frightfully shaken. I told him it would help him sleep peacefully, and he agreed. At least, this way, you won't need to sit on guard all night. He paused, taking a deep breath. He looked as tired as Axel felt. 'Furthermore, I *was* attending the earlier conversation, and need I remind you that I am a doctor? I have no…unsavoury intentions towards those in my care, be they friend or foe.'

Axel felt a tremendous sense of relief that he wasn't alone in having a sense of compassion. 'Thank you, Doctor.'

'I say, Miss Westover hasn't returned, has she?' Whitehall was looking at him over his spectacles and frowning.

'No, Doctor, she hasn't.'

'Confounded women!' Whitehall muttered. 'Ask them to do *one* thing!' He threw his hands in the air in futility. 'And for their own benefit!' He pointed at Axel, 'I tell you, young Axel, I shall pursue the matter with her once I've finished here! She shall *not* escape an examination!'

'Quite,' Axel said noncommittally. He didn't fancy the doctor's chances.

Whitehall stared at him a moment. 'Yes...as you say...quite...' He gave a heavy sigh. 'Come along then, I should need you to assist me to get this other German fellow onto the table. I must still close his wounds.'

'Yes, Doctor.' It was clearly going to be a long night for both of them.

Twenty-seven
Strange Occurrences

Whitehall heard the door close behind him as Axel left the room.

He stared at the body of this German fellow and sighed. This was *less than ideal*. Though he had laid out his equipment readily and carefully, and had adequate lighting, he had no assistance – no nurses – and insufficient anaesthetic, should the man abruptly awaken. A task like this required a hospital, with all its entailed *facilities*. But this would have to do. They could hardly have turned up to a hospital anywhere, in the state they found themselves, with a man shot through the chest, with no questions asked! They would have invariably, and rapidly, found themselves being escorted into Scotland Yard.

Whitehall frowned and began to cut away the bandages from the man's chest. Tired as he was, this would likely take hours. But he had learned long ago to do without sleep and continue working.

He pulled away the bandages. There was very little blood, and none issued from the open wound, despite the beating heart. He struggled to understand it – *it just made no sense*! Taking up the scalpel, he frowned again at the complexity of the coming work. And once he finished one side, he would have to do the other. That would require calling in young Axel to turn the man; though he could clearly see the poor fellow had no heart for this bloody work. He was about to criticise Axel's eagerness to take a life, when he remembered that the opposite was the case: in truth, tonight, Axel had only shot one man.

Three men had died tonight. Three men that he had been unable to save. It rankled with him. He brought the blade to the man's chest, and began to cut with precision. If it were within his power, a fourth would not.

Only when it was too late did Whitehall notice the glow. It had again, begun at the fringes of his vision, but he had been too focused to notice. Now, again, the white light radiated blindingly near his hands. *No! Confound it! Not this again!* he thought.

❧

Axel slumped back into the chair. He was exhausted, both mentally and physically. He tried to think once more on what had occurred over the course of the evening, but nothing came to his fatigued mind. All he could do was stare inanely at the opposite wall.

He dug into his vest and drew out his pocket watch, examining it with trepidation. It had been his father's, and Axel had loved to play with it as a young lad. His father had remembered and gifted it to him not long before his passing. Sitting alone now, in an unfamiliar basement, his thoughts drifted to his father, and for the first time in years, he missed him.

Axel's childhood had not been exceptional or unusual in any particular way; in fact, it had been quite normal for someone from his social standing. Aside from when he had been away at school, he had always been surrounded by his family. Certainly, now that he thought about it, there were those places that had felt uncomfortable or frightening, but at this very moment he couldn't recall a specific one. Besides which, Warner had always berated him at those times for being afraid. That was, in point of fact, the only real contention of his life: Warner. The two of them had always butted heads. Being the eldest, Warner thought he knew *everything*. And Axel especially hated it when Warner would berate his little sisters for being 'silly little girls'. Axel would jump to their defence, and that was the one thing that *always* eventuated in a scuffle.

If that was the worst thing though, he counted himself lucky. Until he had packed and left for America, he had always been close to his family. Now, he felt as though his life had taken such a strange turn that, even though he was so much closer to them geographically, he felt more isolated from them than he ever had in Wyoming or Dakota.

Looking at the watch, he was thankful to see it was undamaged. It was nearly half-past-two. Where had the evening gone? He rested the watch on his lap, stretched out and yawned. The doctor had suggested the surgery would be lengthy. Struggling to keep his eyes open, he wondered how many more hours he would have to wait here.

He folded his arms across his chest, sighed, and closed his eyes. Just for a moment.

Axel was standing in the middle of the floor of the factory at 10 Hamilton Street, South Lambeth, again.

All around him, a horde of walking corpses, Nzambi, were shuffling about in an awkward, ceaseless gait.

The constant sound of gunfire was deafening in his ears, though he could see no shooters, and saw no flashes.

Somewhere above him, on the back wall of the factory were perched two of the Broken Ones, and they were rending men limb from limb. He couldn't look up to see them, but he could hear the sickening tearing of flesh, the hideous screams of the dying men and the silent laughter of the two dreadful aberrations as they glowered down upon him in cold malice.

He couldn't look up to see them because all his attention was focused down the length of his readied rifle. Focused on the translucent abomination with red eyes, a ghastly mouth and pulsating, blood-red body, dressed in a tatty black robe, its arms in the air, shrieking unintelligibly as more Nzambi rose from the floor.

It leapt at him, and he fired, striking it true in its chest. It issued an awful hissing screech and fell forward on its face.

Suddenly, the building was silent. The gunfire was gone. The dying screams were gone. The silent laughter was gone. The Nzambi were gone. The Broken Ones were gone.

Axel moved forward, staring at the floor ahead.

What lay there was not Klaus. What lay there was not a Hollow Man.

What lay there was a supine Lakota Sioux woman, her limbs splayed at odd angles. Her eyes were blank and glassy, as around her formed a pool of bright red blood in trampled white snow.

Beside her stood a child. A young Lakota Sioux girl, no older than six or seven, standing and wailing helplessly beside her dead mother.

He heard a woman's voice just beside him, whispering in his ear, '*Axel*!'

Axel started up in the seat, almost crying out. He looked about him wildly, his heart pounding in his chest, his breathing ragged. He was alone. He had fallen asleep in the chair.

His heart still racing, he was about to reach for his watch, when he heard a sound off to his right. Snapping his head up, he saw Percy approaching.

The other man looked refreshed. His blond hair was combed back, and he wore an ill-fitting robe and pyjamas that were clearly too short. 'I say there, old chap, are you all right?'

At that moment, the door opened, and an exhausted-looking Whitehall stumbled out. He leaned on the door frame, panting. 'It's done,' he said, his voice tired. 'The man will live.'

Axel struggled to understand. How long had he been asleep? He grabbed his watch and looked at the dial. It read two-forty-seven. Axel looked about; it was still dark. *He had only been asleep for about twenty minutes*. How had the doctor finished already?

As they passed the ropes and secured Klaus to the cot, Axel discreetly examined the bandages on his chest. They were fresh, white as fallen snow. Not a single spot of blood was present, suggesting the wounds had been thoroughly closed and cleaned.

Axel was by no means a doctor, but had been injured enough, and seen enough injuries to know this was very odd.

Opposite him, Percy muttered. 'Rather peculiar, what?'

Axel met his meaningful expression then turned to the door. 'I say, Doctor—'

But Whitehall was gone.

Twenty-eight
Disparity

Carnby reeled and swayed in the darkness, the scotch sloshing from the bottle he had swiped on the way upstairs. 'Oi 'ad a 'ot bath!' he slurred to the empty room.

He raised the bottle to his lips and quaffed the potent liquid as if it were water. He stumbled forward and caught himself on a dresser, laughing. 'Now look at me!' He ran his hand along the ridiculously tight, but finely made...made...what had the butler called them? '*Pyjamas*'! He burst out laughing. What a bloody ridiculous word! Pyjamas! Which fool thought that up? 'Look at me! Oi'm a bluddy lord, Oi am!'

He managed to turn and look at the bed. It was to his left. He wanted to go to it, but it was moving in the wrong direction! 'Oi'm a bluddy lord in a bluddy man-shun, Oi am!'

Carnby crashed into a lamp, knocking it over. 'Oh! 'Scuse me, m'laydy!' he slurred, laughing. He held out his hand, ''Ere, let me 'elp you up, darlin'!'

The lamp did not move.

'Bugga ya, then!' He burst out laughing and took another gulp.

He turned towards the corner of the room and began to move. In a moment, he collided with the bed and fell backwards onto it, spilling precious drops of his sweet nectar of the Gods as he did.

Something bad had happened again. People had gotten hurt, or something. But he couldn't for the life of him remember what, and what was more, he didn't care. All he could do was laugh.

Richard Carnby had Chased the Dragon, once. Just once, mind. It had been far too...*enticing*. It made him dull, and he needed to be sharp. It was like being in a bed with an endless stream of women, but without the effort! It was too, too good. He never went near it again; if he did, he knew he would never return.

But this! This stuff was even better than Chasing the Dragon! Carnby had no pain. He had no aches or fatigue. He had no problems, whatsoever. His whole world consisted almost solely of a hysterical euphoria. He would have to get injured more often!

And all he could do was lie there and laugh. Laugh at these bloody ridiculous toffs and their stiff collars, their 'I beg your pardons,' and 'I say's'. Bloody fools.

Percy sat at the desk, eyeing the wall in front of him. Despite the quality of the structural workmanship, and the intervening space of the hall, he could still hear the din from Carnby across from him. And to think he chose the room at the back of the house because he hoped it would be quieter!

There was a crash from across the hall, and he burst into soft laughter, shaking his head. He could hear Carnby blathering away.

It made little difference, as he was not about to sleep anyway. He had been lucky to have been spared a search: in the desk, he found all he needed – paper, pen, ink and blank envelopes.

He had already retrieved the little bible he carried about himself from his jacket. Percy was by no means a religious man; the very idea seemed absurd to him. No. He was far too practical. The bible served an entirely different purpose. He opened to a random page. He wrote that page number at the top left corner of a piece of paper. He followed with a dash. Running his finger down the book's page, he randomly selected a verse. Next, he wrote this on the paper, followed by another dash. Percy counted along the line till he was satisfied, and wrote this as the final number, followed by a full-stop.

After all this time, he had learned to quickly perform the substitutions in his head, and in an educated, and carefully legible hand, he began to write his message.

Once he was done, he would seal it in the envelope and see to excusing himself sometime tomorrow to travel and deposit it at the designated location.

Twenty-nine
Just Over There

Axel was not happy as he stared at the pile of ripped and bloody clothes. These were expensive garments. But more importantly, they were new. He had only purchased them before departing from New York, and tonight was the first time he had worn them. Thinking of his time on the prairies, with his limited resources, he thought it a shameful waste.

Hargraves had asked him to leave his clothes in the bathroom to be attended to, along with the others. He fastened the ill-fitting robe around him and stared at the bottom of his legs sticking out from his borrowed pyjamas.

He stepped out into the small hallway, and then out into the large, dark space of the second-floor landing. To his left was Jane's room – Hargraves had explained to him that this particular bathroom had been prepared as it did not open directly into the ladies' chambers, as the other did into Emma's, at the front of the house. He stood a moment looking towards Jane's door, hoping she was sleeping soundly, and not disturbed by the shocks of the evening. And that perhaps, tomorrow, he would have a chance to talk with her…

As Axel moved towards the large stairs, Emma's door in front of him opened, and Irene emerged with an armful of clothing. She moved in his direction.

As she neared, he saw it was Emma's dark dress, stained with blood. He acknowledged the young woman. 'Irene.'

She glared at him sullenly with her good eye, without saying a word, until she passed. Axel watched her go. He was, quite frankly, unused to staff behaving in such a rude manner. But what could he do? They were not household staff; rather, Emma's personal staff; and he wondered if perhaps, her hostility stemmed from Emma having confided that *he*, in fact, had shot her?

He sighed and began to trudge up the stairs. The bath had taken some of the edge off his body aches, but he was still terribly exhausted.

Finally, he alighted onto the third-floor landing. He had been told there were two rooms at the front of the house, and two at the back. Moving to his right, towards the rear, he saw all the doors were closed. Axel heard a din and laughter coming from the back left bedroom. He listened for a moment, then shook his head. *No more drugs for you, sir!* He gave a short, tired laugh.

He turned back; the door at the front left was closed, but the double doors on the right were open.

Standing in a narrow hall that ran to the right, with the closed doors behind him, he saw at the end of the hall another door open to a private water closet. Moving through a second set of doors, he realised he had somehow been left the largest bedroom.

Discarding his robe on the bed, he moved to one of the two large windows and pulled the curtain open a little. He stared onto the dark and silent square. Evenly spaced street lamps cast a cheery glow off the elegant white façades of the surrounding buildings. The lovely park in the centre of Belgrave Square was mostly in darkness, though the snow clinging to the bare branches of the trees still gave a surprisingly warm and radiant glow from the reflected lights of the street lamps. It was most picturesque.

He shivered as he thought about how far this was from the things they had seen that night. Now, standing here in the opulent tranquillity of Belgravia, it almost seemed impossible. *Had it been real?* Yet here he was, in a house with others who had experienced the same things. Axel looked at the watch in his hand, turning it to catch the flickering firelight. The dial read three-thirty. He sighed. He wanted sleep, but somehow suspected it would be an early morning.

All the questions Axel wanted to ask Lord Renfield flitted through his mind: what *was* this *madness*? How was it possible for such impossible horrors to exist, unknown and unnoticed, in such a crowded and busy place? At this point in history – and for at least the last fifty years – London was very likely the most populated city in the world. People were *everywhere*. And yet, these *things*, these *nightmares* still lurked in the shadows. *What else stalks these streets*? He shivered again. Why had Lord Renfield not forewarned them? Now that he had had time to calm himself and consider the situation, it occurred to him that he simply would not have believed their host. Had someone told him in explicit detail a day ago, or even this past afternoon, that such things existed in the world, roaming the dark, preying on men, Axel would have thought them quite mad. *No*, he mused, *we had to see the truth of the world ourselves.*

He also knew that Lord Renfield would want an answer, and he wondered what answer he would give. What answer would the others give? Aside from Jane, who was already clearly mired in this world, he thought perhaps Percy would say 'yes'; he seemed to think the whole business was rather a lark, and Axel sensed he would opt in for the sheer thrill of it. But the others? If what he suspected about Emma were true – that she was a courtesan –

what did she have to gain from this, other than excitement? Her exceptional beauty and charm guaranteed her a life of ease and luxury that most could never hope to know. Why jeopardise that? Particularly with injury or disfigurement? He thought about the doctor. He could not begin to guess what that man would say. He seemed so irascible, yet so staid; and yet still, so adaptive. And what about Carnby? The man was a burglar, which meant it was all about the prize. He remembered Carnby mentioned he understood this to be a job. Was that what Lord Renfield promised him? Money? And how long could the prize warrant, even for one who came from so little, so much ongoing risk?

What if he himself accepted? What would happen if he were to wake up in the morning as part of the Order of the Steel Rose? What would the next course of action be? To his mind, the next step was to question their prisoners. 'Turn Emma loose on Mathias,' he murmured, considering Percy's 'third' option. What about the other one – Klaus? Would she be able to charm him?

Jane had said these people were amateurs and that they were ignorantly playing at what they thought was power; and yet, they had succeeded in such a profane impossibility. From *where* had they gotten their knowledge? From *whom*? It seemed only Klaus could answer that...if he survived. And he was no doubt hostile, given he had attempted to murder Axel. Would Percy's 'quick' option be required? He prayed not. It seemed profoundly dangerous that there was a source somewhere out there, disseminating such harmful and desecrative knowledge. They would need to find whomever it was and stop them. And then he remembered the Dark Master, too: who was *he*? Axel had vowed justice for the death of von Meyerling, but how would they find him? He stopped himself. He had not even decided to join, as yet. Much hinged on *that* decision, and any consequent ones, yet to be taken in the light of day.

Axel stared at the darkness hovering at the fringes of the light, around the surrounding rooftops. The darkness was always there. '*Just over there.*' The words came back to him from that cold and dark South Dakota night. How had Spotted Elk *known*? And what did that mean for the words he spoke? Were they all true? Was Axel's path predestined?

Axel thought of his two younger sisters, Evelyn and Katherine, safe at their family home. He missed them terribly and longed to see them. To embrace them and hear their stories. Evelyn would be, what? Nineteen, now? Which would make Katherine seventeen. Almost grown up. He wondered if they had *come out* yet, or if they had received any proposals already? If not as yet, then when the season began in April they would no doubt be inundated with suitors. They were both beautiful, like their mother, and he couldn't imagine either of them facing spinsterhood. He thought of their warm, safe world; of the lives they lived; the lives they would live; of the children they would have; and of the glaring contrast to the world out there. The world he now knew with terrible finality, actually existed. *Just over there.*

What answer would he give? What answer *could* he give?

Thirty
They Will Find You

Doctor Whitehall lay in bed with a pillow pressed over his head, staring into the darkness, trying to ignore the pounding pain. He remembered this feeling. He suspected it had happened again.

But he pushed and fought, driving the thought into the distant corners of his mind. He did not want to face that possibility now. He just wanted to sleep.

He closed his eyes. Thankfully, the pain appeared to be subsiding. Slowly, surely, he drifted into that grey world between wakefulness and sleep.

And then he heard it, once again. The thin, trembling voice called to him. 'Docta.'

No, no, no! he thought in outrage. 'No! No more of this!' he spoke without opening his eyes.

'Docta,' the voice called again.

'Leave me alone!'

But the voice was persistent. 'Docta.'

Whitehall gritted his teeth and opened his eyes. The small boy was standing there, again. As always, he was dressed in those poor torn and tatty clothes. His small hand was outstretched towards Whitehall. The boy's hair was dark and wet, his skin terribly pale, and his lips that awful blue colour. His coal-dark eyes fixed on Whitehall, empty and unseeing. Just as they once had. Just as they always did.

'Why do you hound me?' Whitehall pleaded.

'Docta. Yew can—'

'No!' Whitehall hissed, sitting up. The boy's eyes followed him. 'No! I will not hear you!' He turned over and threw himself back down, facing the window.

'Docta. Please...'

Whitehall pressed the pillow to the side of his head, over his ear and squeezed his eyes shut.

But it was not enough to drown out the words. '*They saw yew, Docta. They know yew now. They will foind yew...*'

Whitehall's eyes shot open in alarm. He spun in the bed, sitting up. But the boy was gone. He looked about the room. He was alone.

Acknowledgements

Firstly, as I am no longer able to thank her in person, I'd like to acknowledge the unwavering support of my late mother, as well as her knowledge of the politesse and social dynamics of the Victorian era – she was an invaluable guide through the early drafts of this work.

I'd like to thank my wife, Jess, for her constant support. It is only by virtue of my mother's passing that she is first on this list.

A very deep thank you to my family, and past and present friends and supporters for both their encouragement and their invaluable constructive feedback on the manuscript as it progressed. Particular thanks to Kane S. for Dr Whitehall's *charming* bedside manner.

A special thank you to Dr Juliette Lachemeier, editor and independent publisher from The Erudite Pen. Though I have been writing for years, Juliette's guidance and advice helped me elevate my skills to the next level. I would have been lost without her professional expertise regarding the publishing process.

Thank you Judith San Nicolas from JudithSDesign&Creativity for her amazing realisation of a book cover image that has been haunting me for years, as well as for her additional artwork.

Thank you to Caroline from Sunflower Imaging, who was willing to work with me despite my having to travel to her, and who was able to capture me in the liminal space between light and darkness.

I have endeavoured to be as accurate as possible with my historical and linguistic detail with the research I had available to me. As such, I have taken certain creative liberties here and there, and I beg the indulgence of any historians or linguists who may read this, and to whom any errors may be glaringly obvious!

Finally, and most importantly, I'd like to thank all of you who have taken the time to read this book. I sincerely hope you enjoyed it, and are looking forward to following the adventures of Axel & Co., to whichever dark corners of the world and soul they may lead. If you did, I'd appreciate it if you left suitable ratings and/or reviews on the appropriate sites, or recommended it to your friends.

Dark Masquerade marks the chilling debut of a new voice in supernatural and gothic horror. A lifelong student of myth, language and the macabre, Slater weaves a tale steeped in Victorian intrigue and shadowed secrets. With influences ranging from dark fantasy to horror and the 'man remade', his writing explores the arcane and the dreadful with a dry, grisly wit. A traveller, linguist and obsessive thinker, Slater brings global experience and a haunted imagination to the page, inviting readers into a world where nothing is ever quite as it seems.

With an enduring fascination for arcane mythologies, dark histories and the liminal spaces between the seen and unseen, Slater's work summons the esoteric and the dreadful in equal measure. A master of language and symbol, he weaves tales where secret orders stir, ancient evils awaken and masks conceal more than just faces.

The author has worked across strange and varied fields, yet always returns to the shadows of his imagination – guided, perhaps, by darker muses. Hampered (or helped) by a macabre sense of humour, he writes with a deep awareness that the line between reality and the occult is perilously thin.

Enjoyed the book? You can follow the author at:

Facebook: @R Slater

Email: arxnocturna@gmail.com

TikTok: @arxnocturna – R Slater Author

Instagram: @arxnocturna – R Slater Author

If you liked the book, please leave a review on Amazon, Goodreads or with the author directly. Reviews are invaluable in supporting an author's hard work and are greatly appreciated.